Fidel's Last Days

OTHER BOOKS BY ROLAND MERULLO

American Savior (2008)

Breakfast with Buddha (2007)

Golfing with God (2005)

A Little Love Story (2005)

In Revere, In Those Days (2002)

Revere Beach Elegy (2000)

Passion for Golf (2000)

Revere Beach Boulevard (1998)

A Russian Requiem (1993)

Leaving Losapas (1991)

Fidel's Last Days

ROLAND MERULLO

A NOVEL

Shaye Areheart Books

NEW YORK

Copyright © 2008 by Roland Merullo

Published in the United States by Shaye Areheart Books, an imprint of the Crown Publishing Group, a division of Random House, Inc., New York.
www.crownpublishing.com

Shaye Areheart Books with colophon is a registered trademark of Random House, Inc.

Library of Congress Cataloging-in-Publication Data

Merullo, Roland.
Fidel's last days / by Roland Merullo.—1st ed.
1. Americans—Cuba—Fiction. 2. Castro, Fidel, 1926—Fiction.
3. Havana (Cuba)—Fiction. 4. Miami (Fla.)—Fiction. 5. United States—
Relations—Cuba—Fiction. 6. Political fiction. I. Title.

PS3563.E748F53 2008
813'.54—dc22   2008021278

ISBN 978-1-4000-4868-7

Printed in the United States of America

Design by *Lynne Amft*

10 9 8 7 6 5 4 3 2 1

First Edition

For Gary Pardun, Russ Hammer, and John Recco

AUTHOR'S NOTE

THIS IS A WORK of the imagination, based in real places and guided by actual circumstances. The characters are entirely made up, and I have taken some liberties with the geography of Havana and the workings of the Cuban government.

ACKNOWLEDGMENTS

MY HEARTFELT THANKS to those Cuban Americans who assisted me with certain details of this story, and who chose to remain anonymous. My gratitude also, as always, to my fine editor and friend, Shaye Areheart, and all her staff at Shaye Areheart Books. And my enduring thanks to my wonderful agents Marly Rusoff, Michael Radulescu, and everyone at Marly Rusoff and Associates.

Fidel's Last Days

E rnesto Salvador walked alone down an ink-dark street near the northern edge of Old Havana. In the right front pocket of his jeans was a single yellow cyanide tablet, half the size of his thumbnail, and when he saw the headlights wash across the buildings in front of him, and heard the bubbling sound of truck tires coming fast along the cobblestones, he found himself running his fingers along the outside of his pocket to make certain the pill was there. The truck was less than a hundred meters behind him. In as casual a way as he could, he turned right, down a narrow street, little more than an alley, where the darkness was almost unbroken. He looked for a doorway to duck into, a courtyard, a car bumper to hide behind, but the street was empty and the walls of the buildings offered him nothing but stone and darkness. He listened for the truck, hoping to hear it pass on. But then he saw the sweep of lights again as it made the corner, a flicker of National Police blue, and he heard the sound of the engine closing in, and the horrible squeal of brakes as the vehicle skidded to a stop next to him at the curb.

He reached the tips of his fingers into the pocket of his jeans and then abruptly changed his mind. He thought of his daughters,

Margarita and Ester, and of his wife waiting for him now only a few blocks away. He told himself it was possible to be questioned, even to be arrested, and still survive.

The men were out of the truck before he could see the foolishness of this thought, and they came up from behind and roughly spun him around. There were three of them, none in uniform, bulging shoulders and square necks. "Salvador?" one of them said. "Ernesto?"

Ernesto shook his head. He could not seem to speak. He could not make his hand move farther into the pocket. His legs trembled so violently he thought he would fall down at the feet of the nearest man, but before he could accomplish even that, the man reached out and slapped him hard across the right ear, knocking him sideways. "*No soy*—" he started to say, but the other men were upon him now like heavy dogs, pinning his shoulders against the stone of the building, pressing the skin of his cheek into the grit. He felt someone bring his wrists together and hold them in a fierce grip, and then the sharp metal cuffs against his skin. His captors jerked upward on his arms. The pain shot through his shoulders, and he screamed, and while he was screaming the men were opening the back doors of the truck. They threw him in like a sack. He screamed again when his shoulder struck the floor. The doors slammed closed. In a moment the truck jolted forward and made a tight circle so that his body went skidding sideways across the corrugated metal, and the legs of a bench slammed against the middle of his back.

When the sharpest pain passed, when he could breathe in a more or less normal way again, when the truck was moving in a straight line, very fast now, the siren wailing like an urgent note sung out to his family six blocks away, Ernesto twisted his hips around so that he could get his right hand to the opening of his pants pocket. He bent his body and was able to get his fingers halfway down into the pocket, then farther. With the tip of his middle finger he could feel the yellow pill. He pushed farther, trapped the pill inside the first knuckle of that finger, and dragged it up the inside of his pocket. *Margarita and Ester*, he thought. He could see their faces, the innocence beaming from their eyes and mouths. *Margarita and Ester.*

Just as he had pulled the tablet up to the hem of the pocket, the truck's brakes squealed and he went sliding forward, turning at the last moment so that he did not hit the front wall head-on but took the force of it against his side. He screamed out in pain again as the cuffs cut into the skin of his wrists. The sound of his voice echoed in the metal box around him like the sound of a condemned soul calling from another world. The doors opened. A harsh light flew into the body of the truck. He felt two of the men take hold of his feet and pull, as if he were an animal—worse than an animal—and as his face scraped along the corrugated metal he saw the tablet in the harsh light, half an arm's length away, and then all chance for that was gone forever.

CHAPTER TWO

He was tall, trim, silver-haired, and most people called him by his last name—Volkes. He stood at the picture window of the presidential suite on the top floor of a famous Florida hotel and stared out at the sunny Atlantic. There were two other men in the room. After years of working with them, on what was probably the most delicate and most important project of his life, he had just a moment ago come to the certain conclusion that one of them was a betrayer. This was no ordinary betrayal, not merely a matter of money or power or sex; this would be a betrayal on the grand scale: of him personally, of the project, of the lives and hopes of millions of this man's former countrymen, living now less than a hundred miles away, beneath the boot heel of an aging dictator.

When Volkes understood this—and though he'd had flashes of suspicion before, he saw it now beyond even the smallest doubt—he made himself turn away. He stood, fingertips on the yellow windowsill, leaning slightly forward, in the posture of a great man contemplating the deepest moral questions. Really, though, he had simply not wanted to reveal anything in the muscles of his face. Not surprise, not anger, not the fact that he had dealt with betrayers before and had always somehow managed to spin them around on their own sour axis. He studied the breakers near the golden strand of beach. He thought back over more than thirty-five years spent in the pursuit of a fairer, more prosperous world. The good lives that had been lost during those years. The billions of dollars that had been spent. The hours that had been passed as if in front of an enormous chessboard, figuring eight, ten, fifteen moves in advance. That ability to see far into the future and calculate what others would do—it was, he thought, his one great skill.

So he would have to deal with this fellow now, this Oleg, this man he'd thought of as a friend. But he would have to deal with him in such a way that the friend, the betrayer, believed he was winning, believed he was winning, believed he had won . . . right up until the instant that he lost. Otherwise they would have no chance against him, no chance to defeat the organization that employed him.

CHAPTER THREE

———·-⋀⋁⋀w-———

It made Carlos Arroyo Gutierrez ill to ride in the back seat of moving vehicles. So, as always, when the black Volga pulled up in front of his house on the northeast side of Havana, he opened the front passenger door, not the back, and climbed in.

"*Buenos días,*" his driver, Jose, said. Jose had not shaved this morning.

"Out all night again?" Carlos chided him.

Jose pulled into the road and slid his tired eyes sideways so that they almost met his boss's. "I never stay all night at a woman's place, Ministro," he said. "On principle." And then, when they'd driven half a block, "I found an hour's sleep somewhere."

"You are haunting the tourist hotels again?"

"Some very beautiful foreign women visit here, Ministro."

"You are using protection?"

"I am well protected, Ministro. Against diseases, against my enemies, against despair. Only not against a lack of sleep."

"Let us hope, then, that today you aren't called upon for some difficult duty."

"I already have been."

Carlos heard the tiny catch in his friend's voice. *Ya me lo ha encar—gado*. He had made a career of hearing such things. Amid the vicious infighting of Castro's inner circle, careful listening had saved his career, perhaps his life, many times. "Meaning?"

"Meaning." Jose paused and glanced over at him. "Meaning I received a call this morning, five minutes before I left, directing me to take you to see the Dentist."

"Ah," Carlos said quietly. And then, once he'd let the words digest: "Why didn't he call me himself?"

"An important question, Ministro, no?" *Una pregunta importante.*

They went along through the fragrant morning, out of the Siboney neighborhood where the military officers, cabinet members, and supreme court justices lived, and immediately into the slum that was La Vivora. Already at this hour small barefoot children ran on the broken pavement, waving their brown arms and screeching, watched by stick-thin *abuelitas* on stoops. Above and around them the buildings were crumbling. Each day more pieces of pastel stucco flaked off the walls; each day Carlos expected to see another ochre-colored, overcrowded apartment house that had stood for a hundred years, lying on the ground in ruins. It would be a building that had lived through hurricanes and revolutions, through the salacious gleam of festivals and the dull half shadow of depression. And then, one day it would have had enough, its strength would have finally abandoned it, and in one moment what had seemed cracked and troubled but whole would be lying in a pile of stones, dust, and death.

"Nervous?" Jose asked him nervously.

"My conscience is clean," Carlos said.

"Still. The Dentist."

"The Dentist is not a sane man. Everyone knows that."

"Almost everyone, *sí*."

"Did he call you himself?"

"Yes."

"A good sign."

"Yes. Perhaps." Jose sank a bit lower in his seat, the curved scar on his chin twitching, the wrinkled brown sport jacket hanging from his huge shoulders like a bedsheet draped across two corners of a stone wall. He was brave and wise, educated far beyond his station in life, and Carlos considered him a friend. Six months earlier, Jose's wife had left him for another man—even the Revolution couldn't prevent such misfortunes—and his revenge had been to go on a kind of march of seduction, sleeping with as many women as time and energy allowed. Even with his privileged position—driver and bodyguard for the minister of health—it was dangerous for him to be seen in the hard-currency hotels where foreign tourists stayed. Those hotels were his favorite hunting grounds. It occurred to Carlos, really for the first time, that in Jose's case there were extra risks involved in such recklessness. He wouldn't have behaved that way without the sense that he was protected. But on that warm morning, he was ferrying the man who was his protection to the Montefiore prison. Otherwise known as the Torture House.

Carlos had been there numerous times—for health inspections—though he had never, of course, participated in the torture of anyone, and he had never been summoned in quite this abrupt a manner. Early on, he had spent countless hours with the Dentist, otherwise known as Colonel Felix Olochon Marlos, and had learned to despise him. Olochon, now head of the dreaded D-7, had been with Fidel from the start, had grown up, like so many of Fidel's followers (though not Fidel himself), in the humiliation of the most extreme poverty, his father a cane field worker, a *campesino,* a *machetero,* the lowest of the low, and his mother little more than the town whore. Harvest by harvest, beating by beating at the hands of the foreman and slightly more fortunate children, a kind of monumental anger had been planted and nourished in Olochon, a fury the size and depth of an ocean. When the first whispers of Fidel's campaign had reached the little town that housed the Olochons, Felix—then only seventeen—had required about three minutes to put what he owned into a burlap sack and run off to the mountains to join the great cause. His anger had been like an ugly brother to Fidel's, his ego like a twisted reflection of a twisted reflection. He had been merciless, hacking to pieces the bodies of the *batistianos,* grinning his toothy teenaged grin, spreading a rumor of terror that flowed down toward the capital like a mountain river before the hurricane has quite arrived. There were those who claimed Batista had fled the country, not because of Castro or the sentiments of the Cuban people, but because of the boy who enjoyed killing. Olochon.

Fidel had used him, of course. Brilliantly. And once the Revolution had achieved its aim, there was another use for him. Now the dissidents knew him, intimately. The traitors to the Revolution knew him. The little girl and boy whores of the slums knew him. The sound of his name, merely the sound of his name, ran in cold spirals around the backbone of anyone—even those with the clearest of consciences—who'd ever had a negative thought about the Revolution or its creator. For true conspirators and traitors, for the likes of him now, Carlos thought, the name was a sharp hot spike through the groin.

There was nothing the Dentist would not do, nothing. He was not bound by the thinnest filament of moral compunction, and there was not a soul in the government, perhaps in all of Cuba, who failed to understand that. Carlos had long ago formed the notion that on the day Fidel died, he himself would go to Olochon's office with a pistol and shoot him through the forehead so that he would not become the successor. For the sake of the future of Cuba, even if it meant sacrificing his own life, he would do that.

Beside him, as they rode through the streets and into the heart of the capital, he could feel the apprehension emanating from Jose like a bad smell. In the cool morning, the steering wheel was as slick as if it had been oiled. "Not to worry, my friend," he said, and to his own surprise the words came out with a calm force.

"I'll accompany you inside if you want," Jose offered.

"For what? To make Olochon think we have something to worry about? Wait for me outside, as always. The Revolution is a severe mother, but even severe mothers don't pull out the teeth of their loyal children. Even the Dentist needs his minister of health."

"Absolutely," Jose said, but the tiredness in his voice had been replaced by something else.

CARLOS TROTTED UP the stained steps of the prison's entrance, and, on the broad landing, paused to tug the cuffs of his shirt down from the sleeves of his suit jacket. On either side of the door, muscular, iron-faced guards—D-7 through and through—saluted him. The guards just inside the entrance were creatures of a different sort, just peasant boys, as simpleminded as they were loyal. He'd spent years working among such people, treating their wounds, delivering their wives' babies. They were here because they had been given a clean uniform, promised three meals a day, and told that Olochon himself would come find them if they deserted. There were more salutes. "Olochon," Carlos said confidently, and the guard shouted twice into a half-broken microphone and then pretended to busy himself with the papers on his desk. In ten seconds another guard came into the foyer, saluted Carlos yet again, and gestured for him to step first through the heavy glass and metal-barred doors and into the prison.

It was as it had always been there. Damp concrete walls, the smell of feces, blood, and terror, the sounds of clanging metal echoing down the corridors; cells with lice-infested shadows sleeping in them, and from the upper floors—where the political prisoners were housed—the sounds of screaming and moaning, men and a few women driven insane by hunger, vermin, rotting skin and various unspeakable tortures, wailing out hopelessly toward the vacuum at the center of the universe. To Carlos, this was nothing less than a vision of hell six feet from his face. As he walked he felt an electric anger in his fingers. Those men and those few women had committed such horrible crimes, hadn't they? Maligning the great leader in print, or too often in the street; making one of the wry political jokes Cubans had thrived on before Castro; trying to fly out of the country, or float away from it, or not reporting someone else, a sister or father, who had gone north. Compared to the crime in his brain now, Carlos thought, already in place in his interior world, these transgressions were nothing . . . and look at the penalty. He tried not to think about what they would do to him if the plan failed, but one thin line of fear ran straight up the bones of his back. He lifted his chin and marched on.

"The elevator is broken," his escort informed him at the end of the corridor, and they turned toward the steps. An old woman in a black dress was mopping them. At the sound of the guard's boots on the stone, she cowered against the wall, turning her face down and away. For Carlos, this small gesture was worse even than the screams. Afterward, he told himself, after this thing is finished, there will be no old women cringing in a place like this. Whatever had been done to her would no longer be done to human beings in the nation of Cuba. He vowed that on the souls of his parents and his late wife.

He and his escort climbed the three flights side by side. Though he had turned sixty the previous October, Carlos kept himself in good condition, and at the top he was breathing no harder than the young guard. They went along another dank corridor, to a door near the end on the right. The guard rapped hard, twice, and waited to hear the Dentist's voice before he saluted yet again and marched away.

CHAPTER FOUR

Carolina Anzar Perez was almost sure she was being followed. She turned and backtracked through the streets of downtown Miami, glancing in the rearview mirror every few seconds. A dark green SUV kept appearing behind her, fading away, reappearing.

At last, when she believed she'd shaken it, she drove across the drawbridge to the place she thought of as Brickell Key, pulled her white Roadmaster convertible into the underground garage of its tallest building, and waited several minutes, just inside the door, to see if the SUV would turn in, too.

Nothing.

The garage attendant waved at her impatiently. He was a man about her own age, tall, muscular, skin as black as coal. He commanded her forward with a jerky, scolding movement of his left hand. "How long?" he asked, when she pulled up beside him and stepped out. His words echoed harshly against the concrete, a short string of bad notes, off-key, toneless. An exile from Port-au-Prince, she was sure, full of the anguish of that place. She didn't know why the sound of his voice bothered her so much on that day—maybe it was the sense of some old bitterness he'd carried with him across the Caribbean. Or maybe it was not being fully at peace with what she was about to do.

"*Mwen pap rete' la lontan,*" she answered, trying to soften him up. But the brown eyes stayed on her coldly; his face hardened. She'd spent months working in Haiti, years studying the language; her Creole was nearly as perfect as her Spanish, it couldn't be that. It must be just the sound of that language on the tongue of a pretty, blond, Cuban American woman driving an outrageously nice car. It was misery meeting opulence, the hard world meeting the soft, a story as old as Miami, the hot, roiling city at her back. She turned and walked toward the elevator and thought she heard the attendant hissing.

On the fourteenth floor the elevator opened into the lap of luxury itself: glass doors with *Mandarin* written across them in a flowing gold script, and beyond them real Chinese vases holding calla lilies, a small cocktail lounge of leather upholstered armchairs, and the perfectly calibrated Bach concerto sliding out from invisible speakers. The tables—less than half of them occupied at this hour on a Tuesday—stood before her like white-clothed servants in rows. And when the slim Chinese hostess greeted her with a mellifluous "Good afternoon," there wasn't so much as a speck of world-to-world friction in her voice.

Carolina said, "I'm having lunch with Roberto Anzar," and the hostess tilted her head with a studied mix of dignity and servility, the lick of a smile catching the corners of her lips. She put one of the black menus into the crook of her arm, held it against her breast, and walked between two rows of tables and out onto a balcony overlooking the Intracoastal Waterway. There was only one patron out here on a sunny day, and it crossed Carolina's mind that it would be just like her uncle to have paid off the manager of

Mandarin to keep everyone else out of earshot. Roberto sat far to the right, his back to the wall, of course, his tired eyes gazing out languidly at the turquoise water, the string of small yachts, and the blue and silver buildings of the city beyond, two of which he owned.

When he saw her approach, her uncle got to his feet, took her hand in both of his, and kissed her softly on the right cheek. "*Angelito,*" he said. He tugged the arm of her chair a few inches closer to his and waited for her to sit.

"How are you, Uncle?" She edged the chair back an inch away from him. He was jowly and pink but perfectly shaved, his white hair swept back grandly from a high forehead, his nose just like Castro's nose, an almost exact replica. Such a persistent irony, she thought, because Fidel Castro had been her uncle's lifelong obsession, the man he despised more than any soul on earth.

In answer, Roberto shrugged his sagging shoulders. "Eh, I am a person who eats and drinks anger. I make love with anger."

"You've been that way for forty-five years," she said. "It keeps you young." She watched the quick flash of vanity cross his eyes, and then the waiter was there, and her famous uncle was asking about the specials as if it was his first time at Mandarin, as if there were a hundred foods he couldn't tolerate for medical reasons. It was supercilious, she thought, annoying, just another manifestation of the power he wielded, the privilege in his life. But then he turned to her with all the graciousness of Old Havana, asked if she would mind allowing him to choose their luncheon menu—he knew her likes and dislikes so well. And he put his hand on the waiter's arm as if they were brothers, and listed his desires like a beloved commander—the appetizer, the wine, the main courses spiced in a particular way—so that the waiter left their table feeling as if he'd just been addressed by God.

When they were alone again, Roberto looked out over the water, blinked twice, and faced her. "The position goes well?"

"Thrilling days and boring days."

"Atlanta still suits you?"

"I'm a tropical girl. The winters there are too cool for me. I'm glad you convinced me to buy an apartment here."

"But you hardly use it," he said.

Carolina shrugged and looked away. In a moment, the waiter brought a plate of Peking dumplings, browned in oil, glistening. She and her uncle began to eat.

"You have a man?"

A little twist of pain went scampering through the middle of her. Uncle Roberto had always been able to find the tender places in her, prod and poke them, bring tears up behind her smile. "Three men," she said, and he threw back his head and roared out a laugh that rang across the empty balcony and through the albums of her childhood. Instantly, the sound brought back a chain-link-enclosed yard in Little Havana, women pulling apart cooked chicken meat in the kitchen, men in *guayaberas* playing cards and cursing communism. "Do you have a woman, Uncle?"

She expected him to mention his beloved late wife, but he nodded, surprising her. Then he smiled his devious smile and said, "My woman," and paused. "My woman is the anger we just spoke of."

The dumplings had been served so promptly that she wondered again if he had instructed the people in the kitchen to prepare something ahead of time. Had the ordering been merely a charade? With her uncle, one never knew: Roberto Anzar lived behind a dozen veils; invested his money in a thousand secret places; had friends who devoted their lives to work they could never speak about. Every gesture and word could have been sincere, or it could have been part of some intricate deception, a three-dimensional game of chess in the dark. He loved her, as she loved him, but over the years a shadow of mistrust had found its way into their relationship, the dark lining to a bright tropical garment.

On the heels of their dumplings, the main course followed with perfect timing. Scallops and vegetables in extra spicy garlic sauce for him, and for her the Mandarin's specialty: sesame chicken with mangoes. Uncle Roberto had chosen a California sauvignon blanc, something perfectly un-Latin. She wondered if it might be his way of mocking her. But he raised, as always, a toast to the thing they both dreamed of: a free Cuba.

They ate for a time without looking at each other. Through the warm afternoon a sweet breath of ocean air arose and whisked bits of dust and grit along the edges of the balcony, lifting the hems of the tablecloths as if they were women's skirts. Roberto ate with great delicacy and care. As she sometimes did with men who took her to lunch, Carolina looked at his hands and mouth and imagined him making love with those same manners— precise, appreciative, but with some uncontrolled lust, some danger, at the edges of things. "They say the taste buds gradually die as one ages," he said, "but I have not found this to be true." He lifted his glass a second time. "To the sense pleasures."

She drank and waited, wrestling with one devil of doubt. She had done so many difficult things in her life. But she did not know if she could do this. She consoled herself inwardly, encouraged herself: If what you did ultimately helped people—the Cuban people especially—then it had God's blessing. She had been raised on that belief. It had come, in the beginning, from the lips of the man sitting opposite her.

Still, she hesitated. She watched his handsome face carefully. Intent on the food, he spoke without looking up: "Usually you come to dine with your uncle if you happen to be in Miami." He pronounced it the way all the Cubans of his generation did— *Mah-yammi*. "This time, your uncle thinks you happen to be in *Mah-yammi* in order to dine with him."

"My uncle is either spying on me, or he can read my face like a book."

"Both. Both true, *Angelito*. I have men watching you, you must know that already. I have friends in the phone company listening to you . . . cameras in both your apartments. And you are like a daughter to me, closer than a daughter, so I have always been able to read everything beneath the skin of your beautiful face." There was a pause, one beat—as if to make her think that all of it might be true—then his gentle laugh.

"Well, then you know already why I'm taking you to lunch."

"*I* am taking *you*, *Angelito*."

"Nothing new there. I've never yet paid for one of our meals."

"And you never will. I accept the ways of the modern *norteamericano* man only as far as a certain line." He chewed the last morsel of his last scallop and washed it down with the sauvignon blanc. "And the purpose of our meeting, aside from the love we have for each other and for the ones we knew who have gone?"

She started to look around at the empty tables, at the doorway leading back into the restaurant. It was a reflex as old as her career. Roberto immediately sensed it and put two fingers on her right wrist. "You can speak freely here, *Angelito*. This is my place, my city."

Looking into his eyes again, she thought of a particular summer night in their home, a party for the birthday of some nephew or niece. She couldn't remember who it was now. What she could remember was her father—Roberto's younger brother—knocking on her door and coming into her room, late, when everyone had gone and she was half lying, half sitting on her bed with a book. She could picture, still, her father's powerful forearms and the web of small scars around his eyes. "Your uncle will be president of Cuba someday," he'd told her. "On the day our land regains its freedom, he will be there." The men had been drinking rum, and the women Rioja, and she had been sixteen, restless, without authority, without courage. The name she was about to speak had been haunting them then. It haunted them still. She said: "We have reason to believe that Fidel will not be alive in another short while."

Roberto's face did not change. He seemed to be studying her, curious, perplexed, perhaps disappointed. After a long moment he said, "Forgive me. I love you. You know with what strength and depth I love you. But over the past forty years I have heard this so many times."

"I know you have. But this time is different. I can't speak more specifically, even to you, Uncle. I'm surprised you've had no information from your people there."

He shrugged, giving nothing away.

She tried again: "Have you heard anything?"

"Zero. Other than what has been in the press."

Good, she thought. Perfect. She said: "For the time being this should go no further than between you and me, but he is not long for this world."

"He is truly ill, then," Roberto said, without emotion. "Suffering, I hope."

"Not seriously ill as far as we know. But approaching the end of his life. That's all I can say, though I can say it with some confidence."

"Ah." He raised his glass, half closing his eyes so she could not read them. "A week? A month? A decade?"

"Less than a decade."

"But more than a week?"

"A few months, roughly. I can't say more specifically than that."

"Ah."

"Aside from what the constitution says about Raul—which no one pays any attention to—there are no real provisions for a successor, as you know."

He nodded and went into his Castro imitation, waggling one long finger and shaking his cheeks: " 'I haven't had time even to consider such a thing as a successor' he says, and the world lets him get away with saying it."

"One possibility is Raul, of course, which would mean more of the same."

"Worse than the same," Roberto said.

"You know about the other likely successors. Someone from the Council of Ministers, Crian, perhaps. Or Escalante from Foreign Affairs."

"I dream of them frequently," her uncle said, sipping his wine. "Nightmares."

"But there could be someone else. In the first weeks, especially, there is the possibility of chaos: looting, armed gangs doing battle with his thugs. We expect, at the very least, that there will be a period of instability. We expect his propaganda machine to suggest that the United States government had a hand in his death, which, of course, would not be true."

"Of course not," Roberto said calmly. He held the stem of his wineglass but made no move to lift it. His eyes were a quarter closed, brown as coffee beans, steady as stars. "America has tried to kill him so many times. Why should it be America that finally succeeds? Why not old age? A jealous lover? The Monarchy of Monte Carlo?"

Carolina frowned and waited two beats. "We don't want to find ourselves in the position of reacting to events."

"By 'we' you mean . . . ?"

"The organization I work for now."

"Ah," he said. "The famous White Orchid." And now surely he was mocking her, showing that he knew the nickname only insiders knew, and making it sound foolish, a child's club. "But this 'we'" he went on, "could also mean the United States of America, could it not, *Angelito*?"

She watched him from behind her smile. "We like to think that our objectives and the objectives of the United States of America often overlap."

"Often but not always."

"I love this country as you do," she said.

"But you were employed by its government once and now you are not."

"And you'll never forgive me for leaving. The government, or the husband who recruited me."

He made his classic expression of pretend-hurt, lifting the thicker ends of his eyebrows, turning down his lips. "I love you more than any creature on earth, *Angelito*. Surely you know that."

"Uncle, after Fidel is gone there is the possibility of anarchy. Think about this—anarchy, ninety miles from the American mainland. Think of what that would mean for the United States, for Cuba, Venezuela, for all of Latin America. To the extent possible, we want to control the events of the street. We want, eventually, to give the people a chance to have their country returned to them—"

"And property returned to those who lost it?"

"Some kind of compensation," she said. "It's unrealistic to hope that the million and a half Cubans in this country can return and take up residence in their old apartments, work their old fields, play Mozart on their old grand pianos."

"Ah," he said. "*Unrealistic.*"

"There is an entire mechanism in place in Cuba now, an establishment of fear and lies, and that establishment—"

"You don't have to tell me of that establishment, *Angelito*. Nor of the possibilities after he has gone. I have spent decades contemplating those possibilities, preparing for them, waiting for the moment. You don't have to educate me about my homeland."

"Of course not. I'm sorry."

He was leaning two inches closer now. She could smell the garlic on his breath. "And other than the fact that this mysterious and sudden conclusion to Fidel Castro's ugly reign will mean I shall live to see my country free again, perhaps be able to return and at least look at the property that was stolen from my family . . . other than this, and the love you have for your uncle, why did you call on me, *Angelito*?"

"We want you to assist us with your contacts here and in Cuba."

He nodded, almost seemed to smile. "Naturally. And at great risk to them, no doubt."

"They're already at great risk. There is no hope of anything good without risk. I risk my life every other week. You've risked your life for almost fifty years in one way or another."

He blinked slowly, once, twice.

"You have a web of friends, admirers, and contacts here and in Cuba that even we can't rival. Military men. Political figures. Journalists. In the hours immediately following Fidel's death, we want you to get word to them to maintain order. We want you to counsel Cuban Americans not to expect too much in the way of compensation, not to take any action at first, not to suppose that they can return to their—"

"So that they will be that much more easily manipulated."

She watched him again. She wondered, momentarily, if someone who did not know him at all should have been given this assignment, if they were too close, too aware of each other's vulnerabilities. "You have to trust us or not trust us," she said. "The people who run the organization I work for—"

"Who are these people, *Angelito*? What is their purpose? What are their beliefs?"

"I've worked for them for eight years now, Uncle. I know their philosophy."

"But you don't know the actual people, not even their names, do you?"

"I know they want Fidel gone as much as you do, as much as we all do."

"Gone and replaced by what? A slightly less leftist regime?"

"Uncle. The people who run the organization I work for have the same set of beliefs as you and I. They are motivated by compassion. They want to see people live in freedom. Their worldview is based on one idea: that a free market means a free world. It's a very simple and very powerful idea, and so far it has proven correct everywhere on earth that it has been applied."

"You're giving me lessons in capitalism now, *Angelito*?"

"I'm trying to understand why you're resisting me. If I were a nephew and not a niece, would you resist like this? If the organization had sent a man you didn't know with the same proposal, would you resist? Do you really think we are going to remove a communist and replace him with a leftist?"

He shook his head sadly, but not in answer to the question. She felt as if she were losing him, had already lost him. She was sure, now, that Oleg should have sent someone else on this errand. She hesitated a moment, took a sip of wine, then played the last card in her hand. "If you are not interested, you are not interested, but the other thing I wanted to mention is that my superiors would like you to be part of the interim government, if you're willing. Part of, not head of—that position will have to go to someone who is presently living in communist Cuba."

That finally stopped him. He had heard everything else before. But this idea, that he would be called back, that he could serve . . . it reached him through almost fifty years of bad history, the death of both parents and his brothers and sister-in-law, the betrayal of his closest friends, the torture and murder of countrymen he knew and loved. He struggled for a moment to keep his confident mask in place, ashamed to show anything else to her. He looked at the wine as if afraid to lift it to his mouth. She pretended that the scraps of her sesame chicken with mangoes were as intriguing as a newly discovered Monet canvas, and shifted them this way and that on the plate until he was ready.

"It's real, then," he said. "We won't have to wait for him to die of old age or resign because of ill health."

"Absolutely real."

"You know," he began, then he stopped and bored his eyes into hers. "You know what a sin it would be to give your uncle false hope in a situation like this, at his age."

She knew exactly what a sin it would be, precisely what a sin it would be. She made her face blank, then let some hurt leak into it. "I wouldn't lie to you," she lied. "Ever."

He watched her with what almost seemed like admiration. He said, "No, you would not. I apologize," but she couldn't be sure he meant it. Her bloodline carried a gene for efficient deception. It was one of the reasons she was so good at what she did, and one of the reasons he was. He watched her more intently. She knew that, if he had decided to trust her, he would begin talking about her father and mother, the old days along Eighth Street Southwest, Calle Ocho. He said, "You know, your father was a very courageous man. A brave man among brave men. I promised him I would watch over you, promised I would keep you always from becoming entangled in the web that man has woven around our lives."

She thought, for just an instant, that he was referring to her ex-husband. But that marriage was something Roberto never spoke about. It was Fidel, he meant. The Evil One. Sometimes it seemed to her that Cuban Americans invested Castro with blame for everything from their lost haciendas to the ear infections of their children. "That was never a promise you could keep."

"But I made it sincerely."

"I know you did, Uncle."

"We live in the rubble of ruined promises, you and I and the rest of us."

"I know that. I'm trying to take those stones and rebuild some small good thing. I left the government because they wouldn't let me focus on that problem, because there were too many obstacles—legal, bureaucratic, financial, political. You never understood that I left the government *because* I wanted to work for Cuba. I've devoted the last eight years of my career to preparing for this assignment. And not just to make you proud and happy."

"No, but always you had me in mind."

"Always. And always I thought you put too much faith in the United States government. They use you, Uncle. They—the Republicans especially—use Cuba for their own political ends."

"Only the Republicans have ever done anything for us, *Angelito*."

"What have they done? The man is still in power. The people of the country are still in chains. It's been forty-seven years, Uncle, and how many Republican presidents?"

"Five. I have given money to all of them."

"What have they done?"

He shrugged, looked out sadly over the waterway, and said, "They did not, at least, take a little boy away from his family at gunpoint."

Elian Gonzalez had been, to the older generation of Cuban Americans, a symbol of some imagined old Cuba, the perpetual innocent victim. A symbol of their own stolen innocence. Cuban to the bone, she still could not imagine what it would be like to have had a life like her uncle had known in Cuba, and then to have it torn away from you. Whatever their differences, she always acknowledged that pain in him. "You knew I would act," he went on, "if you asked me to act in this way."

"No, I didn't know that. I still don't. I wonder if your woman will mind."

"My woman?"

"Your anger. I've always wondered if you could keep it out of the room long enough to do something like this the way it must be done."

He looked away and made a series of small nods, and she believed she could actually see a bruise on the huge, proud creature that seemed to surround him like a larger self. She hated that Latin pride, that machismo, the boys on the corner of Calle Ocho with bare arms hooked around their girlfriends' necks. Their swagger, their loud cars, their violence. They were the offspring of a humiliation that stretched back five hundred years, beyond Castro to the cane fields of Camagüey and Oriente, and beyond them even to the Spanish galleons. Those boys, some of them so deliciously handsome, had tried to hook their arms around her and she had sprinted as fast and as far as it was possible to go . . . and then found herself being tugged gently back again, not all the way back, but closer, into her Cubanness, one high-heeled foot feeling around tentatively in the old world.

"How life moves," Roberto said. "Now it is you leading and the old uncle following." He swallowed. Looking into her eyes, he said, "I will risk my own life for you. And I will risk the lives of the men and women I love for you."

Which was all she had come to hear. For a few moments then

she was almost overcome by a wave of guilt. They would perhaps need her uncle's contacts in Cuba and Miami, but not in the way she had promised, not for the event or its immediate aftermath, but much later. He would be part of the new Cuba, yes, but his role would be tiny and symbolic, a bridge to the Miami Diaspora, and she tried to imagine him shrinking his pride down far enough to fit it. Perhaps, when he found out the actual size of his involvement, the actual details of what her employers called the Havana Project, he would never speak to her again.

"We will need that very soon," she said.

"*Claro, comandante,*" he answered, with some irony. It was Castro's title.

"Has the situation in the military changed at all?"

"Not to my knowledge," he said. "Not since they arrested Davos."

Good again, she thought. "But you still have your contacts there?"

"Of course."

"And you could get word to them on short notice?"

"Absolutely. But if I were to do that, if I were to risk their lives in that way, again, I would need a guarantee from you that this time the odds of failure are extremely low."

"I guarantee it with my life," she said.

"How can you, *Angelito*?"

"Because I am going there myself."

"To kill him?"

"The United States will have no part in his death."

"Earlier you said the United States *government* will have no part in his death. You no longer work for the United States government."

"To the extent humanly possible, I guarantee it."

He watched her for a long time without blinking. "Then I shall offer my assistance in any way you ask."

She nodded. They let a silence grow between them, a silence made up of two parts warm family unity and one part pure difference. Old conversations, old hurts rose and burst in the air around her like a silent fireworks display. She willed herself to ignore them. For a minute or two, she and her uncle tried to shift back into lighter talk, but there was too much weight in the air between them now for that. He wanted details—the time, the method, the chosen successor, how the DGI and armed forces would be dealt with—and she could not provide them. He pressed her, gently, seductively; and with each "No," each molecule of misinformation, she placed another layer of hard shell over herself. It was, she could see, maddening to him. Here was a man who, simply by the power of his personality, his fortune, and his family name, commanded the loyalty of people he had not seen in decades. He could buy and sell small cities. After the death of his wife, he'd had a string of remarkable women in his life. And now a rebellious, stubborn, thirty-five-year-old niece was frustrating him like this.

"I'll contact you," she said, when he had secured the check and was holding it down beneath the palm of one hand so she could not look at it. "Indirectly the next time, but soon."

"I am," he said gravely, "the master of waiting."

She kissed him with some warmth, then turned away and walked calmly back through the restaurant doors, rode calmly down in the elevator, and retrieved the beautiful car that did not belong to her. She handed the Haitian man a ten-dollar tip as a sort of apology for her apparent wealth, as an offering to the

Caribbean gods for the sin she had just committed. And then she was driving over the bridge toward downtown Miami, on the verge of tears, glancing in the rearview mirror every few seconds, as if expecting the ghosts of the past to be standing on her bumper.

CHAPTER FIVE

———·∿∿∿∿·———

When Carlos entered Olochon's prison office, the Dentist was washing his hands in a small bathroom with the door open and humming along happily and off-key with a tune on his radio. Carlos looked at his powerful back—which was still, after all these years, the back of a cane cutter—and tried to make out the tune. Olochon was splashing away at first, and then seemed to be cleaning his fingernails. He glanced in the mirror as if he hadn't been expecting anyone, hadn't made any calls that morning, but when he recognized Carlos he smiled, his teeth angling out, hideous even from this distance. Olochon spent a long time drying his hands with a small white towel—as if he might rub away all the suffering those hands had caused over the decades—then turned and came out to greet his visitor.

"Sit, my friend and comrade, sit," Olochon said, showing the teeth again, as if he was proud of them. His face was square as a concrete block, with short-cropped gray hair above a flat forehead. The eyes were large and dark, set over a straight nose. He might have been handsome had it not been for the mouth, but the mouth was grotesque, the lips mashed and scarred from early beatings, the yellow front teeth too large by half and slanting forward as if something had been pulled out from between them by force years before. Olochon was wearing fatigues with the stars of a colonel sewn onto the epaulets, and combat boots—his work clothes. He sat behind his desk and rested his immaculately clean hands on its surface. Carlos sat opposite him.

"Forgive the unusual summons," Olochon said. "I called you at home first but the line was busy, and then no one answered, so I tried Jose."

This was a lie, of course. Olochon opened his mouth and snakes came out, a mass of swirling snakes, hissing and flexing. Carlos nodded and did what he could to maintain a pleasant, slightly distracted expression.

"The phone lines have gotten so bad," Olochon went on.

This was not a lie, but a trick. Olochon was hoping to elicit some complaint, some criticism of the regime. Carlos said, "My lines are fine."

"Yes, in that neighborhood." Olochon, who lived in the same neighborhood, looked out the barred window at the roof of the rest of the prison. His ugly smile slowly disappeared. "Ah, the troubles we have," he said.

"Anything in particular? We had talked about tuberculosis last time. Has there been—"

Olochon chuckled. "Illnesses in the prison don't worry me as they worry you," he said. "Illnesses among rats, among vermin. We don't let the sick ones leave; it's as simple as that. Ever. They don't leave, they don't infect anyone but themselves."

"And the guards?"

"Our guards have little contact with rats and vermin."

"They breathe the same air."

Olochon worked his lips thoughtfully over his teeth, lazily

raised his eyebrows, and gazed around the bare-walled room a moment to give the foolish subject time to leak away. From beyond the door came muted cries and wails. Even the radio music could not quite drown them out. "I didn't call you—that is, *ask* you—here to talk in your official capacity, Carlos, but in your unofficial."

"I wasn't aware that I had an unofficial capacity."

Olochon turned his dark eyes on him and watched without blinking. "As adviser to the regime," he said, at last.

"My advice is not worth as much as it used to be."

The eyebrows went up. "No?"

Carlos shook his head.

"Your passion for the Revolution has been dampened?"

"No more than yours, Felix. Every new move of the *norteamericanos* reignites it. But I don't feel as sharp as I once did. I feel Fidel notices."

"He's had problems with you?"

"We're like brothers, we've always been. He loves and trusts me as I love and trust him. I serve as his personal physician, as you know."

"But?"

"But, outside the field of health, I don't feel I can offer him what I used to."

"Politically, you mean."

"He needs no help politically. I try now to stick to matters of health. AIDS, TB, sexual diseases brought to us by tourists from the capitalist countries. That's more than enough work for a man my age."

"No hobbies?"

"Gardening. Good cigars."

"No new women?"

"One. You know her. Elena. Not a substitute for Teresa, but a good and faithful companion. And you?"

A harsh laugh burst from Olochon's lips. He seemed unable to hold it in, and, once it was out, he seemed amused by it, as by the question. "Women my age have no appeal for me any longer."

"Ah."

"Young flesh now, only young flesh."

"Yes. The beauty of youth."

"The innocence," Olochon said.

"Yes."

"I deal in so much guilt, you see. Guilt everywhere. Stinking guilt all day and all night. For my private life I want the opposite, you see."

"Of course. You're busy then? Here, I mean."

"As always. We have uncovered . . . we are beginning to un-cover a massive web of anti-Revolutionary conspiracy. You cer-tainly must have heard about it."

"Fidel has not mentioned anything specific."

"No, but you must have heard."

Carlos could feel his heart thumping. It was only by a severe exertion of will that he managed to keep the expression on his face from changing. "I haven't."

"Not a whisper?"

"Nothing."

Olochon pursed his lips and looked away as if making it clear he knew he had just been lied to.

A leaden silence filled the air between them. Carlos knew that he should not break it, but sit calmly, looking from his interrogator to the stained stone wall behind him, and rest in an old friendship and comradeship that had never actually existed. He thought of Colonel Davos, who had died in this very prison. Driven insane with electric shocks. For the crime of being a man of principle, an honorable man.

Olochon began tapping the end of one long fingernail on the top of the desk, not quite in time with the radio music. "I tell you this in confidence, of course."

"Naturally."

"Through the diligent work of my men we have uncovered the tip—just the very tip—of another assassination plot. We haven't done enough work to be sure yet, but it seems to have its roots . . . where would you guess?"

"Miami."

"No surprise, is it."

"None."

"But the surprise is that this time it has—again, we are not certain so I probably should say *it seems*—it seems to have reached its ugly tendrils high up into our own government."

"How high?"

"Cabinet level."

"Military?"

Olochon shrugged.

Carlos watched him. "I'm picturing the various generals and colonels and going through possibilities," he said. "None of them believable."

Olochon continued tapping. "This building . . . what I have seen and learned over the years in this building is that the border that separates believable from unbelievable is nonexistent. People do surprising things, Carlos my friend. Believe surprising things. People change."

"Who then?"

"We don't know, but we will know. I have had the pleasure, over the past week, of enjoying a series of conversations with a person, a rat, who was arrested not long after making contact with a so-called tourist from one of the so-called sympathetic countries of Europe. In the course of these conversations I have been able to elicit certain information, very helpful to us, and the information points to an attempt to overthrow our government. This attempt is based, as you guessed, in Miami. The how, the when, the who exactly, this rat did not seem to have been privy to. I believe that, if he had known, he would have been kind enough to share that information with me. We were up all night more than once." Olochon looked at his hands. "Talking."

Carlos nodded gravely, and waited.

"Your name was mentioned," Olochon said.

Carlos shrugged. "I am a public figure."

"Of course. I meant nothing by it, I just hoped that perhaps there might be something, two small dots you could connect. Something you've heard. Something strange or even very slightly out of the ordinary that you've noticed."

Carlos pinched the muscles of his forehead and pretended to give the question some thought. "It's possible. I'll observe more closely. But nothing leaps to mind."

"Fine, then. Thank you. I'll see you at the cabinet meeting at eleven. No doubt you're expected at your office now."

Carlos looked at his watch and feigned mild surprise at the lateness of the hour.

"However," Olochon said after a momentary silence. "I was wondering if there is one thing you might do for me before you go. It's something you might enjoy, as I once enjoyed such things. This rat, you see. Well, there is nothing more to be gotten from him. I thought you might enjoy watching his, well, his departure."

Carlos felt breakfast rise into his throat. There was a slight twitch at the corner of his mouth. He was sure Olochon noticed.

"Nothing too gruesome," the Dentist continued. "The gruesome is behind us now. Something quick, a quick end. He's semidelirious, you see. I thought, I don't know what I thought. I thought that perhaps just the sight of you—a man with a history like your own, a history of selfless service to the Revolution—might squeeze one last drop of contrition out of him. I do this at times. I try to throw the rats off guard, to unnerve them. It is, some people say, my specialty."

As if pulling out their teeth one by one with a plumber's wrench isn't unnerving enough, specialty enough, Carlos wanted to say, but he held his eyes on the Dentist and waited. When the silence became unbearable, he said, "After all these years of trying to heal, I'm afraid I don't have the taste for presiding over an execution."

"A dangerous indulgence, my good friend. A softening that can be fatal. If the enemy came to our shores would you kill?"

"Of course. Naturally."

"You don't believe it's sinful, that you'll be punished afterward?"

"If there's sin, Felix, it's what existed before the Revolution."

"But this rat is an enemy, and he is on our shores, and you'll refuse even to watch as he meets his punishment?"

"I don't see the point in it."

"Squeamishness, is that it? Moral objection?"

"Hardly. Simply not my work."

"Well as a favor to an old friend, then?"

Carlos felt as if he'd been holding a hand of five cards, re-
fusals, all of them, and Olochon had cleverly made him play out
the suit. "Fine," he said, and as he pronounced the word he realized that from the moment he had first spoken openly to General
Rincon of his disappointment with Fidel Castro and the way the
Revolution had turned out, from that moment eighteen months
ago there had been a sort of dim, unbearable tone in the depths
of him, a premonition, something he knew would happen, something he knew he would have to witness, or do. Now it was as if
a curtain had just been moved aside, here in this office, and the
tone was clearly audible.

Olochon smiled. He went to the wall, snapped off the radio,
and took a long and perfectly clean white coat from a hook there.
"Put this on," he said happily. He had started to hum the tune
again, and this time Carlos recognized it. It was a song one heard
sung by the children of the ghetto when the rains ended: "*Viene
calor.*" The heat comes. "It will protect your fine Spanish suit and
fine white shirt. Let us go."

CHAPTER SIX

———— ⟋⟍|⟋⟍ ————

Carolina's departure from government service—the very thing that had caused the trouble between her and her beloved uncle Roberto—had resulted in a quadrupling of her pay. And so, for her visits to Miami, and for investment purposes, she had purchased a two-bedroom apartment in a gated community in Doral, at the city's western edge. She kept an entire second wardrobe there, and duplicates of almost everything she owned— makeup, computer, a complete kitchen. Once or twice since her divorce she'd had men over, and a few times a year she entertained old friends there, but for the most part it was her solitary retreat, the place she went to get away from the life she lived.

After leaving Brickell Key, she drove a short way to regain her composure, then pulled over, put the convertible roof down, and rejoined the highway traffic. The life she lived. The life she lived was a lonely life of constant small and not so small deceptions in the name of a great cause. It had become a life of almost continuous wariness. Not fear. She was rarely afraid. But everything in her working life had a shadow over it now, false fronts, a dimension not visible to the eye of the ordinary world. The ability to live in that other dimension had made her as successful as she was; it had also altered her personal life to the point where she had almost given up on her dream of finding another man, of having a good marriage and a house full of children. Almost.

More than anything at that moment she wanted to take the exit onto State Highway 112, head for Doral, and curl up there in front of the TV. The hour with Uncle Roberto had washed the solid earth out from beneath her feet, as she'd known it would. Something had begun to move inside her when she'd made the decision to leave the federal government and climb into this privatized, secret world. Today, at the Mandarin, that something had shifted into a new gear. She had the feeling, now, that it would not be stopped.

She had been keeping an eye on another SUV—all white this time—that kept appearing in her mirror then fading out of view. She pressed north on the highway, two miles above the speed limit. She was thinking about her uncle, glancing in the mirror every few seconds as if he himself might have charged someone with the duty of keeping a careful eye on her.

She took the exit at Boca Raton and moved slowly and impatiently in the traffic behind the beach. At Conch Street she turned—slowly, innocently, not like a woman trying to lose a tail—and then turned again into another basement parking garage, no attendant here. She waited, watched a white Ford Explorer pull in a minute or so behind her and park far off in the shadows. Why would she be trailed at this early stage, and by whom? Pro-Castro traitors? D-7 agents? Her uncle's people? Employees of the Orchid checking up on her?

She walked to the opposite corner of the garage and took an elevator to the eleventh floor, got off, then walked up the stairs to the fifteenth. No one followed her that far, she was quite sure. If, in fact, the driver of the Explorer was tailing her, he would probably decide to stay down in the garage, waiting for her to get back into her car . . . and it would be a very long wait indeed.

At the end of the hallway there was a window that looked out over Florida's Atlantic coast. She rapped twice on the last door and it was opened for her by a tall, thin man in his early fifties. She had never worked with him before. Spectacles, curly salt-and-pepper hair, eyes that might have been Cuban.

"Evan," he said, holding out a hand for a delicate shake. Last names were rarely used in the Orchid. "Ready to grow old?"

"As I'll ever be."

He gave her a pale green hospital gown, and she went into the bedroom, took off everything but her underwear, and draped the gown over her body. In the kitchen, the man motioned her to the sink, where he had set up shop, and he began by washing her hair, then bleaching the color out of it, then making it into a horrible mass of gray curls. He colored her eyebrows a matching gray. He worked the makeup into her face so thickly that it wrinkled naturally around her eyes and mouth when she smiled or spoke. Crooked blue veins appeared magically on her hands and temples. Real gold marble-sized earrings. A real pearl necklace. The man was a genius, an artist. He worked and worked, even placing tiny short hairs above her lip.

"Hollywood more fun or this more fun?" she asked him when they'd been at it for almost two hours.

"How did you know I came from Hollywood?"

"Lucky guess."

"It was more fun there."

"And you're not there because?"

"Because I like money."

"And the Orchid pays you more than the studios paid you?"

"Three times as much. I was just starting out on my own when they first approached me, and I was worried about that— no security, you know. The man I'd apprenticed for had once taught at Langley, disguises and so on. He gave them my name. I won't get fired here, won't go bankrupt. I'll retire at sixty-two with a nice fat severance package."

"And you will have performed a real service for the world."

"That, too. I have a condo on Eleuthera. A life planned out for myself there."

"With the wife and kids?"

"No wife. No kids."

"You're gay, then."

"No longer practicing," he said. "My sex drive died a couple of years ago. And may it rest in peace."

"There are pills now."

"I know. But I had enough sex in my life, and enough trouble from sex, and I just decided that if my body was telling me it was time to retire from all that, then I wasn't going to fight it. Plus, this kind of work is hard on relationships, don't you think?"

She sighed. *Hard* wasn't the word. His story was not so different from her own: a solitary life, compensated for by a fat pay-check and the promise of saving the world. Though it hadn't yet quite driven her to think about giving up sex. "What about loneliness? You won't know anybody there."

"I'll make friends. I might start a little disguise shop there, a party shop. I might cut hair, you know, just part-time."

"You do it well," she said, and he nodded his thin rectangular head, turned her around and handed her a mirror to show her his work.

She gasped.

"You in four decades," he said.

"A horror."

"You're quite an attractive seventy-year-old. You'll be the belle of the retirement community in forty years."

"I'll be seventy-five in forty years, not seventy. Thank you, though."

"You are absolutely gorgeous, you know," he said. "The real you, I mean. If the opinion of an old queer matters at all."

"I never know how to respond when people say that."

"I have a picture of you in my mind, your whole life—a husband as handsome as a magazine model. Three stunning kids."

"No kids," she said. "One ex-husband, that's all. I don't know about the model part, but he was nice-looking enough last time I saw him."

"What happened?"

Carolina did not want to go there. Her seventy-year-old face in the mirror was a glimpse into a lonely future. "I'm still figuring that out," she said, and Evan got the message, smiled sadly, and turned back to business.

"Your new clothes are hanging in the closet in the room where you changed. There's a handbag for your gun and things. I've sewn something into the dress at the top of your back to make it look as though you have a little hump there, and you'll be wearing special stockings that make your legs look . . . well, like the legs of a seventy-year-old. There's a cane, too. I'll give you a couple of walking lessons, just in case."

"I guess this means I don't get to drive the convertible to the airport."

"No way."

"*Claro,*" she said.

"What?"

"I understand."

"I've been instructed to tell you that your flight is at 6:15 P.M. Someone will meet you out front here and take you right onto the tarmac. Go out the front door and straight across the street to the pearl blue Camry. Someone else will meet you at the plane on the other end. The details are in the pocket of your dress, on a folded yellow sheet of paper in the wallet, in the small purse. You can take your own purse with you onto the plane but leave it there. Destroy the paper when you've read it. You'll have an ID in your wallet and you are to check into the hotel under that name. The person you will be meeting will contact you, so all you have to do is go up to the room and wait. There are mints in the purse in a blue tin. Take two of them a few minutes before you arrive at the hotel. They'll change your voice just enough to make everything believable, but talk as little as you can before the meeting."

"All set," Carolina said. "I can't wait to see the clothes. Who is the meeting with, do you know? Who and where?"

"I'm not in that loop," Evan said. "I'm a disguise master, that's all. No ambitions beyond that. They give me little bits of information to pass on, and I pass them on. Everything works better that way."

"Ever feel like they're testing you? Grooming you for something bigger?"

"Always to the first part. Never to the second." He patted Carolina on the shoulder and she went into the other room to change.

CHAPTER SEVEN

———⸺⁓⁓⁓⸺———

Carolina had been in disguise many times. Not only physical
disguise, of the kind she wore now, but a kind of moral or
psychological disguise as well. Once, still working for the CIA,
she had posed as a prostitute in West Berlin. The other agents had
been delayed, and she'd almost ended up actually having sex with
a vicious former Stasi member, now serving a life sentence in a
Frankfurt prison. Another time, in Mexico City, at the other
end of the moral spectrum, she'd turned herself into a nun for the
purposes of observing a man suspected of helping to arrange the
bombing of Pan Am 103. She spoke five languages almost without accent. She could shift gears from the speech and body
language proper to an elegant restaurant like the Mandarin to the
speech and body language proper to a bodega in East Harlem.
She could put five pistol rounds into the chest of a body-target
from 60 yards. At five foot five and 121 pounds, she could inca-
pacitate a man twice her weight with one kick. Other professional women she knew had trained for fifteen years to learn the
tax code inside out, to be able to negotiate a corporate merger
or convict a drug dealer in a court of law. She'd spent those
years—with two different employers—learning how to change

her identity, how to master deceit, conquer fear, kill or outwit some of the most heinous criminals on earth. She liked it.

The driver did not speak to her, which was just as well, though Evan had, as he'd promised, provided her with the tin of mints that altered her voice. From Boca Raton, they drove south again, hurtling down 95 and turning west into the mile-long ribbon of traffic that always seemed to wrap itself around Miami International Airport. She carried nothing but her own purse and the smaller one Evan had given her. The cane, she'd decided, had been overkill and she'd left it in the apartment. During the short walk across the tarmac to the private jet she sweated lightly beneath the makeup. Once the jet was airborne—she was the only passenger—she opened the new purse, took out the wallet, removed the folded-up piece of paper, and looked at the instructions.

MARRIOT COURTYARD MOTEL, RICHMOND, VIRGINIA.

Register under the name Mary Archibault—A room will have been reserved. Go into the room, leave the door slightly ajar, and wait.

She read the note three times, then used the shredder at the rear of the plane and flushed the pieces in the toilet for good measure. The flight lasted an hour and forty-five minutes, and during that time, sipping a Bombay and tonic from the wood-paneled bar and looking out over the brown, buckled earth of the western Carolinas, she found herself thinking again about her uncle, the famous Anzar, or, as he was known in émigré circles, the Grand One.

Uncle Roberto had grown up in one of the wealthiest families in Havana. His parents had started their married life as owners of sugar and tobacco plantations, and then parlayed money from international sales into a vast real-estate empire that included everything from casinos, downtown apartment buildings, and beachfront villas to thousands of hectares of coffee-growing land in the hills around Santiago. By the time he turned seventeen, in late 1958, Roberto—handsome, confident, poised beyond his years—was already being groomed to take over the family business. He was running a twenty-unit apartment house with only a gentle-handed overseeing by another uncle; he was sitting in as observer/apprentice on meetings of his father's board; on weekends he rode horses with his father in the rolling hot countryside outside of Camagüey and listened to impromptu seminars on the art of attracting and maintaining influential friends (although they despised him, Fulgencio Batista, Cuba's president, had for many years used one of their opulent beachfront villas free of charge).

But—and she'd heard this from family members and nonrelated Cuban émigrés alike—there had always been something different about Roberto Anzar. As a teenager he'd spent time with friends in the poorer sections of Havana. For a while he even had a romantic involvement with a twenty-year-old black woman who lived with her mother in what could only be called a shack. His father had put a stop to that, but Roberto's curiosity about and compassion for the poor persisted. His parents believed it to be a passing fancy, mere adolescent idealism. Four or five times a week Roberto could be found at morning mass in the Cathedral, and actually seemed to want to apply the words of Christ to his own situation, to the world around him.

Two days before Batista fled the country for the Dominican Republic, carrying $600 million in his people's money and riding in a plane supplied by the U.S. government, Roberto's father, two older brothers, and two close family friends were assassinated in front of one of their casinos and before Roberto's eyes, their limousine blown to pieces by some kind of homemade bomb. Four days later, two days after the government fell, when it was already becoming clear how Castro would greet the rest of the Anzar family, Roberto was shipped north—no relatives to meet him in Miami, no family friends, just a representative from the local church. His mother and surviving brother—Carolina's father—stayed behind. For a year and a half Roberto lived in a tiny room in a rectory, awaiting news of his mother, listening to the reports from what was now Castro's Cuba. When his mother and brother at last arrived, she was dirt poor, and she and her two sons rented half of a four-room house on Southwest 26th Avenue. She found the boy changed. Perhaps it was the trauma of seeing his father's body blown into wet bone and crimson shreds of tissue, or perhaps something had happened in the rectory during his stay there, but Roberto had lost his faith, lost his interest in helping the poor. Now he *was* the poor.

While his younger brother assumed the role of good son, Roberto fought, he whored, he ran with street gangs in Little Havana; in his junior year, he dropped out of high school. At nineteen he was working the door at an exotic dance club, while Carolina's father excelled in junior high school and trained in a boxing gym. When Roberto was twenty their mother died in her sleep. At twenty-one he found someone who could provide him with papers saying he had graduated from high school, kissed his younger brother good-bye, and enlisted in the U.S. Marine

Corps. He volunteered to go to Vietnam, where he fought and was lightly wounded in the early years of the American involvement.

He recovered from his wounds but retired suddenly from the Marine Corps under somewhat mysterious circumstances and returned to Miami. Carolina's father had left the city by then, and was training in New York, a light-middleweight with a hard left hook and lots of heart. Soon Roberto married—a woman from a military family, half of which had recently escaped Castro's Cuba—and the marriage squeezed the last of the troublesome rebel out of him. After bouncing around from one menial job to the next, he borrowed some money on the strength of his Marine Corps pension, bought a small truck, some rakes and mowers, and started his own one-man landscaping business, catering mostly to those Cubans who had already made a success of themselves in America. He studied these wealthy former countrymen, sought their advice and listened to them as he had listened to his father on the Sunday rides near Camagüey. And he worked twelve hours a day, six days a week.

Within two years he had a dozen employees, four trucks, contracts with several of the high-priced hotels in Aventura and Coral Gables. It turned out that he and his wife could not have children, a terrible blow to him; more terrible, he sometimes said, than anything he'd experienced in Havana or Nha Trang. This emptiness he filled with a kind of manic devotion to the business, which grew and grew. Twenty employees, forty-five employees, a fleet of trucks, contracts with the city's largest bank. He invested some of the profits in a nursery near Homestead, and then the profits from that in Doral real estate, a tract of marshy land in which no one else saw any promise. Miami, meanwhile, was evolving from a quiet provincial city to a cosmopolitan capital. On his thirty-fifth birthday Roberto sold the marshy lots to a developer for three-quarters of a million dollars, promptly used that to leverage a large loan, and invested in a one-third share of an apartment complex a block from North Miami Beach.

By the time he turned forty-five he had bought out his partners and owned the high-rise outright, along with the landscaping business and the nursery. By the time he turned fifty he owned two high-rises, and had set up all his surviving relatives and friends— including Carolina's father, a struggling ex-boxer and part-time handyman at this point—in businesses of their own: landscaping, Laundromats, motels, restaurant franchises. She remembered him arriving at their modest home in Little Havana, a god in a guayabera and a new Jaguar, glamorous wife on his arm, cigar in one hand, such a gleam of love and need in his eyes when he saw her. She had become the child he never had, and he heaped gifts on her—dolls, bicycles, dresses, private schooling, a trip to Paris when she turned sixteen, riding lessons, tennis lessons, a car.

Throughout these years he was building a reputation in the Cuban American community that was rivaled by no one. He found jobs for friends and the children of friends; he helped troublesome distant cousins avoid jail. He could pick up the phone and have the attention of the mayor and the governor and the state's two senators. He found ways to move illegally large sums of money to his relatives, and his wife's relatives, back in Cuba. He helped more than two dozen people escape—many of them military men fed up with Fidel's lies. His politics had veered sharply rightward, but he'd maintained his compassion for the oppressed, as long as they were the Cuban oppressed. It was natural that he should become involved with people who hated Castro. Natural that he'd give large sums of money to Republican politicians. Natural that he'd form certain mysterious alliances.

Carolina watched all this happen at closer range than most people. He confided in her, to the extent that he was able, hinted at some of the assistance he gave to the CIA, told her of a web of important contacts in the motherland—including a boyhood friend named Alejandro Davos who had risen far in the military ranks. Occasionally, he talked about anti-Castro conspiracies, assassination plots, a gleaming Havana future to match his gleaming Havana past. On the wall of his office he kept a framed list of the names of all the 124 exiles who had died in the disaster known as the Bay of Pigs invasion.

For her, it all became part of his aura—the looks, the cars, the gorgeous wife, the tragic absence of children, the heroic wartime service, the money, the grandiosity; and on top of all that, the intrigue. After her father's death from cancer at age fifty-four, Roberto had become a second father to her. He sent her to college, advising her to major in business. She had no interest in business, but she humored him, adding a minor in political science. She found she had a facility for languages and for the stage. In her senior year her uncle introduced her to Oscar Perez, who happened to work for an organization called the Central Intelligence Agency, and who happened to fall in love with her on the spot. They dated all through her senior year in college, the exotic twenty-five-year-old spy slipping into and out of her dormitory room like the promise of the future. Upon graduating, she was recruited, went to work in Langley, and married Oscar the day she turned twenty-two.

For seven years, while her uncle persistently tried to lure her back into his business empire, she labored away in various

outposts—they sent her to Spain twice, to Mexico City, to Indonesia. The marriage began to deteriorate almost immediately,
and, coincidentally perhaps, she and her uncle drifted apart. He
believed his gifts and love should have been properly repaid: If
she wanted to be a working woman, she should have been working for him. She should have taken over his business, just as he
would have taken over his father's, and those two deep disap-
pointments echoed back and forth inside him. Worse than that,
he believed she should have stayed married to Oscar, when that
marriage, for her, had become only a succession of miserable moments, the travel taking its toll, Oscar's professional deceit creep-
ing into their private lives, his Latino jealousy souring her career
success.

Deep down she believed that what Uncle Roberto really
wanted was for her to live the life of a wealthy Cuban mother
and homemaker, so that he might have his grandchildren vicari-
ously through her, so that he could arrive at her house with boxes
of gifts, let the children crawl up on his lap, kiss him, make a fuss
over him. So that he could groom them, too, to fit his vision.

And then she was approached by the organization she now
worked for—the White Orchid, everyone called it, founded by
men who remained miraculously anonymous. The Orchid was
staffed largely by former intelligence employees, funded—
according to rumor—by an invisible coalition of tremendously
wealthy conservative businessmen and former political figures of
both parties. When she'd left the CIA, her uncle had not even
known about the existence of the Orchid—at least that's what he
told her—and he had never completely trusted her after that.

Her life had become richer, more interesting, no longer
cramped by regulations and bureaucracy, but somehow less

honest. The assignments were strange, sometimes terrifying. Once, in Zagreb, she flirted with one of Europe's largest traffickers in illegal immigrants, for an hour in a bar—that was all. What happened during that hour, what eventually happened to the awful man, she did not know; her assignment was simply to keep him occupied, and she had done that, enjoyed the dangerous thrill. Another time, she was sent to Haiti in the guise of a journalist. Everything was magically taken care of—the false passport and press credentials, a slight alteration of appearance, weeks of training. She worked there as a freelancer for only a few months, just wandering the streets and returning to her dingy office in Port-au-Prince to file stories she was sure were never read by anyone. And then word came that she was to interview the leader of a communist faction—in the north, near Cap-Haitien. The faction was small but growing, the man himself mustachioed and rather unimpressive, though he granted her an interview as if granting her an audience with the Pope. She spent two hours asking him questions in a steamy hut in the middle of the jungle, filed a detailed report about his location, security arrangements, and demeanor, and then learned, a week later—through the newspapers, not through her boss at the time—that he had been assassinated. For a month she felt guilty, went to confess to a priest friend of hers, and considered other lines of work.

But soon after that, as if she had passed some test, her superiors began to show more interest in her. Obsessed with communism, she suspected, they turned her more and more in the direction of what they called The Cuban Question, and her understanding of the importance and rightness of her work returned. Hair dyed black, three bikinis in her luggage, she had traveled to the island twice with a false Italian passport, and was asked to do nothing more than swim, see the sights, note the layout of particular hotels, keep her eyes open, and make a verbal report upon her return. But if she had learned one thing about the Orchid it was that they were an extremely patient group of anonymous world-shapers, planning things for years, sometimes decades in advance. They collected bits of information from a hundred sources and then pulled one far-off string that tripped one gate, that moved one ball, that rolled along a chute, that emptied out in a pool of water, that splashed up on a wall. And that small damp stain changed the world, almost imperceptibly, but in precisely the way they wanted it changed.

After her third visit to Havana she was moved up a rank, paid more. She began to report to a man named Oleg Rodriguez, another Cuban American, a young, dashing fellow who met her at various locations dressed in three-thousand-dollar suits and smiling a great deal. Two months ago, Oleg had finally given her some information about the Havana Project, a few details, a general sketch of the greater plan. A month ago she had been told what her actual role in the Havana Project would be, and what kind of bonus she could expect if she survived it.

Two weeks ago she was asked to pay a visit to her uncle, deceive him slightly, mislead him, make him an offer he could not refuse. His contacts would be helpful, perhaps, but the Orchid would never risk the timing of their plan for the help of Roberto Anzar's people. So she was going to feed him a string of misinformation, a false plot about an assassination attempt, at a different time, in a different location, by different means. And this word would travel through invisible tunnels beneath the Straits of Florida into the minds of her uncle's people there—some of them already known to D-7, the secret arm of Castro's Dirección General de Inteligencia, or DGI. It was possible that a few of these people would be arrested, a few of them would talk, and the misinformation would throw off D-7 just enough to increase the odds of the real plan's succeeding.

Everything was a mask upon a mask. All for a good cause. But using people in that way, using innocent Cubans—using her uncle, especially—made Carolina more than slightly uneasy. She asked herself again and again what kind of end would justify these means. Sitting in the seat of the private jet, made up to look and feel like a woman not so far from the end of her days, she took a moral inventory and felt that the balance had shifted inside her. You did not lie to people you loved and come away unscathed. And so she found herself wondering, just for a few lonely minutes, if her uncle's plan for her life would have been, after all, the better one.

On a whim, as the plane descended, she decided not to fasten her seat belt. She tried to see if just by a small exertion of the abdominal muscles, she could maintain her balance as the floor tilted downward. Everything went fine until, at the moment of landing, a small breeze jerked the fuselage down sharply and she had to hold onto the arms of her seat with all her strength to keep from flying up and banging her gray head on the ceiling. The jet touched down and taxied smoothly to a stop. She shuffled down the portable stairway like an old woman, holding tightly to the rail. She had always wanted to be an actress.

Another taciturn chauffeur met her on the tarmac. The man provided her with a small travel bag on wheels, so she wouldn't check into the hotel empty-handed. They drove out of the Richmond airport without looking at each other, and after a quarter of an hour, he pulled up in front of the Marriott and told her he would wait. No matter how long it took, he would be here when she walked out the door.

"Mary Archibault," she said to the young Hispanic woman at the desk. She had been sucking on the mints, and loved the old sound of her voice. She had to resist the temptation to speak in the clerk's native tongue. When she was settled in the plain, comfortable room, she left the door slightly ajar, as she had been instructed, and lay down on the bed to wait—string of pearls bunched against her throat, pulse pounding in her temples, one doubt swirling in her heart.

CHAPTER EIGHT

E verything Volkes did in his life, he did in a casual way. In his
youth, as a varsity oarsman at Princeton, he had been a student of Zen, and one of the rules of Zen was to never hurry. He
never hurried. He never appeared overly concerned about anything. In thirty years of doing what he now did, he had found
that this approach to life served three purposes: It calmed him, it
impressed the men and women he worked with, and it was an excellent tool for deceiving those he wished to deceive.

Now, for instance, he was meeting one of the cofounders of
the organization to talk to him about a matter of the absolute
highest importance—the betrayer and what to do about him. But
every movement of his still lithe body indicated that he was taking a vacation day to enjoy a round of golf and a few drinks at an
exclusive Ponte Vedra club. He made jokes with the pilot of his
plane, small talk with the chauffeur who took him to the club.
Changing clothes in the opulent locker room, with its teak lock-
ers and plush, salmon-colored carpet, he talked golf and money
with the other members he encountered. Everywhere he went he
threw up these clouds of deception; it was second nature to
him now.

Roberto Anzar met him on the first tee at fifteen minutes after four—they both preferred to walk rather than to use a golf cart. On this day, for obvious reasons, they were both going without a caddy—and Anzar had the same affable attitude going. They shook hands, lit up cigars, stroked their first drives into the middle of the fairway. For five holes they went along like this, pushing their three-wheeled golf carts in front of them, pretending to imaginary observers that they were nothing more than two wealthy older men playing a hundred-dollar Nassau for the pure joy of it.

And then, when they were walking along the manicured sixth fairway, not a soul within three hundred yards of them, Volkes turned the conversation to business: "The meeting with your niece went well?"

"She is a brave girl, my niece."

"It runs in the family," Volkes said.

Anzar grunted.

"She asked you what we expected her to ask?'

"Exactly. Precisely. She offered me a position in the new Cuba."

"And, in return, you enthusiastically offered your services."

"Of course. Anything for family."

"She's the right choice?"

"Volkes, listen to me." Anzar turned to face him and gave him the full force of his eyes. "For her to do that, for a Cuban niece to come to her uncle and make a proposition she knew to be at least partly false, and to do it in such a way that even I, who knew the whole gambit from the beginning, was almost fooled. . . . We are dealing here with an extraordinary woman."

"We knew that," Volkes said, though he was not yet completely convinced. "We knew that from Haiti, from Indonesia. But the physical courage?"

"She's proven that elsewhere, also."

"This is a little different."

"She is the person for this job. I say that not because we are related, but in spite of the fact that we are related. Listen to me: Carolina is the closest thing I have to my own child. Putting her life at risk . . ." Anzar let the sentence trail off. He walked up to his ball, stuck the cigar in the right corner of his mouth, selected his club, and stroked a nice approach shot that bounced crookedly into the greenside bunker.

"Bad luck there," Volkes said.

He walked the few steps to his own ball and flew it onto the front part of the green.

"Putting her life at risk," Anzar went on, "is, for me, a thing that tears out my heart and liver in the nights."

Volkes nodded, allowed the Latin sentimentality to float away on the cloud of cigar smoke. Then: "We have an added complication."

"Oleg Rodriguez," Anzar said immediately.

"How long have you known?"

"Since you knew. Since the meeting in the presidential suite. Before that I had my suspicions, but my suspicions are so widespread now that I buried them. I see that that was an error."

"It doesn't bother you that they could have infiltrated us at that level?"

Anzar shrugged, and Volkes noticed that he, too, had mastered the art of seeming nonchalance. Of course it bothered him. It infuriated him. Volkes knew that it shook his confidence in their background checks to the very core, but he would never show it. "This is what they do," Anzar said. "This is what Castro does. Our job now is to use the information we have as wisely as we can use it. We know who he is. He doesn't know we know who he is. Advantage us."

"You would go ahead with the plan, then."

Anzar nodded. They had reached the green. He pulled the sand wedge from his bag, looked at Volkes, and smiled. "With certain modifications."

Roberto splashed his ball out of the sand trap and up onto the green, but he was still thirty feet from the hole. As Volkes was taking the flag out of the cup to allow his friend to putt, his portable phone sounded. When he said hello he heard a familiar voice: "Volkes, Eddie. Will you please tell your madman friend Roberto to keep his damn phone on. I'm meeting with his niece in a few hours and we need to speak."

"He's right here, Eddie, about to miss his putt for par. A golfer is obliged to turn off his phone when he's on the course. You ought to know that."

CHAPTER NINE

Walking beside Olochon down the damp, echoing corridor, Carlos was almost blinded by the pounding of the pulse behind his eyes. How soft he had become, he thought. And then, glancing at Olochon: how horrible it was not to soften as one aged. The Revolution had been built on a concern for the pain of others. In the beginning the revolutionaries had killed, of course—without that killing they would still be slaves—but always in the name of a glorious future. Now, however, it seemed to him more and more that they killed in the name of a mediocre present, a status quo that kept so many Cubans wanting food, while a few, like him and Olochon, lived well. They had become the men they had once cursed.

Carlos was surprised to see that the dented metal door Olochon opened was unlocked. Inside the almost dark room there was a terrible smell he could not fully identify—urine and blood and something else. A scarred table and chair sat in the middle of the room. Off to one side, shackled to the wall by both wrists, his body sagging so that the metal cuffs cut into his skin, his mouth a ragged, red wound, was something that had once been a man. At the sound of their entry, the man lifted his horribly torn face, and Carlos took in a sharp breath.

"You recognize him?" Olochon asked. "Our Ernesto?"

Carlos shook his head. There was no need to lie here. The man was a complete stranger. Part of another conspiracy, perhaps. Or just someone unfortunate enough to have caught Olochon's attention.

"For a second there it seemed as though you recognized him."

Carlos shook his head again and fought to loosen his dry tongue. "He's a sight," he said. The man's broken teeth and pieces of his gums lay in red puddles on the floor. His shirt and pants were marked with ribbons of blood, and Carlos's first instinct—which he violently suppressed—was to begin medical treatment for the man's wounds.

"Yes," Olochon said. "A conspirator." The colonel had a 9mm pistol in his left hand. He went up to the man and put the barrel end of the pistol against the flesh that had once been his lips. "Just a word from him was all we wanted. A name. One more name." The man was screaming and trying to move his face from side to side.

Olochon took the pistol away. "Anything?" he shouted in the man's ear.

Ernesto was breathing as if he'd run up three flights a moment earlier. His wrinkled jeans were freshly stained at the crotch. He was trying to speak. He made a series of grunting sounds.

"Again?" Olochon said, putting the pistol an inch away from the bloody mess of his mouth. "¡De nuevo!"

"A-ah."

"A-ah? What is A-ah? Speak clearly and we'll let you go. Speak!"

"A-ah," Ernesto said. "A-ah."

"A-ah! What is A-ah?"

"Do you know an A-ah?" Olochon whirled around and suddenly demanded of Carlos.

Carlos shook his head.

"No?"

"No, of course not."

Ernesto sagged against the cuffs and screamed, seemed to lose consciousness momentarily. Olochon was furious with him, livid. He put the pistol up to the man's temple and shouted at him. "Who is Ester? Who is A-ah? Who is Margarita? We'll arrest every Margarita in the country and bring them here. All night you repeat these names and then nothing. Nothing! Rat! Traitor!"

Olochon worked himself up into a fury and began slapping Ernesto's face, this side and that, with the barrel of the pistol. Carlos focused his eyes on a point well to the right of Ernesto's head and tried to think of the future, the reason for this. He willed Ernesto to die, to hold his peace, to be free of his suffering. He said, to Olochon's back, "Kill him, the rat."

"You kill him!" Olochon shouted. "I brought you here to kill him!"

"Certainly," Carlos tried to say. "*Por supuesto.*" But the words stuck against the sides of his mouth for a second before they sputtered out. Olochon stopped pistol-whipping the sagging shadow and turned and looked at Carlos, almost smiling now, the fit of anger flushed from him. He wiped the bloody pistol carefully on his white coat, held it, handle-first, toward Carlos, and said, "Take it."

Carlos took it, wincing at the thought of a stranger's blood against bare skin. The instant the weapon was in his grip he felt an almost overwhelming urge to point it at Olochon's face and pull the trigger. Olochon seemed to sense this; he was watching him through that awful twist of smile. "Against the temple," he said, almost in a whisper, through his protruding teeth.

Carlos's hand was shaking horribly. He raised the gun. All he had to do was make a quarter turn and fire and the earth would be rid of Olochon forever. He could walk out of the building without anyone suspecting, then send a message to his friends here before D-7 could catch him. It would begin. He would begin it.

"Shoot," Olochon commanded. "He gave me all the names he has. We'll figure out who or what A-ah is on our own. Shoot!"

Carlos pulled the trigger and heard a sharp click. Olochon let out a hideous laugh that echoed against the damp stone walls like a flock of mad birds screeching in the jungle night. Carlos pulled the trigger a second time and Ernesto's head exploded away from him in a burst of blood and brain.

CHAPTER TEN

She waited so long in the room at the Marriott that she fell asleep there on the bed with the door ajar. When the knock sounded she was instantly awake and sitting up, embarrassed. The clock radio by the side of the bed read 10:11 P.M., and a woman and two men were in her room—very large men with very large shoulders and short hair. Before seeing them, she'd assumed she'd be meeting with some fairly important intermediary—a "high government official" was all Oleg had said—an aide to some senator on the Foreign Relations Committee, an undersecretary of defense, another of the Orchid's mysterious connections. But all three of them wore earpieces and a certain facial expression she was familiar with: a combination of hyper-alertness and physical confidence, as if there were enemies of the United States behind every door and they would all be taken care of in due time. She revised her expectations upward. A small ball of nervousness formed beneath her old woman's dress.

The trio watched her without emotion. Secret Service, she was sure. There were no handshakes, no words spoken except the name. "Mary Archibault?"

She blinked, nodded. She had been dreaming about her

uncle—that he was a very young man again, and she was old—and she tried to shake off the memory of that image. She looked down at her legs and hands and stood up. They gave her a moment to straighten the dress and hair and gather herself, before the woman—short, unsmiling, and armed—began to check her briskly and professionally.

"There's a pistol in my purse," Carolina said.

"Where's the purse?"

"On the bed."

The gun was taken, with a promise of its safe return. When the woman finished, the men motioned for Carolina to leave the room, one ahead of her, one behind. Eight paces down the corridor they took the doorway into the stairwell—one guard there with a microphone in his lapel and a firearm holstered beneath his coat—and then went through a door and into a plain concrete hallway where an open freight elevator waited. The woman stayed in the hallway. The doors of the elevator banged closed and Carolina rode up with the men to either side of her, looking straight ahead. Top floor, down another short corridor, through another guarded door and into the main hallway. Ten paces there and they were slipping her into a small suite, and then Edmund Lincoln, self-made billionaire and vice president of the United States of America, was standing up from the sofa, walking across the room, stretching out his hand to her as if they'd met a hundred times.

She was nervous at first, and then, strangely, not nervous at all. She thought she smelled gin on his breath. He asked her to sit, asked if there was anything in the way of food or drink they could bring her. She was ravenous, but she shook her head.

"My apologies for keeping you waiting this long. Would you have something, at least? Fruit juice? A Coke?"

"Juice would be fine, thank you. Cranberry if possible, on the rocks, twist of lime."

The vice president smiled and waved a hand at one of the men. Lincoln was smaller than he looked on television, with a soft, fleshy, pasty face and unnaturally pale blue eyes set wide apart. His hair was cinnamon brown—it looked dyed—and pushed straight back from his forehead in the style of her uncle. He was dressed in a plain blue suit and red necktie, polished loafers with tassels, a college ring on his right hand and a wedding ring on his left. He'd inherited eighteen thousand acres of prime Nebraska farmland from his grandparents, parlayed that (with the help of some undisclosed investors) into an agribusiness that dealt in everything from tractors to sweeteners to ethanol, and made a fortune more quickly than seemed mathematically possible. He then spent 15 million dollars of his own money to become governor of Nebraska, serving in the state house for six years—"Lincoln does Lincoln" was the joke. During his tenure as governor, Lincoln had earned a reputation for his pro-big-business decisions, his volatile mood swings, and his ruthlessness with inferiors.

When he grew bored with the governorship, he'd moved onto the Senate—another 25 million—then, after serving in Washington only two terms, he'd been picked for the VP job. There had been a flurry of articles in the liberal press questioning his experience and qualifications, but those small brushfires had been quickly extinguished. Carolina knew his beliefs and some of the rumors; no one seemed to know the full extent of his influence. The only sign of his wealth, in this room at least, was a pair of gold and sapphire cuff links that flashed when he took off the suit coat. He set it neatly on the arm of the sofa, clasped his hands, and leaned toward her. He seemed slightly off balance there, Carolina thought, as if he might suddenly tip forward and end up on the carpet on his face. Meeting the vice president of the United States at a modest hotel like this: it seemed strange to her, somehow not right.

One of the men delivered the glass of juice, and they began.

"Is the disguise uncomfortable? Should we turn up the air-conditioning?"

"I'm fine, thank you, sir."

"Your voice gives you away a bit."

"I took some mints with antithol before I checked in at the front desk. We figured it would be the only time I'd really need them. Antithol makes the voice hoarse. Criminals sometimes use it when they make ransom calls, or phone threats."

"I'm aware of that, thank you."

"Sorry, sir."

"I have twenty minutes. Give me as much of a sense of your plan as you possibly can."

She repeated what Oleg had told her. "Well, we have people in Cuba and here, men and women we've been cultivating for decades. All of them ready to go."

"CIA sources?"

"Mostly not. We have different methods than the CIA. We pay more, for one thing. For another, we rely almost exclusively on personal introductions. There's no cold recruiting involved. We have uncles talking to nephews, aunts to nieces, brother to brother. It means our people are more reliable, which means the likelihood of our plan succeeding is increased exponentially. Because of the closeness of the Cuban expatriate community this is easier than in some other projects."

"Go on."

"We have people in all the important ministries—defense, health—in the countryside, the churches, the police, the military, even someone in D-7. Not many altogether, and most of them have little sense of the larger picture, but they are in key positions. Smart, brave, and utterly loyal. These are people who have hated Fidel for almost fifty years in some cases. In other cases, they started out believing in him and became disillusioned."

"And Mr. Castro himself?"

"Castro's schedule and habits are well known to us, sir. He is not expected to be in his present position very much longer."

"Not, ah, dealt with by our hand, of course."

"Of course not, sir. His own people will deal with him, as well they should. We are just going to act as facilitators, with your assistance, if possible."

The vice president seemed to relax one half of one notch, but his eyes were eager. "What is it you want from us, exactly? Air support?"

She winced. The words were a particular sore spot among the people who knew anything about the Bay of Pigs. "Almost nothing. Benign neglect, for the most part." Deep inside herself, she threw a switch that moved her from the truth to the almost-truth. It was simple for her now; nothing showed on her face, nothing changed in her voice. "At a certain appointed time a small amount of a very toxic biological substance will be released in the most remote part of the Sierra Maestra, where it will do the least harm. A hundred people will be affected, at most. Probably five percent of that number will die, and another five percent will be permanently disabled."

"That's troubling."

"We'll do everything we can to minimize the collateral damage, and avoid risk to children. And what damage we do inflict will be inflicted upon those most loyal to Fidel. There will be a meeting scheduled there, a sort of retreat for his top propaganda operatives in that province, and these aren't people we are particularly fond of. He may be there himself; we aren't sure."

"Of course."

"I haven't been authorized to tell you much more. After the escape of this biological agent, we will have someone leak the official report to the Latin American press, and then the North American press. Once the information comes out, we want you to confirm the accuracy of the report based on satellite surveillance and air-quality monitoring, and then say that you have learned of a terrorist cell there in the mountains. The cell was preparing to carry a biological weapon into the Port of Miami. All the work of this terrorist cell will have been done with Castro's tacit permission, of course. The weapon accidentally detonated while they were moving it.

"Fidel knows the game. He'll fulminate and protest, blame everything on the *yanqui* imperialists. He'll put the country on a state of high alert, round up anyone he feels might be a threat to the regime . . . which is what we want, actually, all those people in one place. At that point we will have to act very quickly to keep our people from being hurt. Shortly afterward, I cannot say how soon, exactly, Castro will be assassinated by one of our agents inside his regime, and then—"

"And then Anzar's people will move."

She almost fell off the couch. This seemed to be a gigantic slip on the part of the vice president, and she was sure then that he had been drinking. There was no way in the world he should have known anything about Roberto Anzar's involvement in this make-believe plan; Anzar himself should only have learned of it that same afternoon. If the vice president did know, it would mean that he had been talking, very recently, with her uncle. Even so, there was no way he should have admitted that to her. But, as she had been trained, she went briskly on, pretending nothing had happened. "Anzar's people complement our people nicely; we couldn't really do it without them. They are already positioning themselves. We have small caches of sophisticated weaponry hidden in various places and it will be distributed to them. We'll take over the prisons where the dissidents are held, take over the police headquarters in a few key towns. We'll kill or arrest key members of Castro's secret police and DGI. We will deal with his brother."

The vice president held up his hand, palm out. On his face was an expression of disdain. "The Cubans are going to see this as a violent coup. They'll blame us. It's no good."

"As a violent coup that some of their own people initiated, and that some of their own good people will have thwarted. The coup will have come from within DGI, not from us—at least, that's the way it will appear. Those responsible will be arrested, or killed . . . by Cubans. What we'd like from you, at that point, is simply to announce that the U.S. military is standing by in case the situation on the ground in Cuba begins to seem in any way threatening to U.S. interests, but that you have no plans to send troops unless there are signs of civil war. Aside from satellite and radar help, that is all we should require in the initial stages."

At first, the vice president had been listening more or less calmly, but by the time she reached this point in her little made-up speech, he was blowing out his cheeks angrily with each new detail. Carolina noticed a sheen of perspiration on his forehead. When she paused for breath he said, "You're going to take over the entire country with what, a few hundred dissidents, some 'sophisticated weaponry,' and a wacky plan? Against what, the entire Cuban army? Which is the largest, most powerful, and most combat-hardened army in Latin America!" He was shouting. She wondered if the man at the window and the man at the door were embarrassed for him. She wondered what the president's reelection chances would be if the American public found out his second-in-command had a drinking problem and such a short-fuse temper.

"With all due respect, sir, the entire Cuban military is not loyal to Fidel Castro. Especially since the arrest of Colonel Alejandro Davos. That one event resulted in a hardening of anti-Castro sentiment within his own forces."

"Says who?"

"Say several of our people inside the Cuban military. Separate, unimpeachable sources, all reporting the same thing. That arrest was what convinced us to move now."

"And what, you are going to assassinate the leader of a sovereign nation and then take over that nation based on the word of a handful of disaffected captains?"

"I think you should give us more credit than that, sir. We never would undertake something like this without first doing the requisite polling on the ground, without having prepared the way for years in advance. Money works small miracles." She almost added "as you know" but thought better of it. She was quickly losing patience with the man and she had to stop herself, take a breath, hold the juice up to her old mouth for a long drink.

"Fine. I happen to know a bit about your organization. You people have done some remarkable work. But you haven't yet told me how it will be fashioned, this little exercise. How, precisely?

Who are these contacts? Captains? Lieutenants? Generals? Little Havana housewives cooking up rice and beans for the new breed of Cuban revolutionaries?"

It was a similar line of questioning to her uncle's, and she deflected it in a similar way. "I can't answer that, sir."

"Then I want to talk with the person who can. Now. Tonight."

"With all due respect, that's not possible, sir."

The vice president's face was the color of a persimmon. He was glaring at her, sweating, trembling. *Another rich man used to getting his way,* she thought. But something was not right—even beyond the drinking and the outburst about her uncle, something was not right. He almost seemed to be acting a role. One, he should not have known about her conversation with her uncle. Two, Oleg had informed her that all she would have to provide was a quick briefing to a high government official sympathetic to their work. As much as possible, the U.S. government wanted to appear to be staying out of this. They wanted it to happen, of course; they'd wanted it to happen for generations. But they wanted it to happen without their direct involvement, which was the beauty of the whole plan. The people who ran the Orchid had understood this a long time ago: Though the U.S. government wanted Castro out, they could not be seen to be ousting him. But if another entity came along with the same desire, and, more important, the means, then the government—this administration in particular—would be anxious to offer whatever kind of clandestine assistance it could and then stand aside innocently and wait.

What also troubled her was the rice and beans remark. It didn't make sense. He knew she was a *cubana*. He must be trying to upset her, to get her to say something she did not want to say. Perhaps he was only pretending to have been drinking heavily.

He huffed and he puffed and he stared at her. She stared back, emboldened now, unafraid. "Without your quiet support we won't act," Carolina lied. "My superiors sent me here because they'd been assured we've had a commitment for that support for months now, that all you wanted was a sense of our timing and a few relevant details. My understanding was that you had been contacted previously by—"

The vice president held up one hand again, and she saw that it was as steady as a stone. "I'm not interested in what you've been told," he said. "I'm interested in what you can tell me."

She took another slow breath. It was a trick. Exactly what kind of trick she did not know, but a trick all the same. And now that she had seen through it, she would be perfectly all right. "I've told you pretty much everything I was authorized to tell you, sir. If you'd like to go back to my superiors, I suppose that could be arranged. But once things have been set in motion like this, a change in your position would—"

"Surely you have to understand my reservations, Ms. Perez. We're putting our reputation at risk here, as the leader of the free world. You fail in this and do you realize what kind of a disaster-waiting-to-happen we have ninety miles off our shores?"

"Yes, sir." She watched him. Something was wrong. He was not quite a good enough actor to pull this off. Something was happening just beyond the borders of her information.

"When does it begin?"

"Two months from today," she said without blinking.

He pursed his lips and brought his eyes down to her half-empty glass of cranberry juice, not seeing it. "There's going to be a popular uprising. There's going to be bloodshed in the streets. What about his maniac brother? Guevara's friend."

"Guevara's friend will be dealt with very early on, sir, as I said. There will be a popular uprising, yes, probably. But we will control it. We have people in the television and radio stations, in the newspapers. There will likely be some resistance to those who assume power after Fidel is gone. There is no line of succession, as you know, and there will be some competition for his rule. We know who those people are and we have plans for them. Fidel's successor, our man in Havana, will make overtures to the dissidents, to the masses."

"The military will allow that?"

"The military will not be a problem, sir."

"Then it's a military man, your so-called successor."

Carolina went on without answering, "We will broadcast demonstrations of people supporting this new leader. We will take the propaganda machine and turn it on its ear. A hundred people can be made to look like a thousand on television, for a brief period of time, and of course there will be many thousands eager to support the new regime. The images will be broadcast around the world. We have news stories already prepared—to discredit the likely opposition, and to bolster our man's claim to power and popular support. The Europeans and others will rush to give aid to stabilize the new regime. We have a large sum of money set aside for the initial days—good works, food, bribes."

"And you are confident that those you'll install in power will have the full support of a majority of the people?"

"Of a significant minority, at first. Revolutions aren't made by majorities, sir."

"Thank you for that lesson in history. But how can you be so confident? How can you gauge the popularity of a man who is untested, unknown?"

"I can't reveal that, sir. As I said earlier. But he's hardly un-known."

"A hero of the Revolution, then," the vice president said. "A hero from Angola. A military man. Stepping in to take the glorious mantle from Fidel."

Carolina shifted her weight and felt the strange stockings pull against her legs. "Except that our man is going to do what Fidel might have done in the earliest days of the Revolution, before Guevara and the communists took him under their influence. He is going to shift the direction from Fidel's direction just enough to co-opt the dissidents, please the United States and its allies, and quiet the unrest that is likely to occur. Those who are uncomfortable with this shift will be taken care of by us, in part, but mostly by our friends in the armed forces."

The vice president looked at his watch. Carolina studied the muscles at the sides of his jaw as they flexed. He drew a handkerchief out of the pocket of his pants, opened it with some fanfare, and ran it across his forehead. "You put me in an awkward position. I have to go back and report to the president after this, naturally, and I'm sadly lacking in hard information."

It was very likely, she thought, that other reports would be made as well. The president was a pretty face, a figurehead.

"I have to report to the president," Lincoln repeated, as if the prospect frightened him, which she was certain it did not. "And there are gaps here; questions he's going to ask that I won't be able to answer."

He paused and looked at her. She looked back. Something about being dressed up as an old woman gave her a certain advantage over him. It took the sexual tension out of the equation. He waited for her to speak, but she calmly held her silence.

"And I'm going to have to tell him the plan seems shaky to me."

"You're welcome to tell him that, sir, of course. I'll carry that message back to my people as well."

Lincoln's face reddened again. He seemed to be working hard now to maintain control. "It's extremely frustrating not to be able to speak with the people who are actually in charge," he said, between his teeth.

"I can understand that, sir. I feel the same way sometimes."

"To whom do you report?"

She could no longer contain herself. "To whom do you report, sir?"

The man standing at the window turned slightly and watched her.

The vice president flew into a rage. He stood up—for a moment she thought he would approach her—and kicked the base of the sofa, twice, then walked around behind it and slapped the palm of his hand hard against the hotel wall. One of the small, framed pictures crashed down against the desk, and splinters of glass skidded across its surface. The taxpayers would be billed. Now both Secret Service agents had turned fully into the room and were watching with more than their customary alertness. "Goddamn it to hell!" the vice president shouted. "It's off. Our participation in this is off. That's all, and that's final!"

"And you don't have to clear that with the president?" she said quietly, calmly. She had not moved. Her hands, with their old woman's spotted and wrinkled skin, lay crossed in her lap.

The vice president spluttered and fumed, paced back and forth. "Off, off, that's it," he muttered once. "The president will concur."

"Fine," Carolina said. "I have a jet waiting for me, and I've been here a very long time, and I'd like to go back, deliver my report, and go to bed, if you will, sir."

"Go," he said, waving a hand in a violent dismissal. "But there are going to be repercussions, I can promise you that. You people drag me all the way down here for some half-baked, tricked-up, rice and beans bullshit! Who do you think you are dealing with here?"

"Sir, I meant no disrespect."

He fumed and huffed, and Carolina watched him closely, trying to penetrate to the heart of the little performance. Inside herself, she took a step back, brought a calm curtain down across her face. When he quieted a bit, she stood, thanked him for his time, and then gave her elderly self over to the company of his protectors.

Without another word being spoken, the Secret Service detail escorted her out of the suite, down the freight elevator, and all the way to the door of her room. She was given her gun back, and they disappeared. She went into the room, used the toilet, checked herself in the mirror, swallowed a mint, took the single empty piece of rolling luggage, and went down to awaken her chauffeur.

CHAPTER ELEVEN

———⟶⟵———

Carlos turned away from what remained of Ernesto's body, from the pulsing arteries and puddling blood, and handed the pistol back to the smirking Olochon. He took off the blood-stained doctor's gown, left the colonel without a word, and went downstairs, through the lobby, out the door, and down the steps, just trying to keep himself from breaking apart.

"You came out alive," Jose said. "That's something."

Carlos could not answer. As they drove through the streets leading away from the Montefiore Prison—Libertad, Cinco de Diciembre, Cabo Rosa—Jose turned to look at him at every opportunity, but Carlos volunteered nothing. "To the office?" Jose said at last.

Carlos was staring blankly out the side window at a stretch of apartment houses built years ago in the pitilessly ugly Soviet style. There was a whole block of them, a blot of Stalinist gray against the ochre of Havana's older facades. "Cabinet meeting at the Central Committee at eleven," he said.

In Vedado, in front of the ultramodern tower where Fidel worked but did not live, Carlos put one unsteady hand on his friend's shoulder, and got out of the car. The monument to José

Martí. The enormous image of Che Guevara on one wall. More guards, more gates, more doors. He seemed to be swimming past them in a river of blood. If he hadn't made this same walk a thousand times, he would have faltered, stopped, looked down bewildered at his own trembling hands. At last, he found himself seated around the oval cabinet table in the sunlit room of the Martyrs of the Revolution, three-quarters of his mind still occupied by the sight of a stranger's head exploding in a splash of bright red and gray.

He was early. For a long time he gazed out the windows at the Plaza de la Revolución, thinking about Elena, and what she would say if he told her. One by one the others arrived: the ministers of commerce and economic development, Lopez and Caudillo, two quiet men who, since the breakup of the Soviet Union and the end of the subsidies, had carried nothing but bad news into this room. Bad news disguised by fabricated graphs, impossible predictions, ridiculous optimism. Expert liars, both of them, they had somehow managed to keep their jobs while the sugar harvest shrank and the nation tumbled toward despair. Lately, things had improved somewhat—thanks to the tourist income, mainly—and Lopez and Caudillo had started strutting and crowing like triumphant delivery boys bringing a hand of bananas to parents whose children had just starved to death. *No more of this,* Carlos thought. *No more.*

Next into the room were the four giants of Castro's personal security detail, who took up places at the four corners.

Then there was Alina Gonzalez Guiteles, minister of education, a woman Carlos considered a friend; a woman who cared about the healthy upbringing of children, a woman who, like himself, had only a secondary interest in things political.

Then the military men: General Augusto Rincon and his only superior, General Emmanuele Adria. Carlos studied Rincon without actually looking at him. The man was laughing when he entered the room. Once he'd taken his seat—just to the left of the head of the table—he started folding a sheet of paper into triangular shapes, then unfolding it, then folding it back again. He was a hero of the Angolan campaign, built like an Olympic wrestling champion, with the face of an Incan god. In time, if everything went as they hoped it would, Rincon would be sitting in the chair to his right, turning the rusting and battered ship that was Cuba away from the rocks long enough for actual elections to take place.

Next came the ministers of propaganda, energy, and labor—a trio of pirate liars in expensive Spanish suits.

Finally, Olochon and Fidel and Raul Castro entered together, with two more bodyguards behind them. Carlos could feel Olochon's eyes on him. When Fidel took his place behind his chair they all stood and saluted, then everyone sat and the meeting began.

Fidel, as always, did almost all the talking. Carlos kept statistics in his head: The record was seven hours and fourteen minutes, in his speech to an international youth group at the Plaza de la Revolución; second place was six hours and two minutes, in this very room. On dozens of occasions, Fidel had held forth for more than four hours, while everyone thought about lunch, their families, the weather, and pretended to listen with both ears.

"This morning the news is good," the Maximum Leader began. "We have a report that . . ." He shuffled through the small sheaf of papers in front of him, looking momentarily confused. "That the Gross Domestic Product is up fourteen percent in the first four months of the year, which means that our reestablishment of further control of the central mechanisms was the proper strategy."

Around the table everyone but Olochon nodded and smiled knowingly, or said, "We knew it would be." Caudillo, minister of economic development, the one who had created the exaggerations contained in the papers in Fidel's hands, nodded most energetically of all. For nearly an hour, Fidel went on about the economy, its surging strength, and how that strength proved that those who had counseled him to allow more private enterprise were mistaken, completely mistaken, caught in the grip of the delusion of capitalism. It had been correct to close down the small private markets. Correct to eliminate the direct selling of a home from person to person, without the government involved. Correct to focus on the project of breeding a species of cattle that could produce both meat and milk. *Correcto. Correcto,* said the Father of Genetics. On and on and on.

As the Great Leader spoke, Carlos watched him. His hairline had receded. There were brown age spots, sprinkled like drops of mud, over Fidel's forehead and the tops of his cheeks, and small scars where two cancerous moles had been removed. His eyes, so piercing and alert in the old days, now wandered and drifted behind thin whitish clouds, and his voice often sounded like a dim echo of the vibrant young revolutionary's, a voice that could make even hungry women with hungry children hand over their bowls of frijoles. His blood pressure was 131 over 81, his heartbeat sturdy and regular. No signs of cancer except for the skin lesions, no high cholesterol, no diabetes, no breathing problems. The man's mother had lived to be ninety-three, suffering from diabetes for decades and not succumbing. Left to the caprices of the natural order, he would live to be a hundred.

When the economic report ended, Fidel glanced at Carlos and turned to the health of the nation. Instead of letting the ministers read the reports they had submitted, Fidel read them himself. More of the same: a further drop in infant mortality, a further increase in life expectancy. Some of it, even most of it, was true. But around the table people looked at Carlos and nodded somberly, as if to say: You lie as cleverly as the rest of us; good work.

Then education, then the military situation—at this point Alina glanced at her watch. Fidel saw her do so and asked, without looking directly at her, if he might be going on at too much length. Immediately there was a chorus of "No, no, Comandante!" He smiled and looked at Alina triumphantly. Any tiny deviation from the posture of adoration was a personal insult now, but Fidel was magnanimous; he forgave such things . . . and remembered them for decades.

At last, the oration seemed to be winding down. Three hours and thirteen minutes, Carlos noted. He wore his watch with the face to the inside of his wrist, so he could pretend to be examining his palms contemplatively, thoughtfully, while actually checking the hour. This time, he noticed one spot of dried blood clinging to the hair of his wrist. He could not keep himself from looking at General Rincon then, just for an instant. Rincon looked back and the tiniest flicker of something passed between them. Carlos felt Olochon's eyes on him.

When Fidel finished, he turned the meeting over to Colonel Olochon, as he always did. As head of D-7, Olochon was charged with one branch of internal security, "a different kind of health minister" Castro had once called him, though some said Castro had no idea of the kind of things Olochon actually did. He was universally hated in the room. With the possible exception of Raul, everyone felt watched by him. Everyone here had known someone—a former ministry official, military officer, friend— who had been denounced by Olochon and his nest of snakes, imprisoned, tortured, killed, never spoken of again.

"We have uncovered another conspiracy against the Revolution," Colonel Olochon began. Though they had all heard it a hundred times, they made their faces into the shape of careful shock. "In fact, just this morning, someone at this table . . ." Olochon paused to sip from his mineral water, and to let beads of sweat appear on the faces of those around him. "Someone at this table . . . was kind enough to assist me in exterminating one of the rats involved in this conspiracy."

Carlos slammed his fist down on the wooden tabletop so hard and so suddenly that Castro turned and stared at him. "And happy and proud to do it," he said loudly. "Excellent work, Olochon!"

"Yes, yes," the others mumbled.

For just an instant Olochon seemed stunned by the outburst. "Carlos enjoys the work so much," he said. "Perhaps"—he turned to Fidel, smiling his hideous broken smile—"he should take over my position."

Fidel went along with the joke. "Not yet, not yet," he said, putting his hand on Olochon's shoulder. "You're still young."

The torturer laughed, then turned abruptly serious. "A web of conspiracy. We've only touched its edges. We believe it has reached its sticky tendrils high up into the government structure."

No one moved. Then Rincon started folding his paper again and said, calmly, glancing at General Adria first, "Give us the names of anyone you suspect in the military and we'll take care of them."

"When I get those names I will take care of them myself," Olochon said. "Personally. And I *will* get them. I am in the process of getting them."

"Good work," Rincon said drolly.

"Yes, yes, fine work," a few other voices echoed. Carlos just watched, still shocked at what he had done in the prison; shocked by his made-up bit of drama in this room. He was not the same Carlos Gutierrez who had left his apartment this morning. He would never be that man again. As if it were a swelling in his frontal lobe, he could feel the enormous hatred that had been building up in him over the past two years. There was the horror of it, the murder of people like Ernesto, the constant fear, the cascade of lies, Olochon's black heart at the center of it all. But there was also something so dull, so repetitive and unimaginative and dull. It was like listening to a song that you had once found interesting, and then being made to hear that song over and over and over and over and over and over and over again, at work, on the television, day after day from the mouths of demons.

The more he sensed that the room was becoming slightly bored with him, the more Olochon embellished his news. The conspirators had imported a small band of U.S. Marines, who were, he believed, hiding out deep in the countryside receiving secret munitions support from Guantánamo. Perhaps some of the Middle Eastern terrorists imprisoned there had been released into the Cuban population. The conspirators were poisoning the food of children in the schools. Two young girls had perished. One boatload of Miami traitors had landed near the Bay of Guanabacoa and been captured.

The best way to get people's attention was to frighten them; everyone had learned that from Castro himself. But Olochon's stories went from terrifying to absurd to inane. Even Fidel seemed bored.

At last, the tale of woe came to its rousing, hopeful conclusion, and soon the meeting ended. But even then the charades went on. Carlos walked up to Olochon and said, "Why didn't you tell me about the schoolgirls, the poisoning? I could have sent a team to investigate. We could have identified the poison and tracked it to its source."

"It's been taken care of," Olochon said.

"But this is a case for the Ministry of Health."

"Done," Olochon said, and turned away.

Fidel left the room with the bodyguards forming a circle around him, and Carlos wondered how the plan could possibly be carried out, how Rincon was going to get inside that circle of muscle and kill him. And what, exactly, would happen once that had been accomplished? It was not as if Raul Castro, Felix Olochon, and the other worshippers of *el Comandante* were simply going to shake Rincon's hand, pledge their undying allegiance, agree to support free elections, and then go happily back to work.

On the way down the stairs, Rincon and General Adria were behind him, chuckling as if one of them had told a filthy joke. Between the front steps of the Central Committee building and the Martí Memorial, the two military men went their separate ways, and Rincon, as if accidentally, fell into step with Carlos. "Another good session," he said heartily. Carlos nodded. He could still see Ernesto's face in front of him; the horrible smells and sounds of that place filled his nostrils and ears. There was traffic noise in this part of the city, tourist buses and trucks, just beyond the concrete plaza. More than a year ago now, General Rincon had started becoming more friendly toward him. They'd always had a mutual

respect and cordial relations, but things had become more amica-
ble, more personal. Little by little, conversation by conversation,
Rincon had sounded him out—how was his work going? What
did he really think of the state of the nation? Were things actually
getting better, or was it all just numbers floating in the air?

Little by little, conversation by conversation, Carlos had
found himself speaking to Rincon with an openness that surprised
him. The only other person he'd ever spoken to this way had been
his late wife, Teresa, and even then only in whispers in the privacy
of their home. But he trusted Rincon on instinct. He'd heard of the
man's heroism in Angola, tales of him standing up to Soviet generals in the old days, refusing to risk his men in the name of some
foolish Leninist triumph. He'd even been rumored to have stood
up to Fidel after the arrest of Colonel Davos on charges of suspicion of conspiracy. Davos, perhaps the most popular figure in the
whole armed services, had been tortured for weeks, then allowed
to shoot himself, and only Rincon had had the moral fiber and
physical courage to raise an objection . . . which was, of course, ig-
nored. Little by little, Carlos and General Rincon formed a secret
bond, and Rincon began telling him of an elaborate conspiracy
that had been under way for months already and that involved certain sectors of the military utterly loyal to him.

As Fidel aged, as he seemed to be losing his sharpness, this
movement had gained momentum. They had been careful to keep
it a Cuban matter, no interference from the outside. They limited
everything to one-to-one or one-to-two contacts, so anyone arrested would have only one or two names to give up. Shocked at
first, Carlos felt himself gradually drawn in. Every time Fidel
ranted about economic improvement while children were going
hungry, every time he spoke about liberty while another journalist

was arrested; every time there was another rumor of a *balsero* taking a raft out into the shark-infested Straits of Florida, Carlos felt himself pulled deeper into this idea of changing things in a radical way.

It frightened him, of course. But gradually he had made a kind of peace with the fear. Now he walked side by side with his fellow conspirator, certain that no one could guess anything from their body language. During one particularly loud honking of horns, Rincon moved slightly so that his mouth was an inch closer to Carlos's ear and he said, or Carlos believed he said, "It is you. You are to do it. How later."

Surprised to the bone, Carlos did not dare look at him. He hesitated one second, two seconds, then laughed loudly, patted the general on the shoulder, and moved through a blood-drenched dream toward his waiting car and driver.

CHAPTER TWELVE

Carolina climbed the stairs slowly toward the door of the jet, staying in character to the last moment. She could not imagine anyone would have followed her here, but this was how the White Orchid worked: layer upon layer of backup, nothing left to chance. When she was inside, and the door was closed and secured, she saw that there was another passenger on the plane for the trip back to Florida: Oleg Rodriguez, her new boss. She sat down beside him, exhausted. It was close to midnight, and the layers of makeup on her cheeks, hands, and legs had become rubbery with sweat.

Oleg's handsome face carried a cheerful expression. "How did your brush with power feel, oh ancient one?"

"Power is the ultimate aphrodisiac," Carolina said mockingly. "I could barely keep my hands off him."

"And I'm sure he could barely keep his hands off you"—Oleg patted the top of her leg—"in that sexy outfit." From the moment she'd met him, there had been some kind of body-to-body tension between them. His family had fled Cuba years before; she had never heard the details. He was a glamorous, impossibly handsome man who had eliminated all traces of a

Spanish accent from his speech, and who liked to dress in ridiculously expensive Armani suits. On the short side, broad shoulders, a wide, clean-shaven face marked by a straight nose, and dancing dark eyes. The eyes were full of trouble, but it was a happy trouble, inviting you to join in. She believed he felt attracted to her, too; he was always touching her shoulder or arm, making little jokes like this. Nothing, of course, would ever come of it, though in certain moods she indulged in a fantasy of the two of them taking a very early retirement, buying a small inn on Key West and raising a dark-haired brood of *angelitos*.

"Everything went smoothly, I trust," Oleg said when they were speeding down the runway toward takeoff.

"Not exactly."

The small jet climbed, bumped through a bit of turbulence, and leveled off. Carolina looked down at the dark grid of lights, then the suburbs, then the black countryside. "Vice President Eddie Lincoln is not happy with our plan. He's not happy at being unable to talk to the man in charge. At the end he threw a kind of hissy fit and said their participation was off. The U.S. government is officially out of the deal."

Oleg laughed quietly and she turned and looked at him full in the face. He seemed genuinely pleased. "Excellent work," he said. "And I must say you are an extremely attractive seventy-five-year-old."

"Seventy," she said. "I'm hurt."

"And how did your uncle react?"

"With a great deal of suspicion at first, and then I softened him up and he came around. The idea of us sending him back there to be part of the government, that's what did it."

"Amazing," Oleg said. It was nice to please this man, nice to do her work well, nice to have the approval of her superiors. But she felt traitorous there, with him, talking about her uncle. She had felt traitorous all that long day. "Here is a man who has everything," Oleg said happily, "literally millions upon millions of dollars, the most beautiful homes, the most beautiful women, the admiration of hundreds on both sides of the water. And the allure of power softens him."

"I think it was the allure of going back and helping to remake Cuba."

"It's a fantasy. A return to a nonexistent childhood."

"I thought it was the point of our entire plan."

"To remake Cuba, yes, of course. To open it. To let it breathe. But to remake the Cuba your uncle remembers? Do you think that's a realistic possibility? Or a desirable one?"

She shook her head. "My uncle and Lincoln had a conversation, I think. Recently. At one point, when I was detailing the made-up plan for him, Lincoln slipped and said, 'And then Anzar's people will move.'"

"It wasn't a slip."

"No?"

Oleg shook his head. He went to the bar and made two gin and tonics and brought them back.

"Would you let me get out of this disguise, please?"

"Not yet. We'll take you to a hotel in Miami."

"Miami? Can't I go back to Atlanta?"

"Not at this time. We're a bit concerned about the Atlanta location, for reasons I cannot divulge right now. It's Miami, for tonight at least. You'll have some clothes at the hotel to change back into. You can spend the night. Sleep as late as you want and then call me and I'll have Evan come by and bring your hair back to normal in the morning."

"I feel like I'm sweating internally."

Oleg smiled, sipped his drink, pushed his seat back and gazed up cheerfully at the jet's gray vinyl ceiling. "Your uncle is a man of the old world. He believes in the Old Cuba and her resurrection, as if such a thing would give him back his youth. He believes in the idea that, when it comes to Cuba, only the government of the United States is capable of acting the way we act. He understands capital and business, you see, but only in its microeconomic sense: the hiring of laborers, the bribing of politicians, the pleasing of customers, the use of the military to support a nation's aims. The larger dimension is lost to him. It would be, I think, his only serious flaw as a true leader."

"And Lincoln?"

"Edmund Lincoln is a more complicated and less trustworthy man. His mentioning your uncle's name was a ruse to get a reaction from you. His refusing to support the plan was another ruse. He'll support it, as will the president. He was just trying to get past your disguise and figure out how much of the truth you were telling him."

"Well, I didn't react. And the whole account was only about forty percent true anyway, right?"

Oleg let the question merge with the drone of the engine. "Lincoln wants to be president someday, you know that."

"Everyone in the country knows that."

"And if he's seen to be a force in the creation of a free Cuba, do you think that will help him or hurt him?"

"Help, of course."

"But because of international pressures, and because of his present position, he can't be seen to be a force in the creation of a free Cuba unless it's a guaranteed success. Your uncle won't risk the lives of his people, again, unless it's a guaranteed success. So naturally, they are both nervous and suspicious and envious. But there is more to it than politics. Lincoln knows, as does your uncle, that there are billions of dollars to be taken from the Cuban sugar plantations, if they could be made to function properly again. Billions to be made from tourism, if the market is opened to the United States and the infrastructure and service industries properly nurtured. Hundreds of millions still in the nickel and gold mines. The difference is that your uncle cares about the old Cuban culture, and Lincoln cares about the money. The difference between them and us is that they see the military as a key ally, when in fact, in this instance and others, the military is going to play less and less of a role in the world in years to come. Do you think it was military or economic pressure that broke apart the former Soviet Union?"

"Both."

"Right. But the military's role was largely passive, which is, increasingly, what it will be: a stick that is rarely if ever used. Look at Libya, for one good example."

"Whereas the economic stick will be used regularly."

"Exactly."

"All right. My uncle cares about Cuba. Our vice president cares about power and increasing his fortune. But tell me, what do we care about? Your boss's boss's boss. What is he in it for?"

"You've been working for us what now, six years?"

"Eight."

"And you just come around to asking this?"

"I've always asked it. The answer I always got was that we were working for a freer, more just world. The rising tide that will lift all boats. An end to war, hunger, and selfishness. It's why I shifted over from the CIA. The Orchid seemed less cynical. Is that what our man at the top is in it for?"

"Men, not man," Oleg said. He paused, and it seemed to Carolina that he was wondering how much to tell her. It was always this way with the Orchid: everything on a need-to-know basis. They fed her information one drop at a time, in conversations like this, in private airplanes, penthouse suites, dusty bars in the Slovenian outback. But it also seemed that they were grooming her, giving her more responsibility, more money, more information. This appealed to her tremendously, more than she liked to admit. Part of her wanted nothing more than to prove to her uncle that leaving the CIA had been a wise decision; sometimes she thought that motivated everything she did now, every risk she took, every discomfort, every lonely day. She was only *thirty-five*, she had her sights set high, though there was a fog of confusion lower down, too. Moral confusion, practical, even emotional—she did not like living alone; she wanted a husband and children . . . and she wanted to be the most powerful woman in any clandestine service anywhere.

Now, though, sitting beside Oleg, she felt the professional ambition rising up over everything else. Usually once or twice in a year she'd be given an especially tricky or dangerous assignment, and that would be followed by a bump in pay, a new boss, a few more drops of information about the Big Picture. She'd become almost addicted to the thrill of these promotions.

Oleg sipped his drink, turned his marvelous eyes on her. "Our bosses care about making the world work as it should work. There are only a few men, a handful of men, who understand, really understand, the way the economy of the world works and where it is headed."

"No women?"

"Perhaps you will be the first," he said, and she felt a warm internal shiver. She could hold her own with vice presidents now. She was being given a key role in the Havana Project.

Oleg went calmly on, "These men, our superiors, are the spiritual leaders of the future, you see, and that is something you have not been told before, I'm quite sure. These people have spent many years, fifty years in some cases, moving the chess pieces into place, thinking two, three, four decades in advance, while people like your uncle pride themselves on looking two seasons into the future. The world is being slowly knit together. In the largest, macroeconomic sense, there is no longer, for all intents and purposes, much real economic distinction between, say, a multinational corporation in China and one in the United States. The borders in Europe have collapsed—militarily and economically— and that collapse will spread slowly eastward. The tariffs that once separated the nations of North America are gone. Take those events and extrapolate into the future—ten years, a hundred and ten years—and what do you think you have?"

"A world market."

"No, a world. One world. You can see it already in its embryonic form. And that world, that unified, democratic, free-market world, will be good for everyone. It is Marx and Engels turned on their heads. Every boat will be lifted, not just the United States' boat, every one."

"The Islamic extremists'?"

"The Islamic extremists are having their day, even as we speak. It will be a short, brutal, bloody day, one or two generations at the very most, but there's really no place for them in the future world, no hope. They understand this perfectly well. It's not an accident that bin Laden attacked the World Trade Towers, you know . . . the symbol of this world economy. The extremists will slowly be squeezed further and further to the margins. In half a century they won't even make the morning news, any more than the Soviet ballistic missile threat makes the news today. Ultimately, it will be financial, not military, pressure that suffocates them." He rested a moment, closing his eyes and rocking his head slightly side to side. Carolina studied the small round scar at his temple, the skin slick and white there. She looked at his full lips.

He opened his eyes and caught her staring. "You see, my beautiful older friend, most people have a poverty-driven mentality, a zero-sum mentality: If this many are rich, then this many must be poor. If this many are safe, then this many must be in danger. Very, very few people understand the growth potential of the planet in all its depth and complexity, the long-range supplies of energy we are capable of producing, long-term communications developments, the sheer amount of foodstuffs. But our bosses, you see, they are visionaries. Buddhas in suit and tie."

"So who is Lincoln?

"A wannabe. A minor player with a huge ego. At the side of our current president, however, he looks like a genius. And he has surrounded himself with sycophants who tell him he is a genius. To your uncle, Cuba is the queen on the chessboard. To Lincoln, she is a bishop. To us, a single pawn. Look at it this way: We find brilliant, brave, deep-thinking people like you and pay them five times what your uncle or Lincoln can pay, so which organization do you think best understands the larger picture?"

It was Carolina's turn to leave a question unanswered. She looked out at the darkness, the world spinning there, billions starving, billions more laboring, a tiny few thinking like this. It all sounded so wonderful. But if she was lying to her uncle and the vice president, then why shouldn't she assume that Oleg was lying to her, that the Orchid had been lying to her all along? They'd seen an attractive, smart, mostly fearless young woman with CIA training and thought: We can use this person. What do we have to say to her in order to make her spiritually at peace? How much do we have to pay her?

"You're not cherishing a doubt, are you?" Oleg asked. "Now, just when we're about to entrust you with something particularly special?"

"Of course not."

"Your visits today haven't shaken you?"

"I get paid very well not to be shaken."

"Good. Because you are about to be paid a lot more."

"Really?"

"And also get a free bonus vacation."

"Where to?"

"To a place called Cuba, via a place called the Czech Republic. You are to deliver certain pieces of the ceramic pistol that will send our friend Fidel into permanent retirement."

"When? I told my uncle we would contact him soon. I told Lincoln it would be months."

"It probably will be several months, but there are certain important pieces that have to be put into place right now. You must simply trust me on that." He put his hand on her knee. "You leave for Prague tomorrow night. Make sure you sleep well." Oleg squeezed her knee once, gently, and took his hand away. She had an urge to tell him to leave it where it was. "Rest now," he said. "We'll talk again before we land."

CHAPTER THIRTEEN

————ⵗⵗⵗ————

Carlos loved Old Havana at night. It seemed to him that the tattered facades of the colonial buildings took on a more dignified aspect once the sun went down. The children on the sidewalks seemed happier. There was always music coming from somewhere, gatherings of friends on the street corners, and, relieved of the weight of the daytime heat, the capital seemed to breathe easier. It was almost a happy place.

Usually, strolling arm in arm with Elena like this in the Plaza de la Catedral, he could let the responsibilities of the day slide off him. For an hour or a few hours he would not worry about AIDS, tuberculosis, malnourishment in the countryside. He would not think about Fidel and his broken wrists and skin cancers and stomach troubles, or Olochon and his tubercular inmates, or the blockade, or the latest *norteamericano* plan to prove to the world that Cuba was wrong and the United States right—at the expense of the daily caloric intake of millions of Cuban children.

But tonight he had no peace. Elena sensed it, he knew that. Tonight he was already a murderer and a traitor, and because of that, because of those sins, an awkward silence hovered in the humid air between them. She had wanted to go to a little place they liked in the former Chinese Quarter, near Paseo di Marti. Ordinarily he'd go wherever she wanted. Tonight, for reasons he could not disclose, he had to be at the Cafe Sierra Maestra at 9 P.M., and he'd been hasty and short with her at the apartment. Now she was paying him back by not speaking.

Elena was also a physician and she served her country in a clinic in one of the city's poorest sections. They had met a year and two months after he'd lost his Teresa. He had been taking a group of visiting Italian doctors and high-level international bureaucrats on a tour of the city's facilities, and one of them—a red-haired woman, impertinent, full of ugly preconceptions—had complained that they were seeing nothing but the cleansed version of Cuban health care that Castro wanted them to see. "Take us to the poor sections," this doctor had said, petulantly, arrogantly. "Let us see what is *not* going perfectly. Let us see your failures as well as your successes."

The failures, as Carlos knew so well, were in the countryside, where the American blockade had hurt most, where even basic painkillers were all but nonexistent and the operating rooms might or might not run short of electricity at any given moment. Cane cutters would come in with a bone-deep machete wound on their thigh, and the doctor—if there even was a doctor—would sew up the wound from the inside, with only a few gulps of rum as anesthetic.

But he could not show the visitors that. So, on impulse, and out of annoyance with the Italian woman, he'd directed the driver of their bus to turn down Calle Cinco de Diciembre. On his morning commute he always passed the clinic there, deep in the slums, but he had never set foot inside it, so there was some risk. But there was also some risk in allowing the woman to complain and complain, because the delegation included World Health Organization observers, and Fidel was sensitive to bad press in Europe.

So they'd pulled up unannounced in front of Clínica 28, and Carlos Arroyo Gutierrez, minister of health, had marched through the front door leading sixteen foreigners with notepads and cameras. It was every doctor's worst nightmare. But the doctor in this case had been Elena Ruiz Mendoza. Dark hair, beautiful figure for a middle-aged woman, fierce eyes with a hint of gold light in them. She'd reacted as if the clinic had had a month's advance notice. There is nothing to be ashamed of here, that was her attitude; you could read it in her posture and voice. The clinic was filled with wailing children, some with running sores, most with lice, a few of them indeed very ill with a violent intestinal flu that had been troubling the island at the time. But the five rooms were spotlessly clean. The morale of the two doctors and the six nurses was high. And though the shelves were not stocked with more than a week's supply of the essentials—zylocaine, penicillin, aspirin, hydrogen peroxide—the nurses called on the patients in fair order, and, it seemed to Carlos, treated them capably, efficiently.

After the Italian delegation had left the country—no loud complaints, no bad press—Carlos dropped in on the clinic a second time, one morning on his way to work. He and Elena talked for a few minutes. He thanked her, complimented her. After that day he began a small campaign to divert medicines to Clínica 28, and then another, more personal campaign: calling on Elena to see that she was receiving the medicines, taking her out for coffee on her breaks, then to dinner, then to bed. She'd lost her husband to pulmonary fibrosis a few years before. Her grown daughter taught at the University in Camagüey. Her grown son was a poor architect for the city of Erlos, not far from Matanzas, and he and his wife had a new baby.

Elena was a brilliant woman, bursting with energy and hope for the work she did, but full of disdain for the politicians—Cuban and otherwise—who built their careers on the backs of sick children.

After a few months of courtship she'd moved in with him, passing on her apartment to a colleague with three young children. Carlos had revealed to her nothing about his extra-governmental political involvement. To protect her, he told himself. To protect her, and others. But, in fact, he was not truly sure of Elena's political leanings. At times, quietly, she voiced criticisms—never of Fidel personally, but of the way things were done. And then, other times, he'd see her watching a television program that was pure propaganda, and there would be tears in her eyes for the great experiment that was Cuba.

Silently, arms linked, they walked along the Paseo, passing a waist-high billboard that read CIA = ASESINOS. They turned down an alley, past a woman and small child begging and a man playing the Peruvian flute, then ducked into the large, noisy, popular Cafe Castro, where you could sometimes get a little chicken or fish with your beans and rice and tortillas, and where you were likely to be seated next to anyone from a government minister to a colonel in the armed forces.

They sat at a table near the dark windows and ordered beer and food. The palms of his hands were slick, but Carlos believed he presented a peaceful face to the world, the face of a loyal patriot, an honest servant of the state. An anti-*asesino*.

"Something's wrong," Elena said, breaking her angry silence.

Carlos shook his head and ran his gaze once around the room. He then pretended to study his palms, as he did in cabinet meetings. Eleven minutes before the hour.

"You're never rude like that with me, Carlos. You never insist on going someplace I don't want to go."

"I needed a change," he lied.

"You've never liked the food here."

"I wanted to give it another try."

She reached out and took hold of his hand, wiping away the perspiration. "Are you feverish?"

"I might be. My stomach is upset. The day upset me. It was an awful day, full of delay and paper shuffling, phone calls and meetings that accomplished nothing, people content to do nothing. I'm sorry. I apologize. I'll make it up to you on Friday night."

She was watching him. A ceiling fan turned lazily overhead. He was trying to count the seconds as they passed.

"If you feel ill why would you come here?"

"It really started to come on when we were driving here. I'll step into the toilet for a moment. Be a different man when I come back."

He tugged his hand from hers as gently as he could manage, stood up, and headed off to the toilet. Four lies already, and the night was young.

General Rincon, he guessed, had chosen this place because there were two stalls in the men's room, and because it wouldn't be suspicious in the least for the two of them to happen to be here for dinner at separate tables. Carlos made his way toward the back, feeling slightly faint. *It's you,* Rincon had told him. But how was he going to find the nerve to do something like that if he could barely walk across a noisy room without losing his balance? How was he going to keep hiding it from Elena? *It's you. It's you.* Carlos had thought about it constantly. Clearly, they needed someone with regular access to *el Comandante*, and, at the same time, someone who would seem the most unlikely of killers.

There was a short wait for the toilet. Carlos stood behind a hugely obese man—how did someone find that much to eat in Cuba?—in the narrow hallway, with waiters squeezing past carrying trays of steaming beans and plantains. His watch read 8:57. He wiped his hands on the sides of his trousers, and, when it was his turn, went into the cramped bathroom. Two toilet stalls, a stained urinal where the obese man stood, a sink. He looked at the shoes in the occupied stall—sandals, dirty feet, not the footwear of the nation's second most senior general—and went into the other one, sat, and waited. In a moment the man at the urinal shuffled back out the door without flushing, without washing his hands. Another moment and Carlos heard a loud flush beside him, followed by the scraping of sandals as the man made his way to the rust-stained sink. Then the door banging shut, then banging open, and what sounded like Rincon's happy voice, humming a tune.

The general took the stall next to him, and, not knowing what else to do, Carlos shuffled his foot as a signal. Nothing happened. Perhaps it was not Rincon. Perhaps Rincon was not who he believed him to be, and it was one of Olochon's men in the stall beside him. Perhaps the night would find him at the prison again, Olochon standing before him triumphantly with his pliers and hideous smile. Carlos coughed. After a long moment a piece of cardboard appeared beneath the metal wall that separated the two stalls. It seemed to be the hand of General Rincon, and Rincon seemed to be holding a note for him, a piece of cardboard tilted up so Carlos could read.

Day after tomorrow. Oriente Hotel Bar. 9:05 P.M.
Make an excuse to be there. Tap twice if understood.

Carlos read the message three times, tapped his shoe twice, flushed, washed his hands at the sink, and went back to his table. The food had already been served and was growing cold, and Elena was watching for him with a smear of hurt on both cheeks.

"Feeling better?" she asked when he rejoined her.

"Diarrhea. Lunch at the Ministry cafeteria. Always a mistake."

But she wasn't so easily fooled. The room was noisy with laughter and talk, and music piped in through rusty old red metal speakers that hung in the corners, but the silence between them was deafening. With his mind spinning in fast circles, and the piece of cardboard and Ernesto's hideous, torn apart face appearing and disappearing in the air in front of him, Carlos asked about her children and new grandchild, about her day at the clinic, talked too much about an outbreak of hepatitis C in La Finca province. Part of his job was to oversee the biotechnology industry, Cuba's pride and joy, and he told her, in great detail, about one Havana lab that was soon to get an international patent on a cancer drug. "Blood cancers," he said. "Leukemia. They've tested it extensively and the white cell levels went from the forty thousand range to the mid-teens."

She listened, watching him. When he had finished his main course—cleaning his plate in spite of the supposed stomach troubles—he came within a whisker of telling her. "Something is happening," he wanted to say. "Something is going to happen." There were three parallel creases in her forehead, and when she was upset, concerned, or tired they grew deeper. He looked at those creases and felt a whisper of distrust in his ears. If he could lie to her so easily, if he could hide things from her . . . then perhaps she was lying to him, hiding things from him.

She watched him. They took coffee in a strained silence. Afterward, they went back out through the alley and strolled down the Paseo arm in arm, but her touch was uncharacteristically cold, and he could still feel her watching him. At the corner where the Officina de Correo stood, two prostitutes dissolved into the shadows. "I have an urge to go over to them and hand out condoms," Elena said.

"Go, if you have them. You'll save a life, perhaps many lives. You'll save the state fifty thousand pesos."

"I have them at the clinic, but they're ours."

" 'Ours' meaning 'Cuban,' *verdad?*"

They were speaking softly, beneath the noise of the bus motors and the salsa music from a third-floor balcony.

She nodded. "*Sí, claro.* The rumor on the streets is that only American or French condoms really work. And American and French condoms are expensive, sometimes twenty-five pesos."

"The price of our dinner. Whereas Cuban condoms are handed out without charge at every clinic in the city."

"*Sí. Pero los nuestros no son seguros.*"

"*Seguros.*" Secure, safe, dependable. The word caught him like a slap on the back of the skull. It had always been a word he'd applied to himself. But he was a certified traitor now; he could be arrested and killed for what he'd just done, for what he'd been doing over the past months.

"I'll send people to the factories for an unannounced check," he said. "Tomorrow. I'll talk to Callata about a propaganda campaign: *Los Preservativos Cubanos—Los Mejores del Mundo!*"

She didn't smile, and he knew she believed it was all slightly abstract to him. He cared, but his work was a matter of reading the statistics, the charts, the falsely positive official reports. It was she who saw prostitutes with Kaposi's sarcoma holding infants at their breasts, a rare sight in Cuba, still, but . . . "It sickens me," he said, very loudly, as if to prove something to her and to himself.

"Shh! Carlos!" She squeezed his arm.

"We can make a drug to fight cancer, but we can't make a rubber without a hole in it?"

"We can. Of course we can. Only nobody here believes that we can." She squeezed his arm more tightly. "And the Americans should sell them to us, in any case. What are we are going do, turn rubbers into bombs?"

"For some things we can't blame them. I mean, we can blame them, but we have to take our own responsibility. Every decent country in the world can make a good condom, but we can't? Cuba can't?"

"But we can, I'm telling you," she said. "We do." She looked over her shoulder. They had turned the corner just as Carlos spoke the last two lines and a group of smartly dressed young men had been passing them, fresh from the Institute. Fresh from having their brains filled with propaganda. One of them recognized him, he was sure of it, he'd been on television recently, promoting prenatal programs. So, tomorrow morning, that ambitious young student would go to the political officer of his section and report that he'd seen *Ministro de la Salud* Gutierrez on the street on Thursday night, and the *ministro* had been spouting anti-Cuban propaganda. Neither he nor Elena said another word until the students were a block behind them.

"Shout it from the rooftops," Elena said.

"Only here would a minister fear a student; only here."

Another cold draft of quiet between them. She loosened her grip. "Tonight," she said, "you are a different man."

"Yes," he said. "The illness. The fever."

But when they were home in bed, side by side on their backs with the sweaty skin of the sides of their thighs pressing together and only a thin sheet covering them against the night air, he decided that he'd had enough of it. Enough lying. Enough deceit. Enough fear. If he were caught and arrested, she would be imprisoned anyway—guilt by association—so there was really nothing to lose in telling her. Nothing . . . except everything. He had known her for five years. In secret, in bed like this, quietly, they had made their timid complaints. They knew who Fidel really was—an old egomaniac, deluded by himself and those around him but sitting on the kernel of a correct idea: that people should be treated equally; that the state should care for those least able to care for themselves; that huge gaps between rich and poor were morally unacceptable.

But it was also true that, from time to time, she said things that echoed the propaganda of their youth. Fidel was heroic. The Cuban people were engaged in an heroic struggle against the cold-hearted capitalism ninety miles to their north. That struggle required sacrifice from all of them, and patience, but on some glorious day in the future they would reap their reward. The Revolution, he thought. The Revolution meant free health care for everyone. The Revolution meant you were afraid to tell your lover what you actually believed. One sentence and you put your entire life in her hands.

He took two breaths, still unsure, then he said, "Elena, I have to tell you something very important and difficult."

He heard her take in a sharp breath and he knew she thought he was going to break off the relationship, just at the point where she'd been hoping he would ask her to marry him. He took her hand and squeezed it warmly, but he felt as if his body were made of concrete. He turned on his side to look at her in the faint light from the street. In the quietest voice he could manage he said, "I am involved in a plot against the government. There are others involved. There are no North Americans involved that I know of. It's not what you think. We have to make a change now and we are the only people who can do it."

Her face was only inches from his, and he could see the spark of gold in her dark eyes. He felt the same deep tremor of fear and hope that he had felt the first time they'd made love, the same vulnerability, the same urge to set aside every separation. He waited and waited and at last could no longer stand it. "Speak," he pleaded.

"They'll kill you," she said, in a whisper. "They're just using you, whoever they are. You're not that kind of man. They'll end up killing you, I know it."

He felt something heavy inside him, sinking now into his depths. "Elena, the people who are organizing this are brilliant people. It is a plan that cannot fail."

"You're sure?"

"Absolutely positive."

She was silent so long that Carlos thought she might have fallen asleep. He found himself answering a question she had not asked, tracing his route back to the point where the most loyal of patriots had started a process of questioning inside himself. The questioning had led him to this moment. *It is you.*

Elena reached up and wiped the tears from her face. Her sobs became audible. He took hold of her hand and squeezed it.

"There is no worry," he said. "None."

She was shaking her head from side to side, almost violently. "Two officers from DGI came to the clinic today," she said, still in a whisper. "They spent an hour going through the files and records, even my personal notes. I thought it had something to do with you, but I didn't want to tell you. I didn't want you to be worried."

CHAPTER FOURTEEN

———⌇⌇⌇———

P art of what Volkes found so difficult about Oleg Rodriguez's treachery was that he had always liked the man. Had a real soft spot for him, in fact. The good looks and confidence, the classy wardrobe, the way Oleg often seemed to be thinking about the world in a grand way, as if all of humanity were one body and he had been entrusted with its care—it reminded Volkes of himself when he'd been younger. Brimming with ambition, energy, shrewdness. Wanting nothing but the best for his suffering species. In those days—his thirties, forties, and early fifties—he'd be in the gym at sunrise, doing a forty-minute piece on the rowing machine, then he'd shower, shave, and have a light breakfast while reading Walt Whitman in the back of the limo on the way to work. He'd functioned like a well-oiled machine then, moving from one pleasure to the next, accumulating money like a magnet in a room of metal filings, courting the most magnificent women, fashioning the grandest plans.

The Havana Project was going to be the culmination of all that effort and ability, all that foresight, imagination, and self-discipline. His swan song, his last great gift to the world. "From those to whom much has been given, much will be asked" was the way the Bible put it. Well, he had been given a great deal, and this was going to be his repayment.

For the last few years he'd been thinking that, when the Havana Project was complete, he was going to retire into the lap of luxury, and watch Oleg take over the organization's reins.

So much for soft-heartedness.

Rodriguez was sitting next to him now on one of the Orchid's corporate jets; just the two of them flying across the bottom part of Florida for what would appear to be nothing more than a relaxing morning of golf at a club he belonged to in Naples. Eddie Lincoln had called him the night before, quite late, all full of enthusiasm for the young Cuban woman he'd just been yelling at. "Volkes," the vice president had boomed, "balls the size of watermelons, this girl!"

"I'm sure she'd consider that a compliment," Volkes had said dryly, but Lincoln was a bit slow on the uptake in the later hours.

"Fine. She's fine. All set by me. We had quite the chat."

Volkes had been happy to hear it, of course. Happy, but not surprised. He sat now with his hands folded in his lap, thinking about Carolina Perez, on whom so much rested, and staring down at the long stretch of alligator-infested swamp that went by the quaint name Everglades. Canals like blue ribbons sparkling in the sun, thousands of small ponds, a few well-spaced Indian settlements, surrounded by some of the wildest land in the lower forty-eight. A person—a betrayer—could be made to disappear in the muck and mosquitoes there and never be traced.

"Penny for your thoughts," Oleg said at that moment.

Volkes turned and regarded the dark eyes and angular cheekbones. There was some Indian blood in Oleg's line, he supposed, and so, in a way, depositing the fellow here would be like returning Oleg to his own people. He said, "I was thinking a couple of things. First off, Eddie Lincoln called me this morning when I was on route to the airport to meet you. He's not happy with our choice."

Oleg's face registered real astonishment.

"Too emotional," Volkes went on. "He said he was hoping for someone with cooler blood."

"Cooler blood?"

"His words exactly."

"The woman has met with torturers, murderers, despots, and never flinched. We've been grooming her, checking her out, for years. If she were any cooler in the blood she'd be—"

"I told him the same thing. He wasn't moved."

"And?"

"And he's one of the partners. We'll have to either convince him he's wrong or move to plan B."

"Plan B might work," Oleg said after a moment.

Volkes could hear the treachery in his voice, the disappointment. Plan B would complicate things for Señor Rodriguez, make him look less than reliable in DGI headquarters, a man who wasn't sure, whose information might not be 100 percent reliable. *What a shame,* Volkes thought. He turned toward the window again, searching for a suitably remote resting place, playing Oleg now like a tarpon on a line.

"And the second thing?"

"What second thing?" Volkes asked, concentrating on a particular stretch of unpeopled swampland and thinking: It would best be done at night.

"You said you had two things on your mind."

Volkes turned to him. "The second thing, my friend, is that

I'm retiring after this. Lincoln and I talked about it this morning. I'm seventy-one. A well-preserved seventy-one to be sure, but seventy-one all the same. I've got ten good years left, at the outside, and I'd dearly like to pass those years enjoying my money. Some sailing, a little travel, lots of golf. If the Orchid wants me to consult, I'll consult, happily, but when this is over I'm most likely to be found on the first tee at Isle of Lakes, Ponte Vedra, Tiburón." Oleg started to object, but Volkes held up a hand. "We talked at length, Eddie Lincoln and I, and it's all set. We'd like you to be the man who takes my place."

CHAPTER FIFTEEN

Carolina slept a deep sleep broken by one flash of dream. In the dream she was in the waiting room of the orthodontist she'd gone to starting at age twelve, terrified. Her uncle was sitting beside her, reading aloud in Spanish, slowly, as if to a child.

When she awoke, it took her a full minute of looking around the hotel room to remember where she was. Her old woman's dress lay where she had left it, on a chair by the desk. The makeup still sat in clumps in the hotel sink, and in the roots of her hair. She made a call to the number Oleg had given her, then stepped into the shower and remained there a long time, scrubbing away old age. Shortly after she was dry and dressed, Evan knocked on her door carrying his hairdressing supplies, and soon she was a blond once more, almost her natural color.

She had a breakfast of fruit and coffee at the hotel restaurant, then went out into the parking lot, young again, or almost young. If someone had been following her since she'd left Atlanta, then at the very least they would be tired and confused. But there were no white Ford Explorers in the hotel parking lot, no one sitting in any of the cars. The Orchid had been kind enough to have another pretty vehicle, a Porsche SUV, brought to the hotel for her, keys with the valet attendant. One ten-dollar tip later and she was driving west in morning sunshine.

Instead of going straight to the Doral apartment to pack, she turned onto Seventy-second Avenue, northwest, drove a ways, then pulled up behind a new, rather nondescript Catholic church. Morning mass had concluded half an hour earlier; the front doors were unlocked. Inside, once her eyes had adjusted to the dim light, she turned into the pew nearest the back wall and sat there, not praying so much as wondering. She believed in some kind of God. The God she believed in would want people to be happy, to be free. If some people had to do evil things in order to make that happen, then she believed her God would forgive such things, to a point. She had done things she was not proud of. Shot a man once, perhaps killed him, she did not know. Working for the Agency she had put the lives of strangers at great risk, served governments that, while friendly to the United States, were not exactly paragons of virtue.

She sighed, and closed her eyes to pray. In the midst of her prayer she heard the exterior doors squeak open and knock closed, a pause, and then heavy footsteps—a man's. She kept her head bowed, but moved her purse onto her lap, opened it, put her right hand inside, and gripped the handle of her 9mm Markus. The footsteps echoed against the church's high ceiling. When the man drew even with the row where she sat, she turned, moving the purse with her, beginning to withdraw the pistol, and saw her ex-husband, Oscar, there at the end of the pew, smiling at her, holding up his hands very slightly from his sides in a gesture of dignified surrender.

She set the purse to her left side, away from him. As he was sidestepping along the pew toward her, a little shiver of feeling

washed over the skin of her arms. Except for weddings and funer-
als, Oscar had not set foot inside a church since his first commun-
ion. He was here to see her; he had obviously been following her.

As she knew he would, he sat down very close to her. She
could smell his aftershave, and another old tremor moved through
her. For a moment, he sat quietly looking forward, as if they were
in the cathedral again waiting for the priest to join them in holy
matrimony.

"You've been following me," she whispered, when she could
no longer stand the silence.

He only nodded, and would not look at her.

"What's going on, Oscar?"

He hesitated, pressed his lips together. Their thighs were
touching. She resisted an urge to slide away from him.

"Do you know who you are working for, Carolina? Really
know them?"

She nodded.

"I don't think you do. I think you were seduced by their
money, and their high-sounding principles, but I don't think you
have a clue as to who they really are."

"We've had this fight, Oscar. I don't want to have it again,
not in church, not anywhere."

"I want to protect you, not control you."

"It amounts to the same thing."

"Right," he said bitterly. She thought he might stand up and
leave. He looked at the altar, ran his eyes over the mural there,
Jesus surrounded by his apostles, with Judas the traitor approaching, leading Roman soldiers. He said in a whisper, almost as if it
were a confession, "Look, I know some things about what you're
doing. I have friends everywhere, Caro, good people, all of them.

I give them a little help from time to time, and they give me a little help from time to time. And the little help they're giving me now is to let me know that my wife is in water too dangerous for swimming."

Ex-wife, she wanted to insist. But instead, she said quietly, "I'm an excellent swimmer." She did not take her eyes off him now. In profile, he looked like some kind of general, an honorable man burdened with the responsibility for his troops. In the great Latino tradition he had always seen her as one of those troops, special perhaps, adorable, but nevertheless subservient. At his temples she saw the first threads of gray.

"Of course, of course," he said, turning at last to meet her eyes. "Excellent. A great swimmer. Better than me. But I've always made it a point to know the people I am swimming with. I'm not sure you have done that. The people you are working for now are reckless. Their aims are not what they claim to be. They'll risk your well-being while keeping themselves safe. This risk might result in your capture, your torture, your death, and I can't just stand by and let that happen."

"I've worked for them for eight years, Oscar, and never once in all that time have they failed to protect me. I have never done anything, or seen them do anything, that was at odds with what I believe. I can't say that about the Agency; can you?"

"No." He shook his head sadly. "But you are at especially great risk this time. They've been preparing this, preparing you, for years, since the day they hired you. I warned you then, and I'm warning you again now. I plead with you to listen to me."

"And what, Oscar?"

"And resign. Take your money. Invest it with me in your uncle's businesses. Together we can agitate for a free Cuba, but not like this."

"You're going to retire, then? Give up a life of chasing terrorists through the alleys in Pakistan and decide to be a stay-at-home Dad?"

She felt as though she could look all the way down into the centers of his eyes and see his soul. They'd been too young when they married. They'd been pursuing careers that would have broken apart any union—weeks without seeing each other; so many things they could never talk about; when they were home in Virginia, the incredible drudgery of working for one of the biggest bureaucracies on the planet. "I might," he said. "I'm willing to talk about it anyway."

"*Bien*," she said, but she could not let herself completely believe him. "All right. I'm going away for a while, a week or two. When I get back, call me in Atlanta and we can talk about it if you really mean that."

"I really mean it. And I really mean this, too: I don't want you to go."

"I have to, Oscar. I get paid to go."

"Tell them you won't go this time."

"Why would I do that?"

"Because Oleg Rodriguez works for DGI."

She blinked. She turned her eyes away, remembering his jealousy, the insinuations, the fights. Suddenly their proposed talk about a future reconciliation did not hold much appeal. "And that information came to you from what source?" she asked him, eyes averted, her voice cold.

"An unnameable and reliable source."

"You know how easy it is to make that accusation. You know how it's used in our community."

"He is using you to expose the entire underground dissident movement in Cuba. You're going there in two months to the day—this is how secret your network is, your Orchid. You're going there in two months with a passport from one of the former Eastern European countries. When you arrive, when you meet your contact at a tourist hotel, you'll both be arrested and tortured. You'll give up the names on the American side. And your contact will be forced to give up the names on the Cuban side. When that's accomplished, there will be more arrests and torture in Cuba, there'll be assassinations here. And you'll be killed, naturally. The whole thing—your hiring, your years of work, all of which this Rodriguez has had a hand in—has been an elaborate preparation, dreamed up by Castro and his men, as a way of decimating the dissident movement."

"And your proof?"

"My proof is that I know the name of the man you report to. I know your assignment. How would I know those things if your organization is as sharp as it claims to be?"

She had no answer for him. "So the entire organization is a front for Castro and DGI? And this front can arrange a clandestine meeting with—" She stopped before she could say "the vice president of the United States?"

"I'm not saying the whole organization is corrupt, Caro. But I am telling you, in confidence, that it's been infiltrated. The infiltrators are brilliant, evil, vicious people who make their plans decades in advance, who will use anyone to achieve their goals."

She was shaking her head. It was a case of crying wolf. The expatriate Cuban community had been so battered by the rise, conversion, and apparent immortality of Fidel Castro that they'd taken to lying about things, exaggerating, bending the truth to fit their own ends, their own anger. It was true, of course, that Castro's agents had infiltrated various organizations on this side of the water. But it was true only about 10 percent as often as the old Cubanos claimed it was.

"You remind me of my uncle," she said.

"I take that as a compliment."

"In the sense that. . . . Listen, Oscar, you can't just keep using Castro's treachery every time you want something. Sure there have been spies, but it's a heavy accusation, the heaviest, where we come from. You can't just lay that on somebody unless you're a hundred percent sure of it."

"It's not jealousy," he said. "I know you think it is, from before. But it isn't. I'm not like that anymore. I'm older. I'm over it."

"All right," she said, half convinced. "We'll talk when I get back."

He pressed his lips together impatiently. She could see him biting back the words. He put a hand on her arm and let it rest there. "Call me if you change your mind. Will you do that? Even if you just want to talk. The number is the same. Will you, Caro?"

She nodded, not blinking.

"Watch yourself," he said, and with that he planted a proprietary kiss near her lips, and left the way he had come, slowly, quietly, just another Cuban Catholic seeking counsel from his God.

CHAPTER SIXTEEN

The next morning an unbearable tension, vaporous and sour, saturated the air of Carlos's kitchen. He sat at the rust-colored metal table watching Elena's back as she squeezed the juice from orange halves into two small glasses. She put one glass in front of him and one on her place mat. She poured two cups of *cafecito* and set one in front of him and the other, again, on her place mat. She had four slices of bread grilling in a pan and she put extra butter on two of them, because that was to his taste, and because, for some unknown reason, there was plenty of butter in the special stores this month. She watched the toast slices for a few seconds, then flipped them over and pressed them into the hot metal so hard that the muscles of her arm flexed beneath the sleeve of her dress.

At last, when she had dragged everything out as long as possible, she sat down opposite him. Her face seemed especially worn out that morning, the forehead furrows deep, the hair dull. She turned on the radio and said, beneath the music: "I want you not to do this."

"It's too late, Elena."

"I want you, for me, not to do this."

He reached across the corner of the table and took her hand. Neither of them had touched their food. "People are depending on me now. Brave people. Good people. Some have already lost their lives for this."

"Who are these people?"

Her voice broke on the question and there was something there, some note he did not like, some urgency. He felt as though thin metal plates, like the plates that held X-ray films, were being slammed down into place between them, one after the next, pushing them farther and farther apart. "You know I can't tell you."

"They mean more to you than I do?"

He shook his head. "I thought you would . . . I thought we saw things the same way."

She was shaking her head more vehemently.

"You don't see the foolishness?" he whispered beneath the music. "The abuses of power? The egotism? The fact that we are all but isolated in the world, living on one of the richest islands on earth and our people going hungry, crops not being grown, or being grown incorrectly? And all of it being blamed on the North Americans? You don't see this?"

"I see everything," she said. "Everything."

"But?"

There was a loud bang outside their windows. Merely a car backfiring, but Elena jumped in her seat and began to weep. "We have made a life," she said in a broken voice. She was not looking at him, her hair hanging down so that the ends just touched the buttery top of her toast, tears dripping into the corners of her mouth. "Here, in Cuba, the people have made a life, in spite of everything, against the greatest odds. You're going to destroy that now? And build what in its place? Do you even know? Could you even tell me the names of the ones who thought this plan up? Even if you wanted to, even if you trusted me enough, could you?"

"No, I could not," he said.

"Are you the leader?" she whispered.

"No, I am not."

"Who then? In whose hands are you placing your life and my happiness?'

"I can't tell you that."

"Can't or won't, Carlos?"

"Can't and won't."

She broke into bitter sobs and stood up. For an instant she seemed to be looking around, as if for a weapon with which to attack him, or a knife with which to do herself in. Then she hurried into the bedroom and slammed the door and he could hear her weeping there.

CHAPTER SEVENTEEN

A fter Oscar left, Carolina sat for almost an hour in the quiet church, her only companion an old woman in black who shuffled through a side door and began quietly mopping the tiles. Carolina thought about what Oscar had said, and the look on his face when he was saying it. He had always been a jealous man. Now, somehow, he had found out that Oleg was her boss— perhaps seen them together somewhere, if he'd been following her—and assumed they were lovers. And he'd reached for a way to discredit him, the easiest way, the way that made all Cubans pay attention: Oleg was secretly working for Castro.

She thought about it and thought about it, and at last it seemed clear to her that there was a perfect parallel between her work and her faith. Doubt was always trying to intrude. In order for anything good to happen you had to banish it completely.

From the church, Carolina drove to a spotlessly clean Guatemalan restaurant on Calle Ocho for a quick, inexpensive lunch, and then to her apartment in Doral, intending to stay just long enough to get her bathing suit, umbrella, sun lotion, and a book, and head to South Beach, as she had been instructed. The apartment door was locked, as usual, but once she was inside she saw that papers were strewn everywhere, her laptop computer was gone, her medicine chest rifled through. So much for the security of the gated community. There was no thought of notifying the police. She used her cell phone to call Oleg on his secure line and tell him. He was outdoors, and when he spoke—she could not help herself—she searched his voice for signs of deceit.

"Did you have any information about the project on the computer?" he asked her.

"Of course not. I don't even have it on my computer in Atlanta."

"Did you have notes lying about, anything—the time you were to meet your uncle, a phone number, anything at all?"

"I've been doing this work long enough to know not to write anything down, Oleg. Even your phone number. The only really important things I keep here are some old snapshots and souvenirs. But they're in an accordion file, and the file was at the back of my closet and has not been touched."

"Fine," he said. "We'll make some small adjustments. Everything else is as we discussed."

"Someone should check the apartment in Atlanta," she said, but he hung up abruptly and she couldn't be sure he'd heard. She wondered if Oleg himself had had the apartment searched, if it was just the Orchid making absolutely sure she was the right person for this job. Or if Oscar had broken in. Or if it had just been common thieves.

None of them would have been this clumsy, she thought, unless they'd been almost caught in the act. Or unless they were trying to send her a message.

THE DAY WAS warm and bright and South Beach was a hive of half-naked bodies and laconic activity. After twenty minutes, she found a parking space in front of a diner on Eleventh Street where she had gone many times with her father and mother when she was a girl. The break-in had shaken her, but she was used to the rest of it, used to knowing things only an hour or a day before she had to know them. She had learned to take things one step at a time, to have faith that the Orchid would provide her with the information she needed when she needed it, would pay her what and when they said they would pay her. Eight years now and not one disappointment, not one broken promise, nothing but good money, high praise, and care taken with her life.

Get some rest, Oleg had advised on the plane. *And while you are getting your rest we want you to go to the beach, South Beach, and lay your towel in front of the Atlantica Hotel. Read, improve your tan, body surf, anything. Just stay there until it becomes apparent that you no longer need to.*

He had been so calm. Even now, on the phone, he had seemed strangely unperturbed about the break-in. Too casual. She thought it likely she'd be contacted soon and told that the Cuba assignment had been given to somebody else. They had backups, she was sure. Their plans were made in multiples of three and four, fallback position upon fallback position. If she was being followed, if Oscar knew so much, if people were breaking into her apartment looking for documents, then the shell of secrecy around her had already been cracked open.

Once she'd made herself comfortable on the sand, she spread the lotion on her skin, vaguely ashamed that she needed it, a woman of her blood. But most of her working time was spent indoors—in airplanes, airports, hotels, cars—and she did not want to sit through a long flight with sunburned thighs. She dozed, she read a travel magazine through her sunglasses, she went in the tepid water twice and splashed around not far from some loud, happy Latin teenagers. The warm sun on her bare skin lit a small sexual fire in her. It had been a long time since she'd made love, and now the sound of the happy teenagers carried her back to Calle Ocho, to a makeshift sofa in a back room. Jose, his name had been. The smell of a teenager's cologne and the trembling of her body, that first incredible sense that she'd been admitted to a secret society of real adults. Jose ran a little restaurant now—she'd checked—had a family, a house of his own. On the sunny beach, for just the smallest stretch of time, she wondered if she would have been happy with him, with a life like that.

At two o'clock she walked across the street for a salad and a sweetened iced tea, then she went back to her towel, ready for anything, or nothing. Ready for the Orchid's next move.

Its next move arrived in the form of a handsome black man. He came and casually lay his towel down next to hers, and she understood she was supposed to act as if they were old friends, perhaps lovers. He barely said hello, made no move to kiss or touch her, just spoke her name, the briefest of greetings—as if they'd last seen each other at breakfast. On the sand near his head he placed a canvas bag—the kind bookstores give away as advertising. He took off his shirt and trousers to reveal a chiseled body, all ripples and sinews. His eyes were green. When he was lying there, facedown in his tight bathing suit, he turned so that he was looking at her, and smiled slyly. "Federico," he said quietly.

She nodded.

"Federico from Oleg."

The Latin boys had come out of the water, shouting and dripping wet, and were throwing a football back and forth on the sand. The ball came bouncing crazily toward her and Federico, and rolled to a stop at the edge of her blanket. Federico turned, picked it up with one hand, half sat up, and fired a perfect spiral into the boy's arms. "*Gracias, Señor!*" the boy called back.

Federico was all smiles. "Rub some lotion on your back or anything?" he said.

"Thanks. All set."

"The tickets are in the bag. We'll leave the beach together in a little while. I'll walk you as far as your car."

"I'm still going?"

"You're going. My job is to get you the tickets. We can swim a little, go out for a meal. You can invite me over to your apartment for the night, for appearances' sake only." He winked at her. She hated men who winked. "But I'm here for the tickets, nothing else. I can't even look at them. I don't even know where you're going. I don't even know who you really are, except that you're someone important."

She nodded and looked out over the aquamarine ocean, huge cottony cumulus clouds drifting past overhead. It was an exercise in trust, she decided. The whole thing, her whole life, was an exercise in trust. But still, some quiet, nagging tone sounded in the back of her thoughts.

They dove into the surf, swam and rode a few waves, then came back to their towels and talked about the weather, the Marlins, music. When the air started to lose a bit of its heat, Federico accompanied her to her car and, as if by accident, tossed the canvas bag into the back of the SUV with her beach chair and towel.

"Tonight I need to sleep alone," she told him, when they'd kissed lightly on the lips and were still embracing. "But maybe another time."

"*Otra vez,*" he said happily. Everyone who had anything to do with the Orchid was happy like this. It was, she thought, merely the satisfaction that came from being overpaid.

———∿∿|ᴅ|∿∿———

Carlos was to meet his contact at the José Martí Bar at the Oriente Hotel in thirty-six hours. The Oriente was hard-currency-only, and for the most part no one but foreign tourists went there. So he would need an excuse. He'd lain awake much of the night thinking of the right excuse, and by the time he kissed his still-upset Elena good-bye and headed off to the Ministry of Health, he was in full deceit mode. It was strange: He'd always thought of himself as a truthful man. Now, lately, lying had become as natural to him as taking a breath.

"Disease," he said to Jose on the ride in, "disease in this country comes primarily from abroad."

"AIDS, you're thinking of," Jose said.

"Primarily, but not only. Rats come in on the ships, and rats carry the plague. *Norteamericanos* sleep with our beautiful prostitutes—"

"Who are the finest in the world," Jose said.

"Who are the finest in the world, and have supplies of the finest rubbers in the world for their own protection—"

"Which are North American rubbers."

"And French. But those foreigners who do not use prophy-lactics—"

"And they are legion," said Jose.

"They pass on gonorrhea, syphilis, the cousins hepatitis. Others bring with them various strains of the flu to which our immune systems are not accustomed."

"If we could isolate ourselves completely, there would be no illness in Cuba," Jose said.

"I would be out of a job."

"But you would never be ill."

"*Verdad*," Carlos said. "Therefore, we must begin a campaign."

"*Por supuesto. Una campaña.*"

"*Sí.* We must begin a campaign of sanitary health, a campaign of cleanliness and tidiness for all areas where the body of Cuba touches the outside world."

"You are going to wash the thighs of our prostitutes with disinfectant. A brilliant campaign, Ministro. I volunteer for service."

They pulled up in front of the Ministry of Health, a modern, ugly building on Calle Virtudes, built on the site of a mansion formerly owned by a mafia chieftain from Coral Gables. Before getting out, Carlos looked across the seat at his friend. He remembered how kind Jose had been to him during Teresa's long illness and after her death; how loyal he had been throughout these years, closer to him than a brother. He fought back a sudden urge to tell him everything. "We are going to begin a campaign of inspections in those areas touched by our foreign visitors—ports, tourist hotels, beachfront restaurants. We will do mandatory blood testing of workers there. I'll draft the order this morning. Raul will approve it with a phone call. You and I will make our first visits this afternoon."

"*Claro,*" Jose said. "Spitting in the face of the outside world, harassing our hard-currency workers, *el Comandante* will love it. This is why you are a *ministro* and I am a driver. You are a brilliant man."

Brilliant, Carlos thought, walking up the grand front steps into the building over which he had presided for almost a decade. Brilliant, probably not.

HE SPENT THE morning drafting the campaign memos and instructing his coterie of deputies on how to get the message out quickly. As a symbolic example, he said, he himself would make some cursory inspections in the coming weeks. He would begin, that very afternoon, with the Port of Havana. Around the table his deputies nodded and dozed. He knew that two minutes after the meeting was adjourned, they'd rush off to telephone their friends at the port: The *ministro* is coming, clean your toilets, wash your faces and hands, take the afternoon off if you can.

AFTER LUNCH, JOSE chauffeured him to the Port of Havana. For amusement, Jose put the blue light on top of the car and set it to flashing, and then pushed down hard on the accelerator and made the siren sound against the fronts of the buildings they passed. A few people turned their heads to look, but it wasn't Fidel, wasn't even the police, just another minister in a black car, his suit new, his belly full, his children protected. As they raced past Elena's clinic, Carlos studied the front door and windows there. One stooped old woman leaving; nothing more to be seen.

For some reason, the port always soothed him: the magnificent old Morro Castle, the beautifully tattered facades near the Malecón, all of it cut by alleys that were inhabited by a ragtag band of workers, whores, con artists, thieves, foreign sailors, and drunks. He wondered if he enjoyed being there merely because the port spoke of the existence of another world, another way of life beyond the horizon. Three freighters were anchored in the filthy waters—in the days of the old Soviet Union there would have been twenty-three.

Carlos stepped energetically out of the car, found the director of the port, made a bit of small talk with him, told one vulgar joke, informed the man about his new campaign, and then marched around in his suit, with two deputies at his elbows, asking questions and bothering people. One of the freighters was from the Czech Republic, bringing in cotton fabric and carrying out—what else!—sugar. In the third car of the three-car convoy, Carlos had brought along a doctor and two nurses, and they set up an impromptu clinic, checking the eyes and pulses of a handful of longshoremen, drawing a few vials of blood for random AIDS and hepatitis C testing. He found the captain of the Czech ship and lectured the man on making sure his sailors used the proper health protection during their visit to the capital. The man listened quietly and nodded, but there was a grin beneath the hard muscles of his face. He was old enough to remember communism; he knew what was going on. Carlos's little lecture would go no farther than the breezy, sunny, salty bridge on which they stood.

When he was finished with the captain, Carlos promenaded back and forth in front of the little bars at the far end of the harbor, stopping at the door of one of them and sending his deputies into the back room to make their inquiries. The chief health inspector of Havana would be furious, of course, but Carlos did not care about the city health inspector. Everything in his life now was a circus playing out on a thin layer of cellophane. Another little while—months, weeks, days—and he would fall through, and then he would either be dead, screaming in Olochon's torture cells, or free. Beneath the ordinary sounds of his life was a droning voice that did not leave him, day or night: It's you, it's you, it's you, it's you, it's you.

When the charade was finished, the three-car convoy rushed back through the streets of the capital, past the Institute of Contemporary Politics, past the statues to revolutionary heroes, past the lovingly cared-for *cacharros,* 1950s-style Chevrolets and Pontiacs parked at the curb. The cars needed gas, the people needed food, but the propaganda billboards were unblemished and the monuments were polished clean. It was no way to live.

In the office again, he half expected, half wanted to find that General Rincon had stopped by or left a message for him, in code, on some pretext or another. Plans had been changed. There had been a delay. The whole thing had been canceled. But no, nothing.

On his way home in the afternoon, he and Jose stopped for one glass of rum at the bar of the Cielo Rojo Hotel—it was good for him to be seen in bars and hotels now, good for him to have been seen by the director of the port.

Warmed by the rum, Carlos was starting, just starting, to allow himself to believe that this plot of theirs was a good and necessary thing, that it might actually work. When Jose dropped him off at his apartment, he climbed the two flights of stairs, opened the door, and found Felix Olochon sitting at his kitchen table. Elena was making coffee for the colonel. When she heard Carlos enter, she half turned away from the machine, and for one instant he saw, in the pretty lines of her face, what seemed to him a flicker of deceit.

Olochon immediately got to his feet and saluted in a way that could have been mocking or could have been the gesture of an old friend and *compañero*. They shook hands. Carlos kissed Elena, who began making a second *cafecito* while he loosened his tie, hung his coat on the back of the chair, and sat. Olochon had his wide, toothy smile working that afternoon. He was always like this in the presence of someone else's woman—grandiose, joyous, giving the impression that if Carlos had not come through the door at that moment, he and Elena might have been headed toward the bedroom, arm in arm.

"A new campaign," Olochon said. "I approve."

"I'm glad," Carlos said, worried that a droplet of sarcasm had found its way into his voice. Elena set the coffee down in front of him, moved the sugar a bit closer to his hands, and smiled unsteadily. He was wrong about the deceit; it wasn't deceit he saw in her face, only a reflection of his own dissatisfaction with himself, his own lack of honesty, his own fear. She was not made like him, this woman; she could not lie.

"You were seen at the port," Olochon said.

"I decided to make the campaign personal, yes. There's far too much sickness on the island; Elena can attest to that. And far too much of it comes from abroad. It occurred to me last month that we're losing millions of hours of productivity because of illnesses brought to us by foreigners. I've been mulling it over. Where are the places foreigners touch us? The ports, the airport, the hotels, and hard-currency bars. Those are the points of entry for these illnesses. If we can keep those places immaculate, if we can educate the workers there, then—"

"Brilliant," Olochon said, as if there were something else on his mind. "The ports, the airport, the tourist hotels. Brilliant."

"We'll see," Carlos said guardedly. Elena had made a coffee for herself, put together a plate of sweet rolls, and she was now sitting at the head of the table watching him.

"To what do we owe the rare honor of your visit?" Carlos asked, between sips of coffee. To show that he wasn't concerned, really, about the answer to his question, he got up before Olochon could answer, took a spotted, undersized mango from the counter, a knife from the drawer, a plate from the cupboard, and proceeded to skin and slice the mango and offer the slices all around.

Olochon smirked into his coffee cup, toyed with the slippery slice between his square-tipped fingers. "Well," he said, twisting the cup in a half circle and running a napkin across his battered lips, "it turns out that you and I are thinking along the same lines. We see the same locations as being places of potential infection. Only the infections you are concerned with are bodily ones, and I am concerned with infections of the mind, the national spirit."

Carlos nodded, wiped his fingers, tried to keep his breathing steady and slow. "How goes the investigation?"

Olochon smirked again, working the muscles around his mouth over the protruding teeth. He turned to Elena and put a hand over her hand. "Carlos is referring to matters of state that cannot be discussed here. Forgive me."

"He tells me nothing," Elena said.

"No?" Olochon somehow filled this question with sexual innuendo. "Nothing of his new campaign?"

"What campaign?"

"It's a state secret," Carlos said to the colonel. "You shouldn't have mentioned it."

Olochon forced a loud laugh. Outside the windows, they could hear the sound of sirens, moving closer. "Those are my men," Olochon said, when he saw that Carlos was listening. "Coming to carry you off, at my orders."

Carlos grinned. Elena looked at him, her mouth tight. In a moment, she stood and went into the bathroom but no noise came from that room.

"A sensitive soul," Olochon whispered, nodding at the bathroom door.

Carlos nodded.

"Concerned for the well-being of her man."

Carlos nodded again. His eyes drifted to the sharp paring knife on the counter.

Olochon sighed, toyed with his cup. The sirens wailed nearer, then reached a screaming pitch and passed on, fading and fading. "We need to take a little ride," the torturer said.

At the words, Carlos felt the muscles of his inner thighs tense. He pressed his lips tightly closed, as if Olochon had already started reaching past them. "I promised Elena I'd take her out for dinner."

Olochon showed his teeth. "It's well before the dinner hour. Perhaps you will still be home on time."

"Where are we going?"

"A secret."

"How long shall I tell her we'll be gone?"

"Not long."

Carlos stood and walked the three steps to the bathroom on unsteady legs. He tapped on the door and Elena opened it the width of her cheekbones, her face streaked with tears. "Take your shower," Carlos said. "Felix and I are going for a short ride. I'll be home in time for our dinner date."

She nodded, unable to speak.

As they were going out of the apartment, Olochon said, "So she was naked in there, when you were talking to her. Perhaps I should let you stay for half an hour longer?"

Carlos didn't answer.

He sat beside Olochon in the back seat of another black, Soviet-made Volga sedan, a thick-necked driver/bodyguard at the wheel. They set off through the city's mild, late-afternoon air. The driver seemed in no hurry. Olochon sat looking out the window. They were headed in the direction of the Montefiore Prison, the Torture House.

Carlos could smell his own sweat, feel it running in a rivulet down his left side. The two men did not speak. Three blocks from the prison, Olochon leaned forward and said to his driver: "Oriente Hotel."

At the words, Carlos's left leg twitched. He reached down immediately and raised the cuff of his pants, checking the skin, pretending something had bitten him. The driver sped out of town on the two-lane road to Matanzas, and for a while they rode in silence.

"Difficult day?" Olochon inquired calmly.

Carlos shrugged. He wasn't sure his tongue would work properly if he tried to speak.

"These are bad times, are they not?" Olochon pressed.

"I see room for optimism."

"Really? Where? Tell me."

The driver glanced at Carlos in the rearview mirror, as if he, too, were hoping for something to be optimistic about.

"The biomedical sector," Carlos said, and he could sense a sag in both the other bodies. "Cuba has some of the best scientists in the world, and our government supports medical research with a vigor you can find nowhere else. I believe that, in the very near future, the curing of disease will come to be the most valuable economic resource, and when that day comes, our patents will be in great demand. We will open a whole new sector of the economy—producing medicines for the world."

For a moment, Olochon watched him across the seat, then he snorted out a laugh. The laugh dissolved quickly into a sly smile. "This from a nation that cannot even produce a decent prophylactic?"

"What are you talking about? Our prophylactics are fine."

Olochon's green eyes did not move from Carlos's face. "You yourself said they were substandard."

"I said no such thing."

"No?"

"No, never. I've used them myself."

"You put out one of your ministry papers on the subject, you don't recall? Last year it was, July or August."

"I don't recall. And, in any case, rubbers aren't made by the biotechnology industry. You are talking about a different type of worker, a different organization."

"I use the North American or French," Olochon said, "when I feel the need to use them, which is rare."

"You should always use them."

"I'm a sensitive man," Olochon said, and Carlos could see

the driver smiling now, at the joke. "Anything that comes between the object of my lust and me is generally unacceptable."

They turned down the access road and pulled up in front of the Oriente Hotel. It sat on one of the nation's finest beaches, all white sand and pearl blue sea.

"Why here?" Carlos said, and instantly regretted it.

Olochon got out without answering. Carlos made a show of checking his watch, as if worried about the dinner date. Olochon strode up the front walk of the hotel, and Carlos had no choice but to hurry and fall into stride with him. They went past the two sets of guards without so much as glancing to either side. The guards were there to prevent ordinary citizens from visiting the premises, which were for hard-currency-paying tourists and a few very well-connected Cubans only. Even the menial jobs here—bartender, maid, clerk—were among the most sought-after in the nation. Doctors, mathematicians, physicists left their practices, classrooms, and laboratories to work in places like this, making, with one week of generous tips, more than they had made in a month of meager state salaries.

Carlos and Olochon passed through revolving doors—they must look like friends, Carlos thought—and entered another world. The lobby was all chrome and shining tiles, the clerks at the desk eager, attentive, perfectly groomed. Here and there Carlos saw foreign tourists standing in small groups or gazing out at the sunlit palm trees on the manicured grounds. He'd seen such people before, of course. He'd been abroad several times—Moscow, Warsaw, Mexico City—though never to the richer capitalist countries. He was no stranger to foreigners, and had, in the past, visited these hotels for international conferences. But now it was as if a film had been scraped from his eyes. In the relaxed expressions and happy faces of the men and women tourists, he saw not decadence so much as a kind of confidence and ease that was almost exactly opposite what he felt. Their world was a safe, predictable world; his was riven with danger, doubt, and want. They had the luxury of trust; he was weighted down with a defensive armor. Almost every encounter of his life now bore the stamp of fear.

Olochon feared nothing, it seemed. He marched into the lobby and commandeered a pair of brown leather chairs that had been arranged around a reading lamp in a small alcove. He motioned for Carlos to sit. From the alcove they could see everything that went on in the lobby, and yet they were safely set aside from it so that no one paid them the slightest attention. Carlos's heart was slamming around in his chest.

"What is this about?" he said, making a show of checking his watch again. "You take me away from a dinner with Elena so we can sit in a tourist hotel and look at the sunburned legs of female guests?"

Olochon had gone into what Carlos thought of as his turtle mode. His eyelids had lowered so that they half covered his eyes. He was resting his elbows on the soft arms of the chairs, his hands palm to palm in front of his chest, as if he were praying. And he had grown very still. Carlos could almost see the shell over him. "Felix," he said, bolder now. Any sign of weakness or worry here and he was dead. Worse than dead. "What is this?"

"This," Olochon said quietly, slowly turning his turtle gaze on the minister of health, "is the heart of the antirevolutionary conspiracy. I'm almost sure of it."

Carlos let out a laugh that echoed in the room. A pretty, blond, sandal-wearing woman, Eastern European he suspected, perhaps German, turned briefly to look at him, before readjusting the small pack on her back and flapping out the front door. "What?" he said. "These young people come here to shoot our leaders after a day on the beach?"

"Why do you say *shoot* our leaders?" Olochon demanded. The eyes were a bit more open now. "Why shoot, exactly?"

"Why? Because I have information that an entire brigade of bikini-wearing Portuguese lesbians is in residence at this hotel. There are twenty of them. Each carried in a small piece of a rifle hidden in her crotch and they are assembling it now in one of the elegant, decadent rooms above our heads." For a moment, Olochon looked at him eagerly, then Carlos watched the anger rise, then the bitterness, then the viciousness, and then the face of false friendship covering all of it. "Come on, Felix," he said. "If you suspect even me—which you seem to lately—then your watchfulness has crossed the line into paranoia. If every time I mention something, you are going to seize on it as the slip of a guilty would-be assassin, then why do we bother with talk? Take me to the cells and beat it out of me, or just shoot me on the spot. But, failing that, I have a dinner date with Elena and I intend to keep it. If you've brought me here to look at German girls in halter tops, you're wasting my time. What is going on?"

Olochon's face seemed to turn to stone while Carlos spoke. When he finished, he met the green eyes squarely, unflinching. Slowly, the stone showed a few cracks. At last, what seemed like a genuine smile lit up the hideous mouth, and Olochon nodded. It almost seemed that he was sincerely happy. "Not the speech of a guilty man," he said.

"I'm insulted that you would ever have thought otherwise."

"Ah, I insult so many people."

"Enough." Carlos made a move to get to his feet. "I'm having dinner with Elena. If you want to stay here and ogle, fine, but kindly have your driver return me to my apartment."

"I'm not ogling," Olochon said, taking hold of Carlos's arm with one powerful hand. "I don't like foreign meat in any case. What I told you was true: I have reason, good reason, very good reason, to believe that this hotel is, if not the center of the plot, then centrally concerned with the plot."

"And you're carrying on undercover surveillance . . . in your army uniform. Come on, Felix, we've been involved in this too long for charades."

"Not a charade at all," Olochon said. "Last night we arrested someone named Jorge Zialos, a musician, supposedly. We had information that led us to him, information provided by another criminal. Zialos let it be known that he had heard something about the Oriente Hotel, and a plot against the regime. Other people work differently, Carlos. And I do, in fact, have undercover men here, as you can imagine. I've had them here since the beginning. But I like to see for myself. I have something of a sixth sense when it comes to these things. I walk into a place like this and a certain kind of music sounds, audible only to me. I can read conspiracies in the faces of the supposedly innocent. I can understand at a level that would not be possible if I were to remain at my desk shuffling papers and attending meetings."

"Fine. And tell me what, precisely, does the minister of health have to do with any of this?"

"I suspected you."

"Again with the insults."

"I had reason to. For a little while a pattern of small pieces of information seemed to be leading us to your ministry. You are the head of your ministry. So, naturally, we suspected you."

"Well, go fuck yourself."

"Thank you. I've tried; I can't seem to manage." Olochon beamed at his little witticism, and ran his eyes—the antennae of his sixth sense—around the gleaming lobby.

"The trail of small details veered off suddenly in another direction, here. I consider you a friend. It would have been a savage disappointment to me if the trail had led to you. So I thought we would come here together and I could get a sense of several things at once."

"Maybe the trail leads to D-7."

"Meaning what?"

"Meaning, if there is, in fact, another plot, it would be logical for the plot to originate among your own people. Perhaps they are power hungry. They have access to state secrets. They have the materials and expertise. They have close access to *el Comandante*."

"My turn to be insulted then," Olochon countered. "To say 'Fuck you.'"

Just as these words were out of Olochon's mouth, what at first seemed to be the crack of fireworks rang out, a strange and incongruous sound among the tile and chrome. Instantly, there was another, stranger noise very close by. Acting on some odd new instinct, Carlos dove to cover Olochon's body, knocking him out of the chair and onto the floor and then pushing him, like a frantic lover, around behind it. Two more shots were fired. The two men lay for a moment on the tile against the chair's back legs, then rolled apart. There was a scuffle in the lobby; three of Olochon's undercover agents had already wrestled a man to the floor and were pummeling his face. One of the rounds from this man's weapon had struck the wooden arm of the chair where Olochon had been sitting—Carlos could still hear the peculiar quick *thut* of the bullet embedding itself in the wood. The other round had ricocheted off the wall. Olochon stood up, smoothed the front of his army coat, made eye contact with Carlos, indicating his approval, his gratitude perhaps, with the smallest of nods, then walked over to begin the first in a series of conversations with the man who had tried to kill him.

CHAPTER NINETEEN

In the rows of dark-upholstered seats near Gate 39 at Miami International Airport, Carolina sat with her magazine and coffee, waiting for the first-class passengers to be called upon to board. A thin coat of fear seemed to lay over everything she could see. She imagined it as a fine white frost, icy and sparkling, and it made her strangely happy. Her father had been a boxer in his youth, an Olympic hopeful at one point, and he had passed his interest in the sport on to her. In her twenties she had been something of an aficionado, impressing boyfriends with her knowledge of different fighters and their styles and records. These days, she liked to watch films of old bouts—Marciano-Walcott, Ali-Foreman, Ali-Chuvalo, Benvenuti-Griffith. Some of the tapes she rented included before-and-after interviews with the fighters, and she remembered watching an interview with Muhammad Ali and being struck by the thrill in his voice when he talked about the upcoming fight. She could not remember which fight he was preparing for—the Thrilla in Manila, it might have been—but she would never forget the light in his eyes, as if running and lifting weights and being bruised by sparring partners and then stepping into a roped-off ring with a man who could break your neck with one punch were the greatest pleasures life offered. Better than sex, or eating, or friendship; better than any kind of artificial high.

She could relate. Looking around at the men and women getting ready to fly across the ocean—for business or vacation—she felt she never could have endured the ordinariness of a life where the biggest worry was whether you'd packed enough underwear, or prepared well enough for a presentation. She needed more than that. She needed to feel the edge of things, that cold breath on the skin of her shoulders. Her uncle had never been satisfied with merely making money and sleeping with beautiful women; he had to have his meetings with Cuban émigrés, his imaginary plots and treacherous DGI agents. And, for better or worse, the same gene thrummed and sang in her cells. The need only grew stronger as she grew older. Pretending to page through her magazine, she thought: *I am going to help rid the world of Fidel Castro,* and it was like an electric current surging in her.

The fear, the risk, rendered her oddly calm. It had always been like this. She made her way past the check-in desk and down the ramp, smiled at the hostess, stowed her carry-on, and took her seat like any other traveler. When the plane lifted off and banked west, then north over Doral, she gazed down at the green bands of the golf courses there, thinking she really must learn to play. And then, as they turned east, she studied the strand of shore shining like a straight necklace of emerald and tropical gold. *Fidel's last days,* she was thinking. *Fidel's last days.*

They were served drinks. The man beside her—lanky, silver-haired, handsome as a film star except for a certain slight sagging of flesh to either side of his chin—turned his calm eyes on her and struck up a conversation. It was the usual thing at first:

Had she been to Prague before? Was she going for work or pleasure? Ordinary enough, until she asked him what he did with his days and he shrugged, offered a gorgeous, bemused smile, and said, "I own companies. A conglomerate, actually. Fairly boring way to pass one's time."

"Boring? I would think it would be fascinating."

"For the first few years, yes. But once you realize the intricacy of things, how large the human situation is . . . then what you are doing for the world seems too small by a factor of a thousand."

"Why are you flying commercial if you own a conglomerate?'

Again the bemused smile. The smile said that he wasn't exactly tired of the world, but that he knew it too thoroughly. It was a kind of advanced, refined boredom, she thought, and it would make him seek the spice in everything, the risk, the adventure. She felt an immediate kinship. "This airline is one of our companies," he said. "Every once in a while I go along for the ride just to see how we're doing."

Soon there was only blue ocean beneath them, and fields of clouds billowing up like misshapen white carnations. They flew gradually into darkness. The conversation went on with a perfect comfort that pleased her deeply. Why did one find one's soul mates on airplanes? Why were they always thirty years older? Everywhere the talk took them—her carefully made-up family back home in LA, her carefully made-up job as a Spanish-language consultant for the Pensacola police and fire departments, her mostly imaginary interests in ceramics and gardening, his children, his country home outside London, his fascination with nineteenth-century oil paintings—they trotted along like two happy horses in tandem. He made her laugh. He seemed genuinely interested in her work. From the tips of his brilliantly shined black loafers to the wide shoulders and gray eyes, the man exuded a supernatural calm, a kind of mastery. Nothing would frighten or surprise him.

Their conversation dwindled as easily and naturally as it had begun. After their meal, the hostess handed them blankets, and Carolina set hers across her lap, turned her head away from him and dozed. When she awoke, the first red shards of light were showing against the smoky eastern horizon, and the pilot was speaking to them—another calm man: "Ladies and gentlemen, we're having a tiny little technical problem, nothing to worry about. I have a very small crack in the windshield here so just to be absolutely on the safe side we're going to drop down to ten thousand feet and then make a landing in Spain, where we can get things fixed up. This is not an emergency landing, just a little detour. We should have you on another plane shortly and back on your way to Prague. We apologize for the inconvenience."

Carolina turned to the silver-haired man beside her and he smiled back tiredly. "And just when you were about to buy some of our stock," he said with a certain irony.

In a matter of minutes the Atlantic came into sharper focus below them. A murky coastline lifted itself into view. In first class, at least, a quick breakfast was served—coffee and rolls, some fresh fruit—and then they were moving into a landing pattern, the gear cranking down, houses, roads, and vehicles taking shape below them.

When the jet had touched down and was taxiing, her gentleman companion said, "I'll arrange for us to sit together going into Prague, if you don't mind. I've enjoyed our conversation."

"I enjoyed it, too."

But as soon as she stepped into the terminal, two Spanish security personnel in moss green uniforms approached her and asked her to stand aside, away from the waiting area. A routine security check, they said, in thickly accented English. She began, quietly at first, to protest. A woman in civilian dress approached them, made solid eye contact with her, and spoke in Spanish: "*Señorita Perez*," she said quietly, "*por favor. Es importante.*" And something in her voice and manner sent a signal.

The woman took hold of Carolina's forearm, and she was led into the terminal and then through a ribbed, smoked-glass door that seemed to be the entrance to some kind of club for first-class travelers. Beyond it, out of reach of the bustle of the terminal, was another door, decorated in gold and red, then a sort of lounge, and off this lounge yet another door. Both burly uniformed security personnel remained in the lounge. The woman kept a firm grip on her forearm and led her through the gold and red door, down a short corridor and into a windowless room where there was a small cherrywood table surrounded by three leather-upholstered chairs, a wooden desk with another chair behind it, and two more chairs in front. The place had the feeling of someone's private study more than of an interrogation room reserved for special threats to Spanish security. Carolina felt herself relax, partly. She was asked to sit and wait. She had the room to herself for thirty seconds, and then the door opened, and her silver-haired neighbor from the trans-Atlantic flight stepped in behind his calm smile. "Bit of a change of plans" was the first thing he said.

CHAPTER TWENTY

A fter one tremendous slap to the face of his would-be, already-bloody assassin—their foreign visitors were getting a show for their money, Carlos thought, though most of them were cowering in various corners of the lobby—Olochon took the man by the throat and shook him roughly. The man's hands were already cuffed behind him. He had a very large nose, which was bleeding profusely now, perhaps broken. He stumbled sideways beneath Olochon's assault. One of the plainclothesmen caught him, forced him upright. They moved him quickly toward the door, Olochon following, barking orders, exuding a kind of perverse, businesslike joy. Carlos was left standing in the lobby on shaking legs, without a ride home. After a minute or so, he went to the main desk, called his secretary on the phone there, and went in search of a shot of rum.

No one else was in the bar. By then, all the tourists had been chased up to the safety of their rooms, no doubt swearing to themselves never to set foot on Cuban soil again. Carlos finished the rum and ordered a second. The bartender seemed to know who he was—no charge for the liquor. After serving it, he retreated to the far end of the bar and pretended to busy himself there, wiping imaginary spots from clean glasses.

General Rincon had told him that things would happen in multiples, all at once. Clearly, they had meant to assassinate Olochon as a preliminary to the greater assassination, as a way of crippling D-7 before the main event. And clearly it had been a very clumsy attempt. Shots fired by an excited amateur from a distance of eighty or ninety feet. No doubt they had lured Olochon into the hotel for that purpose. But they had not expected him to be seated next to one of their own, arms almost touching. Within the hour the would-be assassin would be talking. Which meant Carlos had to get word to Rincon before then, or it would be over before it had begun.

By the time Jose arrived, Carlos had enjoyed a third glass of rum and was a bit unsteady on his feet, but behind the cottony curtain of alcohol he believed he was thinking clearly. The one thing that had troubled him from the start was that there was no dependable way to contact Rincon without other people knowing. He received messages from the general in half-sentence whispers, scraps of cardboard in a toilet. "It's safer this way," Rincon had told him. "If the house falls apart, it will fall apart one brick at a time. We are each only able to give up one or two names. You have my name. I have yours and one other."

"What happened?" Jose wanted to know when he arrived. "I drop you at your house. An hour later Véronique is calling me, saying you are at the Oriente. You look like you've just been run over by a bull." They walked out of the building and climbed into the Volga's front seat.

"Olochon took me for a ride. We ended up here, where some fool tried to assassinate him. I threw him to the ground and covered him."

"Who, the assassin?"

"The Dentist."

"I never knew you cared for him so much."

Carlos reached forward and snapped on the radio loudly. "I despise him. It was all an act. An impulse." Before Carlos realized what he was doing he said: "He suspects me of plotting to overthrow the government. I was trying to throw him off."

"Olé!" Jose sang. They raced out of the Oriente compound and were driving the two-lane highway back into the heart of the city. "Now he suspects everyone, every last person. No doubt, he even suspects Fidel of trying to kill Fidel."

For a minute, Carlos rode in silence. So clear was the view through the window, and the sound of Jose's words, that it seemed to him the effects of the rum had already disappeared. He watched the outskirts of the city sail past, broken apartment blocks and barefoot children. He listened to the familiar shifting of gears. He thought it over for another few seconds, tried to gauge the effect the liquor was having on him, glanced at Jose's face, looked away, and said: "He has good reason to suspect me." Carlos waited for the count of three, then looked across the seat again. Two people now; he had told two people in the past twenty-four hours. If everyone involved in the plan told two people, and those people told two people . . .

Jose was flexing his square, scarred jaw with the stubble of beard on it, working the stick shift, not looking at him. "You can pretend I didn't say that," Carlos told him. "If you want. If they find me out they'll kill you anyway, so if you feel you must turn me in, do so."

Jose did not speak. He chewed the inside of his cheek as he drove. He kept his eyes straight in front of him. "Good reason to suspect you—what does that mean?" he finally asked.

"It means I am involved in a plot with a group of other high officials to stop the madness, to try to bring back a Cuba that makes sense."

Jose glanced across the seat at him for two seconds. He stopped chewing his cheek. He looked at the loud radio. He was nodding. There was an unbearable stretch of silence before he steered the car around a pothole and said: "This is not exactly the surprise of my adult life."

"All the worse for me, then. It shows."

"It shows to me. Enough so the thought crossed my mind once. That's all."

"And?'

"And . . . you have more courage than most people."

"Courage? I'm pissing my boots."

"Where are we going?"

"I don't know yet. To the office, not home. I need a little time, half an hour, before I see Elena."

"Everyone knows what you know, Ministro," Jose said, still not looking at him. "Everyone sees what you see. Not the top se-cret government things, naturally, but the ordinary things—no toilet paper, no cheese, shoes that fall apart, houses that fall apart. People arrested for nothing. Everyone sees it. It makes sense that they, that you, would try to kill Olochon first, because Olochon is the minister of fear, and because of that fear, nothing changes."

"I had the chance the other day to kill him. He had tortured someone, a man, Ernesto, no one I knew. Tortured him worse than you would torture a cat, a tarantula. He asked me to kill the man and I did."

"You did Ernesto a favor then, killing him."

"I could have killed Olochon. I wanted to, but I couldn't bring myself to do it . . . good thing, too, because the first chamber was empty. He thought I might aim at him and hear the click and not pull the trigger a second time."

"This was the morning he summoned you. Two days ago?"

"Yes."

At the traffic light, Jose took a cigarette out of his pocket and lit it. "Does General Rincon know this? About what happened at the hotel?"

"Why do you say Rincon?"

Jose turned to face him, a wisp of smoke curling up between them, and said quietly, "Because Rincon approached me even before he approached you."

CHAPTER TWENTY-ONE

Instead of sitting behind the wooden desk, as Carolina thought he might do, her silver-haired friend half sat, half leaned on the front edge of it, facing her. Before he had a chance to say anything else, there was a knock on the door and a pretty young woman wearing a tight black skirt and white blouse stepped into the windowless room, carrying a tray. On the tray was a silver coffeepot and two china cups on china saucers. Silver creamer, silver sugar jar, china plate on which sat crackers, three small wedges of different kinds of cheese, and slices of apple and pear. Without looking at either of them, the woman poured two cups of coffee—one black, one with cream—and served Carolina first. She then glanced at the silver-haired man, and, after registering his small nod of approval, disappeared through the door.

Carolina was wondering, among other things, how the woman knew she took her coffee black.

"I'm Richard V. Volkes, by the way," the silver-haired man said, holding out one steady hand and enveloping hers in a gentle grip. "Just 'Volkes' to the people I associate with. I'm one of the guys who originally put together the organization you work for. I've heard a lot of wonderful things about you over the past decade or so—at the Agency and with us—and I'm honored to finally meet you."

"The honor is mine," Carolina said.

Introduction accomplished, Volkes pulled one of the chairs up and joined her at the small table. He offered her the plate, then took a slice of apple and chewed it contemplatively. "That was an interesting conversation we had on the flight over. Everything I told you—from my love of Cézanne to the conglomerate work being slightly boring—was true. Everything you told me was a fabrication."

"And yet we got along so well," Carolina said.

"Remarkably well. I felt an instant mutual understanding that's really rather rare with me."

"I'm glad. It's rare with me, too."

"By the way, it took us some work, but we found a person who, with a little assistance, looks remarkably like you. That young woman is wearing clothes like yours now. She will be on route to Prague on the replacement jet in a short while, an empty seat beside her. You'll spend the night in Spain, and then head for Cuba tomorrow."

"Tomorrow?"

Volkes nodded, seemed to smile. "Unless you're having second thoughts."

"None."

"My turn to be glad."

She offered him a slight smile and sipped her coffee. Tomorrow! A hot thrill ran up her spine. She studied her companion, struck again by the otherworldly calm that seemed to emanate from his body. The bright cuff links, the perfectly tailored suit and white shirt, the red and gold silk tie that somehow combined modesty and flair, the neck and wrists that showed signs of being well toned and muscular, even though the man must have been approaching seventy. He had been some kind of athlete in his youth, she guessed, a quarterback, a star pitcher. The sense of calm was something physical, some great confidence in the abilities of his body. But more than that, as well: physical, intellectual, social, almost spiritual. She tried to imagine a situation that would unnerve him.

"I'm here to answer your questions," he said. "Answer your questions, give you a measure of information, then send you on your way. So don't hold back."

"What's the timing? The real schedule."

"The real schedule is that you undergo a small change in your appearance—we have the facilities and the people right here, in the airport. This is kind of a side-specialty of ours, in case you haven't already noticed. You spend a relaxing night at Barcelona's finest hotel. In the morning you fly to Cuba with a group of Spanish tourists on a six-day junket. You stay in another fine hotel, outside Havana, and pass one small item on to a particular person. Then you fly back here, enjoy a well-earned vacation for a week, return to America, and, once this is all over, you meet with me and my partners to talk about future possibilities."

"Why the switch from Prague?"

"We do everything this way. We shift and obfuscate. We change plans, schedules, people, angles of approach. We work the way the most ordinary county-fair magician works—we create illusions."

"Only, in this case, something real is happening beyond the illusions."

"Something very real," he said. He sipped his coffee without letting his eyes leave her face. There was a delicate humor dancing there. She trusted him implicitly. "We're saving the world."

Saving the world. Coming from someone else, the phrase would have seemed preposterous, an absurd boast. Coming from Richard V. Volkes, it carried the weight of fact. "I want to hear more," she said. "Anything you can tell me, I want to hear."

"You've heard most of it before, if I'm not mistaken. It's how we wooed you down from Langley."

"I want to hear it from you."

"In a nutshell, we are three men between the ages of fifty-one and seventy-one. Two of us are businessmen—heads of large conglomerates that are involved in energy and communications work, military hardware, a bit of high-tech, some real estate. We inherited and/or made grand sums of money—our ambitions in that area have long ago been calmed. Our work brought us across each other's paths fairly frequently, and then, almost twenty years ago, we realized we had a common vision."

"Who is the third person? What kind of work is he involved in?"

"Political work. High-level political work, though his profile in our organization has always been rather modest."

"Not a former president or anything like that, then?"

"He's still quite active, that's all I can say . . . not a president, no. Our vision goes something like this: Throughout history there have always been destructive and constructive forces. As the world has grown smaller, those forces have become concentrated. Democracy is on the side of good, as you can imagine. And we support democracy and free-market principles wherever we can. Avidly. At the same time, as you can also no doubt imagine, the democratic process can be cumbersome. The forces of evil know this, and take advantage of it. In certain instances, even the most well-meaning governments act too slowly, or in too much of a mixed fashion. The full might of their goodness cannot be brought to bear. Which is a problem the forces of evil are not burdened by. For instance, our government has a policy of not assassinating political leaders. A moral stance. And yet, think of the lives and trouble that could have been saved if assassinations could be used judiciously.

"Now, I know what you are thinking. Allende. Diem. The trouble that has been caused when this method is *not* used judiciously. Well, without sounding immodest, we believe we are wiser than that. We don't kill people for the lark of it. We rarely kill at all, in fact. Extremely rarely. Most of our projects are more subtle. We have, it is true, gone into Afghanistan and the former Burma and eliminated warlords and drug lords, quietly, efficiently. More typically, when the Soviet Union was first breaking apart, we were able to shift certain resources—oil, mainly, but diamonds and tungsten, too—away from the hands of certain people. Even the well-informed specialist might not notice such a shift. Even government and business analysts might not notice it at first. They'll feel the results, naturally—one piece of one market remains open where it would have been closed. One African or South American nation is more predisposed to democratic principles than it would have been had we not acted to help advance the career of a particular minister or colonel, or discourage the career of someone else.

"Naturally enough, our work sometimes overlaps with the work of our government. You met one of our friends in government, I believe."

"Edmund Lincoln? With friends like that . . ."

"That encounter was what we might call a 'feint.' "

"F-E?"

"F-E. A layer of illusion. A trick."

"Who were we tricking, his bodyguards?" she said, but before the last word was in the air between them she had her answer. Volkes observed her moment of understanding with a keen, bemused interest, then looked away long enough to spread some Roquefort on two crackers. He handed her one, the sly amusement playing at the edges of his eyes. Before she brought the cracker to her mouth she said, "Oleg."

A sunny smile broke across Volkes's face and for a moment he was a young man again, disturbingly handsome, capable of anything. He nodded once, happily.

"What about my ex-husband?"

"What about him?"

"Oscar told me Oleg was D-7. First, is that accurate? And second, is Oscar involved in this or was my little encounter with him just an accident, another feint?"

"Oleg Rodriguez works for and reports, indirectly, to Fidel Castro. If your ex-husband told you that, he is correct."

"And what about my uncle?"

"What about him?"

"Is he part of . . . do you work with him?"

"Roberto Anzar has his own sources—of funding and of information. We know who he is, of course. Some of us have done business with him, but not this kind of business. He does not know who we are—very few people know who we are. And, yes, since he is intimately involved in Cuba and since we needed him not to interfere with this stage of the project, your visit with him was a distraction. Or, more correctly, a covering of one of our flanks."

"Where is Oleg now?"

"Oleg is doing what he has been doing for the past eleven years. We will let this particular line play itself out, and then, at the proper moment, Oleg, unfortunately, will have to be . . . how should I say it . . . retired without pension."

She realized Volkes wouldn't have told her this unless he trusted her absolutely. And he wouldn't trust her absolutely unless she'd been vetted and checked, over a period of years, in a hundred ways. "But he knows I'm going to Cuba."

"Yes, correct. However, he thinks you are going in several months' time. Right now, he believes you are headed to Prague to pick up a ceramic pistol that will pass through airport inspections without trouble. And he thinks you will be leaving Prague in two weeks, after enduring some kind of special training. Which means Castro and his D-7 expect you to arrive at the airport in several months with a gun well hidden in your luggage. Which means that, thanks to Oleg, they have people following you as you make your way to Prague. Only now they will be following this woman who looks remarkably like you. As a matter of fact, fifteen minutes after you were called aside by Spanish security and walked into this part of the airport, your double walked out. Before they realize that she is not you—if they ever realize it—the deed will be done."

"She's wearing what I'm wearing?"

"Exactly, down to the gold earrings. We photographed you when you left your apartment this morning, and had everything prepared."

"She speaks fluent Spanish?"

"*Sí*. We tested her on your ex-husband, if you'd like to know. And from a distance of ten or twelve feet he called to her, using your name."

"Still. D-7 is going to be on high alert."

"The highest."

"They know there is a plot against Castro."

"Yes."

"And they know it will be a woman of a certain age and size bringing something that will kill him."

"Yes."

"So I'm a sitting duck, basically. The only defense is that they think I'll be arriving two or three months from now instead of tomorrow night, and I'll look a little different."

"And have a different passport."

"Why don't we just have someone there shoot Fidel?"

"That's the first thing you've asked that has disappointed me."

"All right. Question withdrawn."

"We have found, over the years, that the best way to fool a sophisticated security organization is to almost not fool it. Any kind of bureaucracy—DGI included—functions in a predictable way. If DGI believes there is a plot against Castro, and if DGI and D-7 believe they have excellent information about that plot, from an unimpeachable source—Oleg, in this case— then there is a fair chance they will neglect to do what they usually do, which is to keep their antennae alert to other possibilities."

"A feint," she said, watching him.

He went on, "The risks—to you, to us—are obvious. However, if everyone does what they are supposed to do, the risks are rather small and the odds of success quite high. If, knowing all this, you wish to withdraw, you have our understanding and your career with us will not be negatively affected."

"A few more questions before my yes or no, all right?"

"Of course."

"How will Fidel die?"

"Topical ointment. Administered by his personal physician to help with some scarring from the removal of cancerous lesions. He'll be told it will help prevent a recurrence. The Comandante, as you know, tends to look for ways to confirm his belief in his own immortality."

"Sounds like a very special ointment."

"Miraculous."

"And I carry the miracle."

"As far as the Oriente Hotel in Havana, yes. You hand it over to a man named Ulises. You go to the beach for few days, see a couple of museums. You leave."

"And he'll die while I'm there?"

"That is our hope. Oleg will die while you are there, also. As will a dozen or so people whom the good half of the world will not miss—Cuban military and intelligence, people who could be troublesome after their leader's death. We want you to stay there because there might be one or two smaller tasks we'll need your help with in the aftermath. And because it would arouse suspicion if you went all the way to Cuba merely for one day."

"Something has always nagged at me," Carolina said.

"Now's the time." Volkes sipped his coffee calmly, but never removed his eyes from her. Another test, she thought.

"Why now? I mean, we've lived with Castro all these years, why not just wait for nature to take him? Especially since he's been having some health troubles of late."

"Two reasons. First, despite the reported health troubles, the man could live another ten or even fifteen years, doing the kind of damage he's been doing, imprisoning people who shouldn't be in prison, ruining a rich, gorgeous land, exerting a kind of influence-by-example on certain sectors of South American politics. Venezuela comes to mind. We don't want to see any more innocent people suffer. Second, some of us might not live another ten or fifteen years. We're at our prime now, in terms of the efficient functioning of the organization, and we want to be proactive rather than sit back and wait to see what will happen."

"The country will be thrown into chaos when he's assassinated."

"We think not, but now you are getting into another area of the operation, and that area doesn't really concern you. We need a yes or no from you now. No, and you vacation in Spain for a week, then head home for a new assignment. No hard feelings. We have alternative plans, as you might imagine. Something else that our Oleg knows nothing about. More confusion for him and the Cuban authorities, more protection for you.

"Another feint."

"Exactly. So, a yes from you and we begin the transformation process."

"What if, while I'm there, something goes wrong? Someone doesn't do what he or she has been trained to do? Someone is captured and informs?"

"You're a step ahead of me; very good. If that happens, then you must get to the cove just to the northeast side of a place called Guanabacoa. There is only one pier there, and the pier has a broken piling. You will have a small, battery-operated, single-frequency transmitter. Activate the transmitter on or near that pier and we will have someone ready to rescue you and get you out."

Carolina took one breath. "The answer is yes, then."

"No hesitation? No other concerns? No moral qualms?"

"None."

"We're set, then?"

"Set."

"Good. Enjoy this wonderful coffee—it's Cuban, in fact. I added that as a special touch. Then we'll get you made over in another little room here we have borrowed from friends, and we'll send you on your way. Other than the instructions about carrying the ointment, you know everything you need to know. You'll get an envelope with the vouchers, tickets, new passport, and so on, as you are being driven to the hotel. Destroy what you don't need, as always. We've spent a lot of time and effort vetting you, as you can imagine. I'm happy to know it's you who will be doing this."

"You know about the break-in, then?"

"Break-ins," Volkes said. "Plural. Miami and Atlanta. Sorry for that inconvenience. We'll compensate you for any damage."

"It's nothing. I just wondered if it was Oscar, my ex, who did it."

"Oscar works for us now. Happily, it seems, though he's at a much lower level than you are."

Carolina looked away and smiled, but the smile was another mask.

CHAPTER TWENTY-TWO

It's good that I'm taking you back to your office," Jose said. They were in the heart of the city now, cutting, in the last daylight, through the small side streets between Avenida Salvador Allende and the children's hospital. "That will look the least suspicious. Like you forgot something and had to finish it before going back home. Olochon will be too busy to notice in any case. Let me go and see if I can get a message to Rincon."

Carlos nodded distractedly. "I am thinking about the man in the cell with Olochon."

"Best not to," Jose said. "We all take our risks."

Somehow, the "we" did not sound genuine on Jose's lips. Carlos could not look at him. Jose had never really said he was working with them, he'd said only, "Rincon approached me even before he approached you," which was odd in several ways. Even the mention of Rincon's name could have been merely a lucky guess, a trick to see how he would react. If so, then he had fallen for it and he was dead, and Rincon was dead, and Fidel and Olochon would win yet another victory. What if Rincon was not really involved in a plot, but working with D-7 to rid the government of those who wanted to eliminate Fidel? Stranger things, much stranger things, had happened. Government drivers reporting to D-7 was almost a cliché now, in Castro's Cuba.

"You're worrying about me," Jose said as they pulled up in front of the Ministry of Health. "My loyalty."

Carlos turned to look at him, hesitated one second, and nodded. Jose appeared to be genuinely wounded. "This is what they do to us, Ministro," he said sorrowfully. "They trust no one, and they teach us to trust no one. It is an infection of the soul."

Carlos nodded a second time. Somehow, with this brief conversation, their roles had been reversed. Jose, unshaven, spending every night out on the town, a simple driver, was now the superior. And Carlos was geniunely afraid.

Hoping to recover his confidence and to make things appear ordinary—just another ordinary twenty-four hours during which he'd dodged a couple of bullets, saved the life of a torturer, told two people a secret that could kill them all—Carlos reached across and squeezed Jose's shoulder, then climbed out of the car and into the Havana twilight. He pretended to brush something off the front of his shirt. He walked past the pair of guards, up the office building's cracked, shallow steps. Past another guard at the door, up one flight of stairs to his office. Everything seemed at once ordinary and absurd. The neat desk of his secretary, Véronique, with her nail polish and cupful of pens. His large desk with the view out over the Museo de Arte. The framed portrait of Fidel on one wall, surrounded by citations and diplomas—it all seemed alien, the accoutrements of another man. In the picture, Fidel was in his early forties, his black beard shining, his eyes intense, wise, fearless, triumphant. He had survived the assault on the Cuartel Moncada, survived prison and exile, chased Batista off the island, repulsed the worms at the Bay of Pigs, stood up to Kennedy over the missiles, avoided a string of CIA assassination attempts, survived, somehow, the withdrawal of billions of dollars a year in Soviet aid without the economy completely collapsing, repaired relations with the European Union after his crackdown on dissidents. He had, in other words, won every battle he'd ever engaged in, with enemies more powerful and more sophisticated than the ragtag group Carlos seemed to be a part of. How could he kill a strategic genius like that, in person, in cold blood?

In case his phone line was being bugged by Olochon and his men, Carlos called Elena, intending to tell her not to worry, he'd be home shortly, they'd still have time for their dinner date. But the phone just rang and rang.

THIRTY MINUTES LATER, when he went outside to meet Jose, he thought he sensed a change in the posture of the guards at the door. Word of the assassination attempt at the Oriente Hotel had spread like a fire through the city. There had even been a rumor—briefly, he'd heard the cleaning women in the corridor whispering—that Olochon was dead, but he knew where Olochon was, and what he was doing, and he could not force from his mind a vision of a bleeding, big-nosed man, hanging from iron cuffs in the Montefiore Prison, saying the name Carlos Gutierrez through splintered teeth.

In the front seat of the Volga the air was stifling and the radio still playing too loudly. Jose seemed to be tormenting him with a purposeful silence, making him wait. They went four blocks before he spoke, and by that point Carlos wanted to reach across the seat and strangle him. "Rincon is in Mallarta Province, supposedly inspecting the troops. But the person I spoke with said, when I told him what had happened at the Oriente today, 'That man is not ours.'"

Carlos leaned closer to him. "Who is the person you spoke with?"

"I am not allowed to say, Boss."

"Even to me?"

"Even to you."

"He's reliable?"

"As reliable as any of us now," Jose said, and they did not speak another word to each other until they were almost at Carlos's apartment. There, just before he stopped the car, Jose said, "Your meeting at the Oriente has been canceled. It's still you, though. But now you will meet your contact at Elena's clinic instead. Day after tomorrow. Eleven A.M. His name will be Ulises. He will give you a cigar. You can light it, but don't smoke it more than an inch or so down. When you are in a private place, carefully cut it open. There will be something inside."

Carlos nodded once, tersely, and shook Jose's offered hand. Suspicion between two people was a poison, he thought, climbing the steps to the third floor. As deadly as any bullet.

Inside the apartment there was no sign of Elena, which was very strange. Whatever her duties at the clinic, she was usually home for lunch on Tuesdays, and always home by six P.M. on nights when he'd promised to take her to dinner. He went into the bedroom looking for her, and saw a book—one of her sentimental novels, a story of the great revolutionaries—set out on his pillow in a way she would never have left it. When he picked it up he noticed a scrap of paper protruding from the pages. He opened to that page and the note said: "I have gone to my son's. I left you the car. I called one of my colleagues at the clinic and told her that he is ill. Do not contact me." And nothing else. He lay down across the bed, touching both her side and his, and watched the ceiling fan turn in a breath of air.

CHAPTER TWENTY·THREE

---···-w\|\w-···---

Carolina wondered how much more dyeing, bleaching, and redyeing her hair could take before she'd have to cut it all off and grow a new crop. They had made her a brunette now, with highlights of chestnut brown here and there. They'd given her green contacts to wear. They'd cropped her hair short—it would take months to grow back this time. They'd darkened her teeth a shade and exchanged her stylish skirt and blouse for a lime green pantsuit, so that now, flying back over the Atlantic again in the opposite direction, she felt like some kind of Spanish American butch executive sneaking off to Havana for her winter tan.

When she'd awakened at the hotel that morning, a sense of nervousness had come over her all at once. She'd looked in the bathroom mirror and it seemed that even with all their miraculous work, she did not look different enough. Without Volkes there, laying out her duties in his calm voice, the plan seemed faulty to her, dangerously flawed. Oleg knew too much. Castro's people would be too wary. She was flying, as always, on faith, on a love of risk, on buried old feelings for Cuba.

The deadly ointment was contained in an ordinary-looking collapsible tube the size of her little finger. The tube was printed with a prescription label identical to those used in Cuba. The whole thing fit neatly into a hard plastic container and the container was inserted into one of two lipsticks she kept in her purse. Light red and dark red. She had to remember: Dark red was deadly.

Sitting beside a sleeping pensioner, in tourist class, she'd resisted the urge to open her purse and check the lipstick tube, which was slightly wider and longer than its twin. She limited herself to two drinks with the rice and beef dinner. She tried to sleep but could not.

One thought gave her comfort: If they suspected her, they would suspect her right from the first glimpse. If there were DGI agents in the customs line—and of course there would be—and if they were on the lookout for a woman who fit the description Oleg would by now have given them, then she would be picked up right away; or, at least, her bags would be searched with special care. If she made it through customs without too much fuss, made it through the check-in at the hotel, then she would have a fighting chance.

The night wore on, endlessly, the drone of the engines vibrating against the tiredness in her body. She wanted more than anything to sleep, but the medication she had taken could not make any headway against the rip currents of her fear. She'd slept for half an hour after taking it, and was now painfully wide awake, listening to her neighbor's snores.

At last the sun rose and the plane began its descent into Havana International Airport, the fuselage bumping on the tropical air like a truck on a rutted dirt road. Her neighbor, nervous about the landing, babbled on and on in Castilian Spanish about some television news anchor who had been involved in an affair with a high official of the Spanish government. Carolina nodded and nodded in response, but her eyes were on the emerald island beneath them, a land full of silver, nickel, and copper, a land where coffee, tobacco, sugar, and almost every kind of fruit and vegetable grew, a land that had been drenched in blood and misery for half a millennium.

The jet bumped hard on landing. The brakes squealed and screeched, sending vibrations up through the bottom of Carolina's seat. They taxied quickly—too quickly it seemed—toward the terminal, and the nervousness rose into her chest and made her take short, tight breaths. When at last the doors opened and she worked her way down the aisle and then stepped out onto the top of the portable stairway, the nervousness disappeared for a moment in a soft breath of morning air. Cuba. In Spanish it sounded softer, more feminine: *Coobah.*

The new, Canadian-built terminal and the luggage trucks seemed to be glistening in the fragrant air. By the time she'd retrieved her bags and was standing in the customs line with her fake passport in one hand, currents of excitement and terror were racing through her fingers and forearms, and it was all she could do to still the trembling of her jaw. *Just get through this*, she thought. *Just get through this part.* She was fifth in line, fourth, third. There was some fuss up ahead, a magazine being confiscated. Freedom of the press, Castro-style.

The man who took her passport was a sleepy-eyed, light-haired descendant of the Spaniards who'd come here to find gold and work the Indians to death. He flipped open the passport with a practiced thumb and read over her new name, Angela Vera Miranda, very slowly. Very slowly he raised his eyes to her newly colored hair, and ran them across her cheeks and mouth, and then down over her breasts. He looked at the passport again. He frowned. He raised his eyes to her eyes and stared into them, noticing the green contacts, she thought, perhaps noticing the sweat on her forehead. He thumbed through the pages, then returned to the photo, studied it for at least the count of ten . . . and handed it back. Waved her through.

There were some women working the customs lines—that had not changed since her last visit, two years ago. One of them, thin and dark brown, ran her hands through Carolina's clothes, with some envy, it seemed to her. The silks there, the fine cotton cloth, bathing suits and bras and gossamer skirts, two and three and four of everything. Carolina had a strange urge to say, "You can have that one if you'd like." But she stood still, trembling in the core of her torso, watching, not speaking. There was a tension in the air here, it was almost like Haiti in that way, though the two places were as different from each other as night and day, sorrow and sin, ingrained poverty and enforced poverty. The female customs clerk found and opened her makeup case—black leather. She moved her index finger around as if it were a spoon in soup, pushing the razors, lipstick tubes, and lotions this way and that. She zipped up the case, then turned to her colleague and made a hand signal, and Carolina was free to move forward with the other tourists in the direction of their bus.

Soon they had left the crowded edges of Havana behind and were in the lush, poor countryside. The bus moved toward Matanzas along a two-lane road that ran not far from the coast. Her seatmate, a Madrid schoolteacher visiting for the first time, sat at the window, gawking at the tin-roofed houses, the beautiful children in the road, and the bright colors of laundry drying on lines. The world was a Spanish-speaking world now—it had been for the past twenty-four hours, and was not so different from the world she had grown up in, ninety miles to the north—and the woman kept saying, *"Increíble! Increíble!"* Carolina didn't ask her what was incredible—the gorgeous shoreline blinking blue and green beyond the houses; the palm trees leaning as gracefully as dancers, their fronds glistening in the sun; or the poverty, so obvious, even as the government guide went on with her propaganda into a microphone a few feet in front of them: *"Y el gobierno de Fidel Castro suministra . . ."* Fidel's renowned health care for all, and a guarantee of education and employment, and the sustainable farming programs to which even the *norteamericano* students had turned their attention. The sanitation initiatives that had reduced infant mortality; the elimination of prostitution; the medical research sector and its new drugs. All true, of course, at least in part. But the price of these improvements was never mentioned.

In just under an hour they made a left onto a long access road—their guide also failed to mention that it was guarded by soldiers to keep ordinary Cubans from approaching the foreigners, or making use of their clean stretch of beach. They bounced along the dirt road past the tall thin palms and the banana plants, and, after a mile and a half, pulled up beside the glass and red stucco of the Oriente.

They checked in as a group and were given an hour to rest and wash up. Carolina had, of course, been instructed to pay extra for a single room, so she rode up in the clanking elevator, used her key in the shiny wooden door, closed and locked it behind her, and tried to get rid of the nervousness by staying busy. She immediately unpacked her things. The two lipstick tubes—dark red was death—stayed in her toiletries bag on the edge of the bathroom sink.

The morning would be devoted to a tour, a visit to the Museo de la Revolución, lunch, and then some promised beach time in the afternoon. At night they would be free. She would dance, meet a man named Ulises at the hotel club, make the transfer in any way she saw fit. Everything would be over then, from her end. Almost everything. The nervousness had retreated to a small film of sweat on her palms, and a low, steady vibration in her abdomen. She thought of Volkes and his supernatural calm. She thought of the assignments she'd had over the past eight years: never a problem she hadn't been able to solve. She thought of her parents and her uncle and the rest of the Cuban community in Miami. She would be a heroine there, if they ever learned the truth. It occurred to her, briefly, that all of this—her work at the CIA, at the Orchid—all of it could be traced to a certain kind of wound all Cuban women knew about. It was nice to be distinct from men; she liked that. She liked the fact that outside the Versailles Restaurant in Miami on Sunday mornings, the men stood off to one side, smoking and waving their hands, while the women and children formed a warm circle of laughter and care. But from the time she was nine or ten, she had not liked being told she could not do certain things because they were not the kind of things good Cuban girls tried. Could all of her adult decisions be traced back to that?

The telephone rang—its strange elongated tone sounding like a memory from childhood—but when she lifted it to her ear the line was dead.

—⁓⁓⁓—

CHAPTER TWENTY-FOUR

Carlos could not eat breakfast, could not even bring himself to make a cup of coffee. The empty apartment reminded him of the months after his wife had died, and he realized that, had his beloved Tete been alive, there would have been no thought of doing this, no thought of risking their life together even for a cause as important as this one. Maybe Elena had sensed that, and taken it as an insult. Maybe she'd left for other reasons, less personal, worse.

He went down the three flights of stairs and out into the morning sunlight, trying to remember how he walked and stood and greeted the neighbors on ordinary days. Jose was late, which never happened on ordinary days, never, not ever, not once. Carlos waited on the sidewalk in the stink of diesel exhaust, in the noise of the morning traffic, in the rising heat. He looked once at his watch—9:07.

At twenty past nine he saw the black Volga turn onto his street, and when Jose pulled up beside him at the curb he glanced into the back seat, half expecting to see Olochon. "Sorry, Boss," Jose said cheerily when they were moving. "A detour in front of the Montefiore. Colonel Olochon is no longer allowing motorized vehicles to pass on any of the four sides of the building. And since the building is in the heart of the city, this is causing us trouble."

"Olochon is safe, then. We can be thankful for that."

"Safe, safe. *¡Gracias a la Revolución!* The word in unofficial circles is that his good friend, *Ministro de la Salud* Carlos Gutierrez, pushed him out of the bullet's path. Fidel is said to be pleased."

"I'm scheduled to give him a physical today, just before lunch. Fidel, I mean."

"I know."

"You're not supposed to know."

"I know that, too."

They rode along in silence for a few blocks. Carlos felt like a man walking in complete darkness, waving his arms around to find something familiar to hold on to. He tried to puzzle out the facts. If Jose knew about the timing of Castro's physical—a state secret—then there was someone else very close to the dictator who was also in on this. But who was that close? A bodyguard? Raul? He looked over at Jose but could not bring himself to ask.

"It is still the same?" Carlos asked, at a particularly noisy intersection. "Eleven o'clock tomorrow at Elena's clinic?"

Jose gave a nod without looking at him. "It's going to be done with ointment. You put some on and wipe it off. Put more on and leave it."

Carlos could barely concentrate. "She went away," he said. "Elena."

"To where?"

"To her son in Matanzas. She left a note. Told me not to call."

"You told her, then."

"*Sí,* as I told you."

"Anyone else?"

"No one."

"Did you mention Rincon's name to her?"

"No. She left out of hurt, Jose, not because she disagrees with what I am doing. She would no more betray me or you or Rincon than she'd betray her son or daughter."

"*Claro,*" the driver said, but he sounded unconvinced. The assassin himself, their main player, had told at least two people he should not have told. Carlos watched his friend's face for a moment, then looked away. At the gates of the Ministry, he met Jose's eyes and saw a sliver of doubt there. He could not think of anything to say, any message for Rincon, any good reason why Jose knew Castro's schedule, or why he had worried about Rincon's name being mentioned. Was Rincon more important than the assassin? Weren't they all in equal jeopardy if Elena turned out to be more loyal to the Revolution than to him? He squeezed Jose's shoulder, as he always did, said, "We leave for the appointment we cannot mention at a quarter to noon," and stepped out into the light.

During the morning hours the phone did not ring. In all his years of sitting behind this desk, in this sunlit office, Carlos could not remember that happening more than half a dozen times. He wondered if all calls were now somehow being routed through Olochon's office, through D-7. Véronique seemed distracted; he wondered if someone from D-7 had spoken to her, if she'd been told to watch him carefully. Twice he called her in to be sure there had been no messages. He thought of making another trip to one of the places where Cuba touched the outside world, conducting another inspection, but he could not bring himself to go out again, to face the sunlit city so soon. He tried to steady himself by reading through reports from the various clinics, inspectors, and directors of enterprises that had any connection with the nation's health, but it all seemed like so much froth to him now, bubbles upon bubbles, lies upon lies, piles of ridiculous folders on his desk with one truth running beneath them.

At fifteen minutes before noon he told Véronique he was going home to have lunch, and walked downstairs and out to his waiting car. Jose was smoking. He seemed relaxed, unconcerned. On the ten-minute drive to one of Castro's semisecret residences, his driver and friend talked about baseball, some new shortstop in Matahambre who was said to be the best player the island had produced at that position since Renteria. "The *norteamericanos* steal our finest. They dangle money and women in front of them and steal them away."

"They steal everything," Carlos said. "They have always stolen everything."

It was a kind of game they were playing, Carlos thought. It was meant to relax him, get him into the proper frame of mind for his meeting with Fidel. Jose was more clever—and better connected—than he had ever imagined.

At the former *palacio,* Carlos went confidently through the grand doors, carrying his black medical bag. He had an appointment, of course—but Fidel varied his schedule constantly, revealing it to only his closest aides and those he was actually meeting with, sometimes keeping his promises, sometimes not. Carlos was concerned, for a moment, that the guards were going to ask to look into his bag, something they had never done. There was nothing to hide there, not yet; still, it would signal a change. But they only saluted stiffly and went back to their half-bored watchfulness.

Up the grand, sweeping marble stairs he went, carrying his great burden. At the top of the staircase were more uniformed guards, and then, beyond them, as he approached the doors of the Presidential Suite where Fidel sometimes slept and where they often met for these monthly checkups, two bulky thugs wearing no uniform. Olochon's men. These men did not salute, and there was not a scrap of boredom in their expressions. They eyed him calmly, giving away nothing. They stepped aside to let him pass, but it seemed to Carlos that they did so reluctantly, without respect, without affection, without the smallest bit of warmth in their Cuban blood. Where, he wondered, were such creatures bred? And after Fidel was gone how would anyone ever get past brutes similar to these, to kill the paranoid Olochon? And who, he wondered, what fool or hero, would be charged with *that* task in the hours ahead?

Beyond the doors was an opulent living room with long red curtains closing out most of the midday sun, armchairs, a thick carpet, and propaganda oil paintings on every wall. With Olochon's men following at a discreet distance, Carlos approached a set of gilded, three-meter-tall doors and knocked three times in a slow rhythm. There was a long pause—too long; unnaturally long—and then Fidel's voice, calling him in.

Fidel had become the prince of contradiction. The communist who lived in luxury like this. The octogenarian genius of strategy who refused to prepare for a successor. The man who had always boasted of his strength and unshakeable good health, and yet insisted on frequent checkups and medications for illnesses he did not have. His stomach troubles were nothing, really, a bit of diverticulitis, common enough in a man his age.

When Carlos closed the doors behind him—even Olochon's men would not dare to follow him into one of these medical examinations—he found *el Comandante* in his usual posture: pacing the carpeted floor with his hands clasped behind him, upper torso tilted forward, eyes searching the colors beneath his feet as if the key to his life and death lay in the various shades of red there.

"*Buenas,*" Fidel said, without looking at him.

"*Buenos días, Comandante.*"

Fidel looked up abruptly. Carlos wondered if something in his voice had already given him away. His palms were perspiring; he waited for Fidel to look at the floor again, and then rubbed them, one by one, on the cloth of his pants. When he spoke he tried to make himself sound optimistic, garrulous, another hopeful and fierce defender of the Revolution. "Feeling well?"

"My health is unblemished," Fidel said. It was his favorite term. Unblemished. *Sin mancha.* He seemed to believe the word would cleanse even the faintest stain of doubt from those around him, and from the people he ruled. Perhaps he even thought the word would chase off death itself.

"And may it always be so," Carlos said. He walked over to the desk and set his medical bag down there, trying to pay close attention to every movement. Tomorrow he would have to do this again, and do it exactly this way. "Let us begin the examination."

Reluctant as a boy expecting an inoculation, Fidel removed his combat-fatigue shirt and then the undershirt beneath it. Carlos put the stethoscope around his neck, placed the two plastic knobs in his ears, and listened to the pulse of the nation. It thumped there with the steady rhythm of history. The Supreme Leader was remarkably fit. His lungs were sound, even after years of cigar smoking, his blood pressure 124 over 88, excellent for a man his age.

"No blood-taking today," Fidel said.

"We should check the cholesterol."

Fidel shook his head. He was not a fan of needles.

Carlos tapped along Fidel's spine, looked into his ears and mouth and nose, helped *el Comandante* remove his boots and socks and felt of the slightly swollen feet, running his thumbnail across the tough skin to be sure no feeling had been lost. "My mother had diabetes," Fidel told him, for the thousandth time. "No sign of diabetes?"

"None. Any tingling in the hands and feet?"

"Absolutely nothing."

"Good."

Carlos then went carefully over the skin of Fidel's face, neck, and forehead. *El Comandante* was bored with the ritual by this point, or pretending that he was bored. The skin of his forehead, especially, was spotted, a few moles growing there. Eighteen months earlier, he'd had a surgeon remove some cancerous lesions from the hairline, and afterward, Fidel had not used the required medicine and the scars had not healed well. That piece of information had been, as it turned out, the kind of small fact the conspirators had been waiting for. Carlos had mentioned it to General Rincon, in passing, carelessly, before Rincon had been anything to him besides the deputy head of the Glorious Cuban Armed Forces. And with that remark, it seemed, everything had started. A few days later, Rincon had taken him on a walk and had begun the series of strange conversations, probing gently, carefully suggesting small complaints about the state of the nation. Every other day or so they had another conversation, more probing. Two weeks of this and Rincon had raised the idea of a change.

During this part of the examination, with Fidel beneath his hands, Carlos emitted one small grunt of concern.

When Castro was dressed again, Carlos half sat, half leaned on the front of the carved mahogany desk in a posture of confidence. Fidel resumed his impatient pacing. "What?" he said at last. "Something's wrong."

"You are in superb health. Almost unblemished."

"Almost," Fidel said, turning his eyes up to him finally. "*Casi*. What is this 'almost'? What was that noise you made?"

"There are some small new growths on the skin of your forehead, just at the hairline."

"Show me."

Carlos took out a hand mirror and held it so that Fidel could examine his own skin.

"These?" Fidel snapped. "This is worth talking about?"

"Your heart is as solid as a young stallion's. Your lungs, the same. Your blood pressure is better than mine and your spine and musculature also those of a much younger man. But these moles are things we cannot neglect. Cancerous cells double in a week. Next week there will be twice as many as there are now. The following week, four times as many. We are seeing this kind of thing with more frequency now because of the deterioration of the ozone layer."

"And who do we have to thank for that?"

"Yes. Still. It seems like a very small thing to you, and it is, in a way. These kinds of cancers are usually relatively weak, in the systemic sense. But they are cancers all the same, and I would be neglecting my duties if I didn't counsel you to treat them. Immediately."

"Fine," Fidel said distractedly. "Treat them, then. I am here. You are here. Treat them."

"It will take me some hours to get the proper cream."

"Why?"

"It is not commonly available. And, frankly, I didn't expect to see the moles at such an advanced stage."

"Didn't expect? You see me four times a week."

"I don't always make a close inspection of your hairline, Comandante. We can have the medicine prepared by the end of the day. Tonight or tomorrow I can apply it."

"I can't apply it myself?"

"Not as well as I can. There's a certain technique. You dab some on, wait a bit, wipe it off with a clean cotton cloth, dab on a second time, so that it sinks in deeply. But if you'd like—"

Castro waved an arm. "Fine, tomorrow. Noon again. Here. So much bother over nothing."

"There are no major side effects. No danger to you whatsoever."

"Fine, tomorrow."

Carlos put the stethoscope back into the bag and zipped it closed. He stood and was on the point of leaving, when Fidel stopped him with the wave of one hand. "Sit," he said. "Sit opposite me."

They occupied two of the high-backed chairs, a few feet from each other, facing at a slight angle. "We need to talk about something."

"My campaign?"

"Not health. Something. How long have you been with me?"

"Since just after your visit to Nuevitas. The stomach flu."

Fidel nodded as if he didn't remember the stomach flu. "How close have we been?"

"Brothers."

Fidel nodded. "Only Felix and Raul have been with me longer, in so close a capacity."

"Yes. Felix, your brother, and Augusto Rincon."

Fidel nodded again. "Rincon is away. Some sort of organizational troubles in Pinar. But what about Olochon, my other close associate?"

"What about him?"

"Yesterday you saved his life. Is this true?"

"I reacted spontaneously. We were at the Oriente as part of my campaign. A mental patient there—"

"Foreign?"

"I don't know. A mental patient there fired two shots. I reacted. Pushed Felix behind the sofa. I doubt the man would have hit him in any case."

"But it was very close. I've heard the bullet nearly struck him."

Carlos shrugged in what he hoped was a modest way.

"Is he good?"

"Who?"

"Olochon."

"Good in what way?"

Fidel bore his eyes into Carlos's eyes without blinking. Carlos felt the twitch in his left leg again but Fidel did not seem to notice. "Good in the sense of what?" he repeated.

Fidel seemed disappointed or angry. He tugged at his graying beard, narrowed his eyes. He let the silence press in against them for a few seconds. "Loyal. True."

"Olochon?"

Fidel nodded.

Carlos tried to run his mind over all the possibilities that could stand behind a question like this. Fidel did not blink, did not move his eyes. He had to speak. "Absolutely, in my opinion. Sometimes, I think . . ."

"What?"

"Sometimes, perhaps, a bit too enthusiastic, bordering on the paranoid. There are dangers, of course, naturally; we all know this. But he sometimes, I think, sees dangers where there are none."

"Better to be safe."

"Of course. I didn't mean it as a severe criticism. His loyalty is unquestionable. His judgment is good, sound, with the occasional excess."

Fidel nodded, but some evil new wind had entered the room. Carlos cursed himself. He should have been absolute in Olochon's defense. They did not need complications now.

"And Rincon?" Fidel said suddenly.

"Rincon? Loyal?"

Fidel nodded, staring into him.

"In my opinion, beyond a doubt. Beyond the tiniest shadow of the smallest doubt."

Another nod, more tugging on the famous beard. Fidel looked away and seemed to ponder for a moment, his eyes clouding, his mind drifting. He had what Felix Olochon only claimed to have—a sixth sense for danger. Everyone knew that. It had gotten him through the first arrests in Mexico, through the disastrous landing at Santiago de Cuba, through the battles of Sierra Maestra. Again and again, he had cheated death.

At last he waved his hand and Carlos stood. Before turning his back he said, "Tomorrow, then. Noon, if that suits you. It will take me all of two minutes to apply the ointment." He gave a short bow, and left the room with a cool sweat breaking out beneath his shirt.

CHAPTER TWENTY*FIVE

W hen she had to, Carolina had the ability to put herself into a state of semi-hibernation. In this state, she almost stopped thinking. It was as though her spirit took her outside of time for a few hours, gave her a kind of deep rest in preparation for the moment when she would have to act.

It was that way in the Museo de la Revolución in downtown Havana, where their muddy-haired guide nattered on about one politicized painting after the next, a series of tributes to the Revolution and its courageous leader. The only relief came in the form of acrid comments from one member of their tour group, a young man with a thin moustache, who kept asking questions like: "Excuse me, but if things are so wonderful in Cuba, why do people so often risk their lives to flee to the United States?"

"Those are mental patients," the woman replied. "Every culture has them."

"In a few years I'm sure you won't," the young man persisted. "You will have found the cure for that, too."

After all this charade of tourism—the bus rides and diatribes, even the decent lunch—the relative solitude of the beach was a great relief. She could feel herself come part of the way out of her hibernation there, feel a lining of nervousness beneath her hot skin.

She thought about the lotion in the lipstick tube, how it required a little time to penetrate the three layers of human skin and work its way into the bloodstream. Twenty to forty minutes, Volkes had told her. The more surface area it covered, the better its chance for effectiveness, so if you had some on the tip of your finger you'd likely experience only a brief dizziness and disorientation. Spread more widely, however, it would reach the blood in sufficient dosage. The chemical would first paralyze the digestive system, then thicken the blood; a few minutes later, clots would form and travel to the brain and heart, and the body would cease to function. Which made her a murderer, or at least an accomplice to murder.

She swam out into the surf to keep from thinking too much about it, but the idea nagged at her. "Nothing is accomplished by violence," her priest, Father Ricardo, often told her. "Nothing but the creation of new anger, and anger is the soil from which more violence grows." She felt torn, at moments, between his pacifist view of the world—a view in which each individual soul had to seek its own salvation—and the worldview she'd grown up with and embraced: One had to struggle against the evil forces in the world, and sometimes that struggle meant doing things a priest would not approve of. In certain moods she nourished a fantasy of setting her professional ambition aside, taking early retirement after one last great accomplishment, and living the life of a domestic would-be saint, a life filled with love and tenderness, not killing and deceit.

Now was not the time for a dream like that.

They ate dinner as a group: rice, beans, and fresh tilapia in a private dining area that was all gleaming wineglasses and white linen napkins. It seemed to her like a display of all the things the average Cuban did not have. She watched the women who served them. Whom did they know, she wondered, what hero of the Revolution were they related to, in order to have landed a plum job like pouring wine for well-off Spanish tourists? What kind of anger roiled behind their dark eyes? Or had all that been crushed long ago?

Once the meal was finished, the ability to hibernate left her completely. She could feel her heart working, feel herself climbing into a cold steely persona, setting aside all fear, all compassion, all softness. She went upstairs and changed into her dancing clothes, the bright crimson shirt and patterned skirt. She removed the contact lenses, slipped the dark-red lipstick into a pocket in her skirt. The phone had not rung again.

She had stayed at the Oriente on previous visits, and she knew that the bar/nightclub was located on the hotel's lowest floor, partly below ground level. As she stepped out of the elevator there she heard a decent mambo band playing, and saw some of her acquaintances from the tour group sitting at a table near the bar. Some of them had already had more than a little to drink. Carolina joined them, nursed one mojito and watched everyone in the room without seeming to. She was curious now, completely alert. How, she wondered, would Ulises find his way to her here, with the free-form dancing, the asking and accepting, all the getting up and sitting down again? And how could he have access to the hotel in the first place? Any Cuban who managed to get into this bar would have been carefully screened by the guards. Or would have had to bribe his way in. Or would be working for the Dirección General de Inteligencia. Or would have some high-level connection that protected him. "He will approach you and you'll know immediately that it is he," Volkes had told her. No other information given—not his looks, no code word, nothing but his odd name, which, she was sure, was not real.

One of the men in the group, another teacher, twenty years her senior, asked her to dance. He was a capable dancer, and they stayed on the floor for several numbers until she pleaded tiredness and wandered back to the bar for a drink. The older man got the message. Standing at the bar, sipping a mango juice and watching everything in the mirror behind the bartender's back, Carolina saw a stocky man with short hair moving toward her across the room. He was handsome in a rough-looking way, and carried himself with confidence, like an athlete. She watched him in glimpses, and then, when he was a few feet away and obviously approaching her, she looked directly at his reflection. There was a scar slicing across part of his cleft chin, some kind of fire in his eyes. If this wasn't Ulises, she thought, then she was going to be in trouble.

The man tapped her on the shoulder and she turned. He introduced himself as Jose, said he had seen her as soon as she came into the room, smiled, and asked her to dance. The band was playing rumba, and she twirled and touched Jose and let her eyes run across his face. DGI certainly, she thought. So they knew who she was.

They danced two numbers, and when the music slowed, in spite of what she knew she should do, she stayed on the floor with him and let him hold her loosely and close. He put his mouth near her ear and said, "You dance well. What is your name?"

"Angelita," she said.

"And you are an *angelito*." He pulled her closer.

At the end of this dance, she would find some excuse to get away from him. What a foolish plan it was, not totally controllable. She'd get away from him and let Ulises find some other way to contact her. She wondered if the phone call had been from another conspirator, warning her about this man, warning her away. She cursed Volkes and his excess of confidence, tried to move one hand down and casually brush the pocket of her skirt to be sure the lipstick was in its place. But then, just as the song was ending, the man put his mouth to her ear again and said, "Jose Ulises de Madrid, at your service, *angelito.*"

So she danced two more numbers with him, and let him accompany her back to her mango juice. She talked to him over the music, about nothing, trying to listen behind the words, but he might have been any Latino romancing a pretty woman in a bar. He was handsome in the rough, unpolished way she had always liked. His laugh was quiet but sincere, seductive, as if, in spite of all the evidence to the contrary, he himself found life to be a happy adventure. She sipped her drink and cautiously observed him. There were two possibilities: He was the real Ulises, the contact to whom she was supposed to pass her lethal dose of lotion; or he was from State Security and they had broken the conspiracy and were playing her for more information now. Either this man would accept the dose from her and disappear into the Cuban night on his treacherous errand, or he'd find a way to get her away from the group and they would arrest her, cart her off, torture her, and then, eventually, kill her.

But something else was going on. From the beginning of her career, from the first days of her CIA training in a windowless room in northern Virginia, she had been taught the most essential lesson: People are human beings first, and spies second. Human beings first, and soldiers second. Human beings first and government officials second. The greatest of mistakes was to forget the fact that in addition to their official duties, men and women were motivated by their individual psychological makeup, their need for sex, love, admiration, money, revenge, protection, security, approval. Bush, Clinton, Castro, Hussein, Kennedy, Mussolini, Hannibal, all the way back to Pontius Pilate and the Old Testament kings—there was the title and the office, and then, beneath that, buried in the mystery of the human personality, something else. History was the sum total of these "something else's."

And now she felt it in herself. She was there to do a job, and she would do it. But she was a person, a woman, not just an employee of the Orchid, and during that half hour in the bar something was rising up in her from beneath the layers of her own history. Jose Ulises was a bit on the macho side, a bit overly confident. His mannerisms—the sweeping hand gestures, the way the eyebrows and mouth worked together, even the sound of the beautiful language on his tongue—it all reminded her of the boys of Little Havana in Miami, so full of sexuality, so smooth, and yet, where women were concerned, so easily threatened. But he was smart, and tender with her, courteous, respectful. The kind of man who would not feel less of a man because of her career successes, her abilities with a pistol, her courage.

She decided to trust him. And then it seemed to her during the half hour after that decision was made, that she understood her whole life in a different light. Her attraction to and repulsion from the Cuban culture floated before her in the loud, warm room. If Uncle Roberto wanted the Cuba of his imagination, a place of family warmth, money making and music, then she wanted the Cuban man of her imagination, masculine but yielding, confident in himself but allowing her the freedom to be who she was. Oscar had almost been like that. Almost.

Jose asked her to dance again, and by then she had made her decision. There was more than one way to pass on lipstick to a man.

She pressed herself gently against him. She let one hand slip down just beneath his belt along the back of his trousers. It was all right: To anyone watching she would seem like just another European tourist letting herself go in the tropics, having her fling before heading back to the routine of home. But she was serving two masters now.

When the band took a break, she held onto Jose's hand and tugged him in the direction of the short stretch of hallway where the elevators were. There, for appearances' sake, and for the sake of something else, she put a hand behind his head and pulled his mouth down to hers. Jose seemed surprised, but only at first. It had been a very long time since she'd kissed anyone; years, a lifetime, since she'd been kissed like this. When they separated, she saw her neighbor from the bus ride walking past, trying not to look at them, and then looking, catching Carolina's eye and offering a conspiratorial smile.

Perfect, she thought.

Then she and Jose were alone in the elevator. Carolina rubbed the seat of his pants—there were cameras trained on them, perhaps. They said nothing. Upstairs at last, she fumbled with the key at her door. Inside, she wondered again about cameras, about microphones, so she whispered to him when they were in the room with the door locked: "Quiet."

"*Sí,*" he said. But his voice was thick. He had not expected this kind of good fortune.

She kissed him again and he unbuttoned her skirt and let it fall. She put her hands inside his shirt, took off his pants, pushed him toward and then onto the bed, and sat on top of him, moving in a slow rhythm, without haste, without violence. She pretended to herself that this was going to be the last night of her life, the last man she would ever make love with, and that he was her dream lover, future husband, father of her as yet unborn *angelitos*. He seemed to be pretending, too, turning her into someone else in his imagination. Or perhaps not. When her shirt was off and she leaned down so he could take her breasts in his mouth, he kissed and sucked as though they had done this together many times. There was fire there, but not the harsh flame of lust.

When it had burned itself out, she was surprised to notice that a deep warmth remained. She lay down on top of him, then beside him, and he turned and put his mouth against her ear and said, in that beautiful language: "*Una cosa hermosa.*" Something beautiful.

"*Sí,*" she said. "Something beautiful in the midst of pain."

"I cannot stay," he said, after some time had passed, enough time. "I want to."

She rolled over on top of him and kissed him, the damp skin of their chests pressing together. She dropped her mouth close to his ear and said: "In the pocket of my skirt. On the floor next to the bed. A lipstick container."

He squeezed her against him. He said: "*Acuerdate de mí.*" Remember me. And then she lay there alone with her face in the pillow and listened to him sit up and rustle the cloth of her clothes for a moment in the darkness. He went into the bathroom, used the toilet, quickly washed himself, and dressed. He touched her once on her bare back before he left, the touch that had been missing from her life, and then the door clicked quietly closed and it was done.

It was done. But a sadness washed over her. She could still feel the warmth between her legs, and something else. The steel shield she had set up around her heart wasn't working the way it usually did. She had seen too much of the evil of the world, too much deceit. It had infected her, but the touch of Jose's skin had been like a cure for that. The lotion that killed all pain.

She drifted along on a sea of memories, not quite awake and not exactly asleep. She did not know how long she lay there like that, half an hour perhaps, before the phone rang next to the bed. *Another hang up,* she thought. *More treachery.* She did not want to answer it, did not want to be pulled back into that world. It rang again, then a third time. She rolled over and lifted the receiver to her ear. Jose's voice. "Get out," he said. "Now. Immediately." And the line went dead.

CHAPTER TWENTY*SIX

———ᴡᴨᴨᴡ———

Carlos ate his first meal of the day alone in the apartment, just as darkness fell. He did not know how he was going to get through the night and the following morning. He believed now, after his hour with Fidel, that he would probably be able to do what it was he had been instructed to do. Shoot the man, no, he could not; he did not think he could ever shoot anyone again, after what had happened with Ernesto in the Montefiore Prison. Certainly not at close range like that, in the head. But rub lotion on an old forehead, knowing it would kill the person who had once been his hero, knowing what that hero had become, how he had failed his people? Yes, now he believed he could do that. He just was not sure he could live through the hours that led up to doing that.

For a time, he paced the four rooms of his apartment, but the memories there—of Teresa, of Elena—haunted him. He took a cigar out of the box on his bureau and smoked it, something neither woman had ever wanted him to do in those rooms. He paced, smoked, felt the visions rise up around him like a circus of demons: Rincon would be the new president, and he, Carlos, the great national hero . . . or he would remain in his current position in anonymity; or the plot would fail and he'd become a national disgrace, imprisoned, prodded with electric shocks in the Havana Psychiatric Hospital until he gradually lost his mind. Elena and possibly even her son would be thrown in jail, the grandchild taken by the state so that it would have a proper upbringing. Jose would save him; Jose would betray him. Fidel Castro would prove to be immortal. Olochon would somehow twist things around and become president for life and the island would sink into despair, another Haiti. The United States would invade, again, or the change in regime after Fidel's death would mean only a return to a different kind of slavery in which most Cubans would still be living in poverty. They would be serving a different elite, democracy on its lips, and a chosen few, a different chosen few, would have every imaginable luxury.

These images swirled around him like acrid smoke. When he thought they would suffocate him, he went down the three flights of stairs and out onto the street. He heard sirens in the night. A child crying through an open window. Music. He walked to his car and opened the door, thinking, at first, that he would only sit there, and then, that he would only drive around the city for a while to calm his nerves.

But once he was actually behind the wheel and moving, he knew where he was going. Elena's son lived in Matanzas, an hour east of Havana along the northern coast. He did not know if she had gone to denounce him, to ask her son whether she should denounce him, or just to get away from him, but she had been the only real warmth in his life these last years, and he could not do what he was about to do without seeing her one final time.

In order to get to Matanzas, he had to drive along the road that led to the Oriente Hotel. That could not be helped. In the event that he was stopped, it would be natural enough to say that he was going to pick up his woman, who was visiting her son and grandchild. The Revolution had not yet outlawed such gestures of familial love.

He drove through the dark city—men and women and a few children on the corners talking, playing music, having a simple meal outdoors in order to escape the heat of their homes. Such things had not yet been outlawed.

Soon he was in the country, the moon rising amid a wash of stars in the black sky, dark little huts by the side of the rutted road, shadows of palm trees, and banana fronds waving like arms warning him to go back, go back.

As he was passing the access road to the Oriente Hotel, he saw a twinkling of lights there, the famous pale blue lights of the National Police. His stomach tightened. He drove on. He thought he saw something large moving in the dark foliage by the side of the road, just a flash of something, he could not be sure, a soldier on patrol, a beggar ducking into the shadows, a peasant selling mother-of-pearl, a thief. He slowed for just an instant, but the shadow disappeared. There was nothing to do but drive on. If the plan had already failed, they would soon find him. If he knew they were looking for him, he would tell Elena to denounce him, save herself. Perhaps it was already too late for that gesture.

Elena's son, Julio, lived with his dark-haired wife and their infant son in a two-room flat on the outskirts of Matanzas. Carlos had offered, more than once, to use his influence to get the family a larger apartment, closer to Havana. But Julio was as idealistic as his mother. He'd become an architect with the intention of improving the living conditions of the poor, designing buildings that weren't ovens in the middle of the day, that didn't start falling apart the moment they were completed. Julio and his mother were real revolutionaries, real communists. They were, Carlos thought, what he had been at the beginning.

He parked a block away from the building and sat there, staring through the windshield, waiting to see if State Security had followed him, or anticipated him. But the street was quiet, only a radio playing a rumba faintly in the distance. If Elena had revealed anything about the conspiracy to Julio and his wife, then Carlos would be the devil walking in on them, a kind of deadly plague threatening their calm lives. He thought back to the years when he and Teresa had been idealistic and newly married. He'd gone to medical school, the way Julio had gone to architecture school, with the intention of treating the poor. He'd spent two years on a sugar plantation in Nuevitas, near Camagüey, where the Party leader had been a woman—a good woman, not one of these ubiquitous officials out to line their pockets, but someone who wanted to make the lives of those who labored a bit easier. This woman, Liliana Morro, had encouraged him to become active in the Party. People liked him, she said, admired him. He was a natural leader.

He worked hard. Teresa, a nurse, had worked hard beside him. They'd turned the tragedy of their childlessness into a passion for helping others.

Because health conditions at the sugar collective improved so dramatically after his arrival, someone in some director's office had new statistics to boast about, and a newspaper reporter had been sent to do a story on the young, idealistic doctor-and-nurse team. The story had caught the eye of Alejandro Fernandez Lella, who had then been in charge of health for the province of Camagüey. Fernandez Lella had offered Carlos a job as his assistant, convincing him by telling him how much good he could do and by creating a position for Teresa. After a few days of doubt, Carlos had accepted. They worked hard, they believed in the principles of the Revolution—sharing, helping the workers, defending the nation against outsiders who wished them harm; they believed Fidel Castro was a kind of Latin saint. When Fernandez Lella took his pension, Carlos—only thirty-three—had been promoted to the head position. The health of the province became a national bragging point. There were more newspaper articles, more awards, accolades, even international attention. Fidel visited the area and asked for an interview with the young doctor who was doing so much good. On that day, during a visit to Nuevitas, the Maximum Leader had been troubled by a stomach virus. Carlos met with him, accepted his praise as modestly as he could, took the small risk of prescribing ginger tea and boiled tapioca, an old folk remedy. Fidel had trusted him and the remedy had quickly gotten rid of the symptoms. A few weeks later Carlos was summoned to Havana to work in the Ministry of Health, a midlevel position in charge of overseeing the web of rural clinics. Little by little, without especially trying to, simply by working well, causing no trouble, and developing an instinct for office politics, he had climbed high up on the government ladder. So high that the ladder itself began to wobble beneath him.

It was then that the first seeds of doubt, planted long before, began to sprout. From his high post he had a clearer view of what he had not allowed himself to see earlier: how Party officials and members of the National Police lived, and how most of the workers lived. In some places there was not even enough painkiller for the simplest procedures. All this was blamed on the blockade, naturally—what North Americans called "the embargo." And the blockade was, in truth, partly to blame. But there was blame to be spread everywhere. Carlos began to think of approaching Fidel directly, personally, telling the great man what he had seen. But he was saved from this error by the first assistant minister of health, a man named Baleste, who did exactly that and for his efforts was reassigned to Niquero for ten years of giving injections to prostitutes near the port there. Carlos was promoted to first assistant in the outspoken Baleste's place. He did what he could. He kept his mouth closed. He watched Fidel in the meetings, talking and talking, grandiose, charismatic, tireless, sly, shrewd. He started to become aware of the steady tone of falsehood behind everything the man said. His naïveté was replaced, day by day, meeting by meeting, with a nagging cynicism. He had heard of Olochon, of course, but now he came to know him well.

Then Teresa fell ill with breast cancer. And nothing, not even the best care the nation afforded, could save her. He watched her wither and die in front of his eyes, and his thoughts were only personal then; everything was secondary to this slow, agonizing decay. It wasn't until she had been gone for more than a year, it wasn't until after he'd met Elena, that the slow-building anger in him reached a boiling point. He heard about the dissidents being arrested, then starved or beaten in prison for a few words of criticism. He saw what happened to the *balseros,* the raft people, desperate enough to risk dying of thirst, drowning, or shark-bite in the Straits of Florida.

And slowly, gradually, unstoppably, all of that had brought him here, to the dark front seat of a car on a street near Matanzas.

Wearily, fueled only by the anger now—he felt sure he'd wasted his life—and by a desire to see Elena's face one last time, he stood up out of the car and knocked lightly on the door of Julio's apartment. Elena herself answered, her cheeks streaked with fear. She stepped out, closing the door behind her, and walked away from him along the street, quickly, her shoes tapping in the night like a song of omens. Carlos followed her. She turned down an alley. They passed a pair of lovers there, the man pushing the woman into a doorway, kissing her forcefully, almost violently. Elena went on, out behind the buildings to a dusty playground where the faint moonlight illuminated broken swings and a sagging metal fence.

She stopped by the set of swings and whirled around. "How could you come here?"

"I had to."

"How could you put us at risk?"

"You're already at risk. I wanted to see you. I wanted to tell you that if it seems like I will be caught before it happens I will try to get you a message, through Jose if I can, through the clinic. I want you to denounce me."

"Denounce you! I couldn't denounce you. Never! How could you think that?"

She burst into tears and turned away from him. In the darkness he could see the curve of her back, and he remembered, in a rush of feeling, all the things he loved about her—the tireless efforts to heal, the deep warmth, the brains, the beauty. He put his hand on her shoulder blade, currents of guilt running up and down his arm. He thought: *This is what they do to us.* "I'm sorry. Sorry for everything, Elena. I thought . . . I wanted to see you before . . ." He moved his hand up to her shoulder and turned her around so that her tear-soaked face was close to his. "I am supposed to do what I am going to do tomorrow," he said in a whisper. "I am supposed to kill him. I wanted to see you first."

"How can you?" she whispered back, but the whisper was a shout in his inner ear. "A man of healing. A man who loves to garden. How can you do such a thing?"

A thousand words of explanation leapt to his lips. The things he had seen that she had not, the hypocrisy, the opulence, the special fruits, meats, and canned goods for the military, for Party officials, for factory directors, for the likes of him. The jails. Olochon's cells. He wanted to tell her about Ernesto but she would be disgusted by it, and with him. He said, "When it is over, tomorrow night, please come back. What do I have to gain for myself from doing this? Nothing. I have no ambitions. I don't want any luxuries. I want the same thing I have always wanted: I want some measure of truth in my life, some measure of goodness in my country. Is that impossible to understand? Does that make me evil?"

"Killers are killers," she said. "You can't kill in the name of goodness, in the name of healing. It rots the soul."

"Tomorrow night, come back. If my soul is rotten, you heal me. If things don't get better, leave me. But don't curse me yet. I need you not to curse me. I have no one else close to me in this life."

She turned away, turned back. He moved to embrace her but she put the palm of her right hand flat against his chest and pushed him firmly away. "It will be the same," she said in a hoarse, angry whisper. "Whoever is leading you to do this, don't you see, they will end up the same, or worse. We know what we have now, we can function, we can do some good. Later, afterward, we don't know. Go. Go away from me. Don't come here again and put my child and grandchild in danger. Go!"

Her hoarse, awful "¡Lárgate!" rang in his ears all the way back through the alley, where, in the smell of rotting garbage, the lovers were still half wrestling, half kissing in the doorway. Who was with him now? Who was close beside him? Rincon? Jose? Who were Rincon and Jose? He drove back into the city through a moonlit Caribbean darkness.

———⸎⋀⋁⋀⋁⋀⋁⋀⋁ⁿⁿ———

C arolina had her clothes on and was out the door of her hotel room within thirty seconds. She found the staircase, sprinted down two flights, pushed through an emergency exit (the alarm sounded for three seconds, then stopped; that was communism, things not working) and slipped across the sandy stretch of brightly lit decorative foliage between the back edge of the hotel and the beach. Staying in the shadows, she circled slowly around to the front side of the building, giving it a wide berth, stopping in the protection of a breadfruit tree or banana plant and then scurrying sideways again into the next patch of shade.

She had taken only the lipstick tube—lighter red—with the transmitter in it, some money, and the cyanide tablet she had been given, all safely stowed in her skirt pocket now with a handkerchief pressed down on top to keep them in place. As she slipped through the darkness, she tried to step away from herself and analyze things calmly, as she had been trained. The fact that Jose had had a chance to get to a telephone and call her must mean two things: first, he'd gotten safely away from the hotel with the lethal dose; second, to some extent at least, their cover had been blown. State Security had information that had led them, if not directly to her, then at least to the Oriente Hotel.

Then, as she crouched in the foliage watching the front of the hotel, other possibilities arose in the darkness: Jose was working for State Security but the lovemaking had given him a fleeting moment of sympathy for her. Or it was some neat trick he was playing so she would be apprehended outside the hotel, away from the eyes of the hard-currency-paying tourists. Or he himself was running now, and the dose would be thrown out the window of his car as it sped along some dark coastal road, and Castro would survive again, and all of this—the incredible risk, the expense, the sacrifices of dozens of people on both sides of the Straits of Florida—would have been for nothing.

She stayed in the trees near the hotel only long enough to see the telltale blinking blue lights of the National Police as the lopsided-looking small trucks pulled up to the front door. When uniformed figures leapt out and hurried along the walk—so much for protecting the tender sensibilities of their foreign guests—she was gone like a deer in dancing shoes.

She wished only that she had a weapon. They should have thought to let Jose pass a pistol on to her. But, most likely, carrying such a thing into the Oriente would have been almost as problematic for him as carrying it through the Barcelona airport would have been for her. And what would she have done with a handgun anyway, left it as a tip for the chambermaid? Made her living by giving shooting lessons under a new identity in the Havana suburbs? Still, a weapon would have given her some comfort right about now.

She'd gone only a few hundred meters when she realized that the shoes were going to be a problem. She thought of taking them off and moving along barefoot, but decided against it. Keeping the hotel to her back, and angling away from the access road, she moved deeper into the jungle, swatting at mosquitoes and banana fronds, letting the voices and engine noises fall away behind her and be replaced by the sounds of the Cuban night: a soft wash of surf, the sharp calls of birds she had no name for, the rustle of dead leaves beneath her feet.

The moon rose. She could not see it yet, but she could sense it. To her right, east, the quality of the darkness changed, making it a little easier to see the large, sharp-edged leaves before they slapped across her face. The western promontory of the Bay of Guanabacoa, the abandoned fishing pier there, the transmitter—in the safety of the Barcelona airport it had all made sense. Here, it looked like a plan riddled with trouble. The pier was five and a half miles away, for one thing, and she had no shoes for walking in the underbrush. And the police were surely in her empty room by now, though they might waste some time searching the rest of the hotel before deciding she'd fled. They might also have had only a general sense of the plan, not tied it to her specifically. Which would be nice.

She came, abruptly, to a road. It might have been the road from Havana or it might not have been; if it was, it meant she'd already moved too far away from the coast. The headlights of a car surprised her, approaching fast around a curve. She ducked into the trees and dove flat on her face in a musty, soft bed of decayed tropical flora. When the car passed she stood, brushed herself off, then changed direction slightly, using the moon as a guide, keeping it just off her right shoulder, adjusting as well as she could for its steady swing south.

The going was very slow, exhausting. The footing was uncertain; branches and brambles scratched at her, holding her back, as if they, too, had been charmed by Fidel Castro. Every few minutes she stopped to catch her breath, check her bearings, listen for any sound of pursuers. Her shins, ankles, cheeks, and forehead were already badly scratched. Her dancing dress was torn. Her underwear lay tangled in the hotel sheets. For a moment during one of these pauses, it occurred to her with a sharp stab of pain that if she failed to make it out of Cuba alive, she would not be especially missed. Her parents had passed on; her uncle would know she'd deceived him and would feel a wave of sadness, but the sadness would probably be overwhelmed by his bruised pride and by the sense that he had been correct, that she should have listened to him from the start; the people at the Orchid would replace her with only a little more trouble than it had taken them to find a body double. A few girlfriends in Atlanta might grieve for a while, but there would be no memorial service with teary tributes, no children at her grave. Despite his claims of enduring love, Oscar would quickly move on. Assuming Jose lived, and assuming he wasn't in the employ of State Security, she'd be nothing more than a wisp of sweet memory in his brain cells, fading month by month.

Her life—all that education, striving, risk, all that inherited beauty and brains—would amount to one quick exhalation of the universe, one grain of sand among trillions. A quiet sadness wrapped itself like a climbing vine around the fear on her skin. She told herself that if the dose reached Fidel, if she had played a role in ending his reign, then it would have been a good life all the same. Not the worst thing, to die quickly of cyanide poisoning on a beautiful beach, having sacrificed yourself so that people wouldn't be tortured and enslaved. Not the worst way to go.

She plowed deeper into the trees, startled once by a flock of birds screeching in the night with a madman's hilarity. The humid, dense landscape seemed endless, a place that existed beyond the eyes of the Maximum Leader, a secret place known by no one but the native people who had hunted and fished on this soil a thousand years before it was called Cuba. At one point she was slapped on the shoulder by a dangling mango. At another point she heard something crawling or slithering close to her, a low rustle that came within a meter of her ankles, and then, when she scuffed her feet, hurried away. Jutia, lizard, *rata*, she couldn't know. If she could get to the pier before sunrise and activate the transmitter, her chances would be slightly better, but as she stumbled along, fighting the dense undergrowth, she grew tired very quickly. It was one thing to train on a track in early-morning Atlanta; something else to work like this in Cuban humidity, with the fear pushing her heartbeat up and the unpredictable earth shifting beneath the wrong kind of shoes. The mojito and the lovemaking and the jet lag didn't help either. Her breaks—to rest and to listen—began to last longer.

She wondered if it would be better to stop here, where no soldiers would follow, sleep as best she could, get her bearings by the sun, and make it to the pier by midafternoon when half the island would be at rest.

After another hour—it was the heart of the night now, three or four A.M. (she never made love with a watch on, that was one of her rules, and she had left it on the bedside table)—she saw a glint of light through the trees. She took a few quiet steps and could see that it was a metal roof touched by the tropical moon. She crept closer. No lights on, no car, no road. It was some kind of fisherman's hut; maybe she was close to the shore and could work her way along it to the bay. But as she moved toward the hut she heard a small dog start to yap inside the house, then a voice. She waited a few minutes, then crept farther off to the right, north she hoped, toward the water.

Soon she heard the sound of the surf grow more distinct. The moon had climbed high and begun to tumble off toward the opposite horizon. She was completely exhausted, bloody blisters bubbling out on the soles and sides of her feet, mosquito bites on her face, neck, and arms. A faint light, first whisper of the Latin American dawn, touched the sky above her head.

She felt as though she could not go another hundred yards. She scooped out a depression in the cool matting of broken leaves and stalks, broke off three banana fronds to use as a kind of blanket, then lay there curled up like a fetus, covered in green and a cool layer of fear, to wait for what the morning would bring.

CHAPTER TWENTY‑EIGHT

———— ∿∿ ————

Carlos did not sleep but lay twisting in the too-large bed, tormented by the enormity of what he was about to do. Every second, the deed seemed to grow more real, its edges sharp, its center a dark purple-black, a monster gnawing at his soul. To keep himself from going completely insane, or letting the fear chase him back into the safe shadows, he thought of Ernesto's mouth, the man struggling desperately to speak a name that might rescue him. "A-ah. A-ah." Who was A-ah?

Eventually he dozed in a fitful, unsatisfying way, his rest torn into strips of horrifying dreams.

He awoke at the usual hour, bathed, shaved, dressed. At exactly nine o'clock, Jose pulled the black Volga up in front of the building. As usual, he looked as if he hadn't slept the night before, and Carlos wondered if he'd been spending all these months conspiring, sitting up late with Rincon and the others, whoever those others might be. The stubble on Jose's cheeks resembled a darker version of the cane stalks after they had been cut and rained upon. The scar on his chin glistened like one loop of river in a jungle, seen from above.

"*Buenos días, Ministro,*" Jose said, as he always did, but

aside from those words, the driver did not speak until they had driven several blocks. There, just as they were crossing the Río Almendares, he turned on the radio, loud music interrupted by government reminders to participate in the Great Victory by keeping the rats out of the apartment houses and old-age homes.

"Boss," he said, at last. "The plan has changed again. I have a present for you."

"Good. I could use a present."

"You didn't sleep well, I can see."

"Hardly at all."

"I have just the thing then." Jose reached inside his sport coat and brought out a large cigar.

Carlos frowned. It was not exactly the kind of present he'd hoped for at nine A.M. on the morning he was going to assassinate the man millions still thought of as a hero. Jose was smiling at him, glancing back and forth between his boss's sour expression and the road. "It's a good cigar," he said.

"This morning I can't joke, Jose."

"A fine, a special cigar. Look." He took his hand from the wheel for a second and pointed to the thin slits down each side. "See?"

Carlos took the cigar out of his friend's hand and turned it this way and that. He examined what appeared to be two hairline cracks running on either side of it.

"You can smoke it, but only a few centimeters down, then put it out. Open it up when you are alone, and you will find the present."

"*Claro*," Carlos said. His hand had started to tremble. He looked up at Jose, who was not smiling. "Everything went well then?"

"Not exactly. Someone at the Oriente was arrested. I don't know who, or how high up. But someone."

"That someone will give them someone else, who will give them someone else, and so on."

"Exactly," Jose said, not the smallest trace of optimism in his voice now. His eyes stayed on the road ahead of them, the craziness of the Havana morning spelled out there in the desperately overcrowded, Czech-made, red buses and an odd fleet of old, half-broken cars, some of them well-cared-for *cacharros,* Fords, Chevies, Studebakers, built in American factories in the fifties; some from Soviet factories in the eighties; some, part of the newer fleet of Italian Fiats.

"How long do you think we have?" Carlos asked him.

"Long enough."

Their route took them not far from the Torture House. Neither man looked in that direction. When Jose pulled up in front of the Ministry, there were a few more soldiers there than usual, but otherwise the place looked the way it always looked—men in white shirts holding briefcases and mounting the stairs, the guards, the star of the Cuban national flag barely moving in the warm morning air. Carlos could not make his hand rise to Jose's shoulder, could not force even one note of good cheer into his voice. "We have to be at the old residence at noon," he managed to say.

Jose moved his eyes so that they rested on him, the weight of the world there. "We will be."

CHAPTER TWENTY·NINE

———— ·····ᴡᴡᴡ···· ————

Just before dawn a hard rain fell for ten or fifteen minutes, huge drops smacking against the leaves and palm fronds, waking Carolina from a deep, messy sleep in which she had dreamt of her mother. She scrambled to her feet and tried to take cover against the wide trunk of a breadfruit tree, but it was a tropical downpour, and within seconds she was wet to the skin and shivering. When the rain passed, the air was cool for a short while, then it took on the temperature and consistency of steam. She stopped shivering, but her dress and hair did not dry. She tugged the damp handkerchief out of her pocket and found the cyanide and the lipstick tube and the Cuban bills. Undamaged.

She drank some of the water that had pooled up on the wider leaves, and found a not-quite-ripe mango for breakfast. Eating it, the sticky juice on her fingers, she thought back to her meal at Mandarin with Uncle Roberto, the texture of the fine tablecloth and napkins, her uncle's cuff links and starched shirt, the waiter pouring water with a studied deference, the spices of the sauce so perfectly balanced. Such luxury seemed a thousand miles away now, the colorful flickering of a lost world. She was living, at the moment, closer to the way Castro and his tiny band of Sierra

Maestra revolutionaries had lived. They had survived on the locals' generosity—beans, rice, and water—a ragtag, starving, ridiculous group that would, by some improbable twist of fate, chase a strongman dictator off to Santo Domingo.

History, it seemed, was composed of just such unlikely events.

From where she stood she could clearly hear the surf washing up on shore. It was easy to get her bearings from the sun. There were no houses in sight. No sound of traffic. Even with her battered feet, she could make it to the coast now without much trouble, she knew that. Once she reached the water the only question would be whether she should turn right or left; whether she'd traveled more than five miles during the night or less.

Though her face, arms, and legs were badly scratched, it was her feet that really concerned her. As an employee of the Agency, and later of the Orchid, she'd had all kinds of training, everything from using handguns to resisting interrogation. She'd studied languages and Okinawan karate. But there was no way to practice being in pain like this. The shoes pinched her feet so badly they'd rubbed raw lines on either side.

She forced herself to stand and begin walking, hoping the pain would diminish after a while. When she'd traveled only a few hundred yards she came upon another house. She saw it first as colors between the trees, flashes of white, red, and gold there in the distance. She crouched and approached it, a few feet at a time. No dogs barked out an alarm. The metal roof sparked into view. Another fifty feet and she saw that the colors were pieces of clothing strung on a line to dry in what was now a fierce sun. She went only another few feet then remained still, hidden behind some kind of flowering shrub, the smell of which made her think of

Miami. A heavyset woman in a red bandana was hanging the clothes to dry—shirts and dresses. Carolina remained absolutely still, watching. When the woman was finished, Carolina crawled another fifty feet closer, still hidden by the dense undergrowth. She heard a wooden door slap closed, then slap again a few minutes later. She watched the red bandana moving off away from the house, along a road or a path she could not see.

When the woman had walked out of sight, Carolina crept closer. It would not do to go promenading on the beach in broad daylight in her ruined, expensive dress. People here, trained by a lifetime of poverty and suspicion, would notice such things, would spot her as a foreigner from half a mile away. If the National Police had sent out any kind of alert, if they were combing the area questioning residents. . . . She crept forward, only a hundred feet from the clothesline now. After watching for a while, she crept still closer, picked up a stone, and flung it into the yard. Nothing; no barking dog, no sign of people. She tossed another stone so that it clanked on the tin roof and rattled down its slope. Nothing. Hurrying now, wincing with each step, she crossed the small, rutted path, stepped over a low wall made of coral stones, pulled one of the dresses off the line, pinned some money to the rope, and was back in the trees in under a minute.

She pondered for a long moment, then decided to leave her shoes. She'd be on the beach very soon, and then on the Orchid's boat, speeding north to safety. The shoes meant only more pain now.

Barefoot, she made straight for the water, going along at a turtle's pace, stepping gingerly, splinters of pain running up her calves. Soon the undergrowth thinned. Not far from the edge of the trees she stripped off her ruined, $485 dress, crawled into what seemed like a rainbow-colored tent, then took the contents of her pocket into her hand and transferred them carefully into the huge pocket. The owner of the dress had to weigh three hundred pounds, Carolina thought, but it was better this way. She tore a large enough piece off the good dress to make a bandana. She found a length of branch that would work as a cane. She fashioned a crude pair of sandals from two folded-up breadfruit leaves wrapped around her swollen feet with more ribbons of torn dress. She rubbed dirt on her legs in the hope that they might seem, from a distance, older, more like an islander's, then she hobbled across another small road and onto the bright, burning sand. Not two hundred yards to her left, she saw a pier with one broken piling. Guanabacoa Bay. Limping, leaning on the cane, she set off toward the pier, looking, she hoped, from a distance at least, like an indigent Cuban woman hobbling off to gather some mother-of-pearl to sell, or to scrape for edible sea snails in the shallows.

She reached the pier, her feet screaming with every step, the blisters broken and already infected, oozing pus. She opened the tube of lipstick and pressed hard on the transmitter inside. Its red light flashed . . . the battery had not died. That done, she hobbled around the end of the pier and sat crouched in its meager shade, staring at the blinding sea, a woman waiting for the spirit of death to come and fetch her.

CHAPTER THIRTY

O leg thought it slightly strange that Volkes had been keeping him so busy over the past several days. He wondered if the schedule had been speeded up. He'd flown back and forth to Atlanta twice, carrying sealed documents, and was now going across the Everglades, after dark—in what he had been told was a former U.S. Army helicopter—with yet another envelope in the inside pocket of his suit jacket. This particular document was going to be delivered to someone from the Department of Defense, he knew that, but how important a someone he wasn't sure. The secretary or an undersecretary, he guessed, judging by the bodyguards in the seats behind him. The message he was carrying would have something to do with the U.S. government's actions in the hours and days following Fidel's murder, and he was curious about the envelope's contents to the point of distraction. If he'd thought he could have gotten away with it, he would have slipped into the bathroom at the back and had himself a quick read.

But things were going along well. The gullible Carolina, half in love with him, out to rescue Cuba from itself, was in Prague now; D-7 had someone tracking her movements. Volkes and the others were so confident in his loyalty that they were promising him what amounted to a partnership. Decades it had taken him to earn this kind of confidence. Years of leading a double life, of setting up an absolutely secure and secret line of communication back to DGI, of watching every word he spoke, controlling every facial expression and emotion, constantly looking in his rearview mirror. It would be over soon enough, and they would find a place for him back in the motherland, and when Fidel did pass on, who knew to what heights Oleg Rodriguez might climb? Head of D-7 maybe, or even something larger.

He looked down at the utter blackness of the central Everglades. Panthers still ran there, or so he had heard. A dozen varieties of poisonous snakes called the place home, alligators, the huge and vicious Belizean crocodile. He did not like such places. He would be glad when the lights of the Gulf coast came into view.

He was looking for them through the vibrating windshield when he thought he heard—over the *whump-whump-whump* of the rotor blades—a shifting of weight behind him. A shifting of weight, and then a sound like a whisper in both ears, and he felt something brush his chin. Too late by a fraction of a second, he reached up his powerful hands to try to get them between his throat and the piece of cable. But the man behind him was immensely strong, and then so quickly, so terribly quickly, everything in Oleg Rodriguez's world turned the most hideous shade of red.

CHAPTER THIRTY*ONE

Fidel Castro was a man of moods, a sinking soul wrapped in paranoia and the past. Carlos had been Fidel's personal physician for six years, and in that time he had seen the Great Leader fidget and complain like a young child over the smallest discomfort, and sit stoically and endure his skin being sewn up without anesthesia. The man had not a milliliter of patience, but he had a massive pride, and sometimes the pride was enough to keep him still.

Carlos walked past the guards, gave his signal knock on the tall doors, and could tell, instantly, just from the sound of *el Comandante's* voice, that his noble leader was in a good mood this hour. "Ah, Doctor," he said, when Carlos entered the room carrying his black leather bag. "You slept well?"

"Perfectly, Comandante, and you?"

"I was tossing in the bed all night worried about this injection."

"It's not an injection, just some topical ointment."

"Ah, yes; let me see."

Carlos tried to keep his hands steady as he opened the bag and took out the small tube. What in his past, a past of healing and complicity, had made anyone believe he could kill his president in cold blood? But it seemed that he could. He handed the small tube over for Fidel's inspection as calmly if he were handing over a new toothbrush.

The first thing Fidel did was open it and lift it to his nose. "Smells of tobacco," he said.

"My hands. Jose and I had a smoke on the ride in this morning."

"A smoke? And you a physician?"

This was as close as Fidel came to making a joke. Always his humor involved a slight meanness, a joust to keep the other person off balance.

"A few puffs."

"Ah." Castro sniffed at the tube again and then spent a long time examining the label with his glasses. He never wore the glasses in public anymore the way he had when he was younger, never admitted to even the smallest frailty, rarely allowed his illnesses to be reported in the official Cuban press or mentioned aloud in his presence. His famous stumble and broken wrists had made the news, of course, but had quickly been followed by absurd reports that he'd undergone surgical treatment and bone-setting without anesthesia. His health was always "unblemished," always, every day, every hour. He narrowed his eyes and asked, "So what is involved?"

Carlos lifted his eyebrows once as if having to work to call to mind the treatment regimen from the jumble of his other duties. "I rub it on. We wait two minutes; I wipe it off. Then I rub it on again and leave it for one hour and you can then wipe it off yourself, though most of it will have soaked into the skin."

"Aha. And its purpose again?"

"To reduce the size and density of the moles in preparation for treating them with a mild dose of radiation. Also, to help the healing of the skin where other moles have been removed."

"And the side effects?"

"A bit of drowsiness during the second application. If you need to take a short nap, you can. Two hours after it is applied, you will no longer feel these side effects."

"Ah." Fidel would not release the tube. There were, in total, four or five words and perhaps ten numbers printed on the label, but he kept going over them, studying them. He was famous for his intuition. Some people talked about his great luck, but it wasn't luck, really, as much as a kind of sixth sense that alerted him when his life was in danger. Carlos could feel small rivers of sweat dripping down the sides of his ribs. His left leg was trembling. Fidel did not seem to notice; he was nodding his large head, eyes closed as if the drowsiness had already come over him. "Very good," he said. "*Muy bien. Muy bien.* But I want . . ."

He paused, lifted his eyes to Carlos and held them there, unblinking, for what seemed like half a minute. "But I want you to take the treatment first."

"Happy to," Carlos said. "But I have no moles."

Fidel was waving his empty hand in a grand sweep. "No matter, no matter," he said. "For the protection of the head of state, it's part of your job, no?"

"Of course."

"Who knows what demon might have had access to this tube before it came into your possession. For the protection of the head of the Cuban state, you rub it on your forehead exactly the way you will rub it on mine. We'll wait and see what happens, and then proceed. There's enough for both of us, isn't there?"

"If I don't use too much, yes."

"*Bien. Vámonos.* Let's go then."

Fidel was holding out the tube. Carlos took it in his hand and to his horror he saw that his fingers were shaking slightly. "Coffee and cigar for breakfast," he said. "Not wise." The words came out beautifully, perfectly, just the proper combination of self-deprecation and humor. He squeezed a bit of the yellowish cream onto his fingertip and wiped it briskly across his forehead, trying to keep the layer as thin as possible. Fidel was watching him, staring at him. Instead of immediately taking his turn he swiveled on one boot, marched toward the window and stood there looking out at the morning. Carlos was tempted to wipe off the cream when Fidel's back was turned, but he did not.

"What you said about Olochon yesterday, I won't forget it."

"What did I say?"

"That he is too, how did you put it? . . . overly enthusiastic. I disagree."

"He's loyal; he's a friend. In his position I would do the same."

"Ah. But you think him sometimes too enthusiastic. How can someone be too enthusiastic in protecting the Revolution?"

"Now I will wipe off the cream and then reapply it, just as I will do for you."

"Wait a few more seconds. You said two minutes. I have a clock in my head, you know. Eleven seconds more. . . . And you didn't answer me."

A clock in his head. Fidel had never been on time for an appointment in his life. If he had a clock in his head, the clock had ninety-second minutes. "Here's what I meant," Carlos said. And again, to his astonishment, the words came out of his mouth with a clarity and force, a confidence that he did not know he possessed. "If you respond to too many false threats, it eventually hurts you in responding to real ones."

"But how do you know the false from the real?"

"A question of judgment."

"Ah. Well, you risked your own life to save Olochon's. You must have at least a fairly high opinion of him."

"Very high, Comandante. Now I shall wipe this off. It does smell a bit, makes me want to have another smoke." Smiling, Carlos took out his handkerchief and rubbed the cream away.

"Any effect?"

"Nothing."

"Good. Now rub it on again and we'll leave it for a while."

Fidel watched him put the second small dollop onto his finger, watched Carlos smear it across his forehead. Now, already, he thought he felt a small warmth there, and a tiny change in his perceptive abilities. The powerful poison was already working its way into his bloodstream. All his university training came back to him, the layers of epidermal cells, the permeable lining of the capillaries, the chemistry of blood absorption. Fidel watched and watched, turned away, paced to the window and back. "Anything?"

Carlos smiled. "A warmth. Perhaps the smallest bit of sleepiness. If I can't wipe it off I'll have to go back to the office and nap."

"No wiping it off," Fidel said, and there was a slight hardening in his voice. "If you have to sleep, sleep. You are the *ministro*. Who is going to report you for sleeping during the working day? And to whom?"

Carlos laughed. Again, it came out in the most natural way. So natural, in fact, that he started to finally comprehend what General Rincon had seen in him, something he had not seen in himself. He was capable of doing this. More than capable. If it meant that he had to die, he would die, but he would not give himself or anyone else away; he would not waver now. Several minutes passed. Fidel began musing aloud about the sugar harvest, then about the copper mines. It seemed he would go on forever. But then, abruptly, he stopped and waved Carlos over. "Apply it," he said bravely.

Carlos smeared on a thick coat of the ointment, rubbing it into the dark moles and finding imaginary scars to treat. He checked his watch. At exactly two minutes he vigorously rubbed the cream away.

"Are you rubbing it off or rubbing it in?" Fidel asked. He raised a hand to his forehead and peered at Carlos. "Do you feel anything?"

"Nothing." The warmth remained, but the sleepiness seemed to have been an illusion. The drug was supposed to take between twenty and forty minutes to work. He wondered how long it would be before irreversible damage was done. The digestive system would go first, Jose had told him. Then the heart. After that, the final sleep.

Fidel waited. His eyes shifted back and forth along the carpet. At the point where Carlos thought he was going to tell him to leave, that he'd do the rest of the application himself, he motioned to his forehead. Carlos approached. Squeezed out as large a dose as he thought he could get away with, and applied it liberally to the Great Leader's skin.

"*Bien,*" Fidel said.

"Feel anything?"

"The warmth. Nothing. I'll have a coffee. Tell them outside to bring me a coffee. You can go back and nap, but I need to work."

Carlos closed his medical bag. Just as he was preparing to take his leave, Fidel spoke up: "The campaign goes well?"

"It's just begun. It's a matter of propaganda, of raising awareness. The results will take time to materialize."

Fidel watched him without speaking. There was something different in his eyes, and Carlos wondered if somehow he knew, if he sensed the truth in the same way an animal senses it is about to be slaughtered. For a few awful, endless seconds nothing was said, and Carlos felt a flood of sorrow seeping through his thoughts, a river of guilt. At one time, this man, this man whom he was now in the process of murdering, had held the hopes of millions of people in his hands. In a world where the rich did not look twice at the poor, this man had been a kind of messiah, and Carlos had been one of the worshippers. Even with all his flaws, Fidel had at least spoken for the poor. Who would speak for them now? The lunatic Chavez?

Time seemed to stall, as if one immense note was about to be struck in human history. At last, the great Fidel Castro, slayer of dragons, saint to the poor, betrayer of his own cause, said "*Gracias*"—something he never did after a medical procedure— and nodded his dismissal. Carlos made a quick salute, turned, and was out the door. He did not tell the guards about Fidel's coffee. The instant he was past the first set of them and trotting down the curling stairway, he took out his handkerchief and, careful to use a dry patch, careful to make certain that no one could see, wiped away the cream that had not yet been absorbed.

Jose was waiting at the curb, just as they had planned. Except that General Rincon sat in the back seat. Carlos did not see him until he'd already opened the front passenger door. Rincon and Jose were making a show of talking very loudly and joking with each other. "We're having lunch together," Rincon said, loudly, when Carlos greeted him. "The occasion is my thirty-fifth year of service. I am taking you out for lunch, Ministro."

When they were out of sight of the residence, the joking immediately ceased. "It went as planned?" Rincon asked.

Carlos turned around so he could look at the general's face. "Almost as planned. He made me apply it to myself first."

"On you? You put it on you?"

"I had no choice. I wiped it off as soon as I was out of his office."

"Are you feeling anything?"

"A small dizziness. Nothing serious."

"And on him, how long will it take now?"

"In half an hour he will begin to feel nauseous. If the dose was sufficient, fifteen minutes later he will be dead."

"And nothing anyone can do?"

"Not now. Nothing. Unless he wiped it off, too, when I left him."

"Fine," Rincon said, and there was something in his face Carlos did not want to look at. He turned around, facing forward, and heard: "To the Dentist's, Jose. We have one piece of business to conclude there before our celebratory lunch."

CHAPTER THIRTY TWO

E ven in the meager shade of the pier, Carolina could feel the power of the tropical sun. She had been sitting there for at least two hours, possibly more. She'd pressed the transmitter button six times, but now, from the fading glow of the small red light, she could see that the battery was nearly exhausted. She was terribly thirsty, her feet felt like nothing more than shards of whipped flesh stuck to throbbing bone, and her eyes burned from continually looking out at the horizon. The ocean seemed to be on fire, lit up with dancing flames. Even the palm fronds were like knives of light.

At last—it must have been past noon—she saw, or thought she saw, a dark spot on the horizon. Not on the horizon, exactly, but well out in the bay. The boat, if it was a boat, had not come from the open ocean, but seemed to have circled around the promontory of land to her left, west. So this would be a local operation, then, more Cubans risking their lives for her. She wondered if Jose Ulises himself would be piloting the craft, and if he would head it straight out to sea, north through the porous defenses of the Cuban navy, toward Florida, toward safety. Or maybe they had some other place of refuge closer by. Moved by an old reflex, she checked the huge pocket at her hip for the cyanide, then stood and walked to the end of the pier. The craft approached at a fast clip. It seemed like a small yacht, well appointed. But it was moving too quickly for any ordinary yacht. She decided it had been outfitted with about four times the horsepower required of a pleasure craft that size. Enough speed to outrun the Cuban destroyers and make it safely to Key West.

The boat was coming straight at her. She stood in her peasant's dress in the broiling sun, her face scratched, her feet swollen, her belly all but empty. She tried to maintain her concentration, but it was undercut by the exhaustion, the hunger and thirst, and the night of fear. Somehow, even the garish tent of a dress and tattered leaf-sandals conspired to put her off balance.

The boat churned steadily toward the dock and then stopped short, sending a wake splashing through the pilings and onto the beach. A skiff was dispatched, piloted by a muscular brown-skinned man in a straw hat. The man was a master. He sped to the dock, turned the bow, and cut the engine at the last instant, so that the gunwale swelled up to the pilings, barely bumping against the wooden ladder.

The man gestured for her to climb in, but did not speak. Once she was seated, he opened the throttle and they were back beside the yacht in seconds. The rope ladder pressed into the torn soles of her feet as she climbed. She saw that, with the help of a small crane on the back of the ship, they were lifting the skiff back into place. She climbed over the top, into the luxury of the boat, and everything seemed fine at first. Someone—a servant— was moving toward her with a tray on which a bottle of water rested like a gift from the hand of God. But then, as she was reaching for it, as the yacht turned and sped back close to shore, down from the bridge came a man in uniform. The man was in his late sixties, she guessed, and she thought he was handsome until he smiled at her, showing teeth that bent outward away from his lips. Something in the smile was all wrong. Something in the man's posture. He walked up to her calmly and she thought for a moment that he might reach out his hand to greet her, but when he was close enough, he hit her across the right cheekbone with a ferocious backhand.

The force of the blow knocked her hard to the floor, and there she spit out a piece of bloody, broken tooth. She could see only the man's boots, and she thought he was about to kick her in the face, but he spoke a word, one very foul word. The man spun on his heel and went back up the stairs, and she felt herself being hand-cuffed from behind, and then shoved over against the hard ribs of the boat's gunwales. The craft bounced and tilted, each slap of the waves a jolt of agony through the bones of her face and skull.

The ride was endless, the sun smashing down on her, the men ignoring her, the bumps blinding her with pain. She lost consciousness. When she came to, nothing had changed, but there was blood on the deck in front of her face, and an almost paralyzing fear running through her. Over the years, she had imagined many times what it would feel like to be tortured. She had worked with someone in Uzbekistan once, posing as a tourist then, too, but carrying something out, not in. She remembered the mosques with their sky blue domes, the dry mountains rising up beyond the Soviet-style housing, the bustling markets with women in bright kerchiefs selling watermelons and apricots—another potential paradise made into hell by a mad dictator. She'd gone in and out safely, bringing back a few documents to her boss at the time, but she'd heard that moments after she boarded the plane for Moscow, her contact had been arrested. Later he was tortured and killed. That was as close as she'd ever come. Until now.

The pain in her face was terrible, sharp at first but then a deep throbbing ache that burned the bones of her jaw and scalp and radiated up through the broken tooth. She could feel her face swelling. She could feel that the boat had left the rough water and was moving closer to shore again, perhaps into port. In a moment, the man with the awful teeth came down the steps in his tall black boots and colonel's stars, and pushed the tip of one of boot against her breasts, then into her crotch. He was wearing a side holster with a pistol in it. He held the boot there and wiggled it around, and the harder she tried to squirm away from him, the more force he used, pinning her against the side of the boat. He laughed his horrid laugh, then turned away and she could hear him giving orders in a tone of absolute, unquestioned command.

She had the dose of cyanide in the pocket of the huge dress, but even if she could have reached it she would not have taken it, not quite yet. Through the fog of pain and terror she had the thought that, somewhere, Volkes must know what had happened. The Orchid prided itself on never leaving one of its own to be devoured by the wolves. If there was any possible way to do it, they would get her out. The trick—for them, for her—was not to wait too long.

After another two minutes the engine noise changed again. The boat came slowly to a stop. She was lifted to her feet, blood dripping from one side of her mouth and down onto the front of the dress. Havana. She saw the crumbling façades of the Malecón. Off to her right, the famous Morro Castle stood like the battered hopes of all of Cuba's glorious pasts. There were a few large freighters tied up to their left. One of the men took hold of her elbows and maneuvered her forward on unsteady legs, down a sort of gangplank. The makeshift sandals slipped this way and that but remained on her ruined feet. Through a fiery cloud of pain, the world seemed to swivel and tilt. They were moving toward a car. Someone opened the back door and she was thrown roughly, facedown, onto the floor of the back seat. She heard the door slam behind her, then the passenger and driver's doors open and close, and then she heard the voice of the man who had struck her. He was sitting in the passenger seat. She tried to raise herself up far enough so that she could see him.

CHAPTER THIRTY-THREE

"Put your light on the roof," Rincon told Jose in his general's voice. "Engage the siren." They went through the streets of the capital beneath a blinking blanket of shrill noise. The city Carlos loved passed beyond the windows like a dream: the arched facades and columns of the buildings along Paseo del Prado, the Museum of the Revolution, the university. He shifted his eyes to Jose, but his friend was busy turning the radio dial to improve the reception, and would not look at him. There was nothing on the news, nothing at all. It was early yet: Thirteen minutes had passed since he'd walked out of Fidel's quarters.

"Feel anything?" General Rincon asked as they were shrieking past the university.

Carlos shook his head without turning around. His body felt fine, almost normal, but he did not like the atmosphere in the car. The lack of sleep, the massive worry of the last few days, the thing he had just done—it was all working on him, twisting his thoughts into knots of wet rope. He did not like the fact that the cream had seemed to have no effect on him. None; zero. It had been several minutes before he'd been able to wipe it off; if the drug was as potent, as lethal, as he'd been told, then even the small dose should have caused him to feel something. Perhaps it would strike him all at once, and instead of killing him, the diluted dose would mean only a minor heart attack, or a stroke, or chronic digestive problems. He'd spend the rest of his life in a home for the *ancianos,* or he'd die in the prison here. Or perhaps the cream had been fake, and the so-called conspiracy had been fake, an elaborate ruse dreamt up by the prince of paranoia to see which of his ministers he could trust. Who was the betrayer? Olochon? Rincon? Gutierrez?

Jose screeched up in front of the Montefiore Prison and turned off the car. He and Rincon leapt out as if acting roles in a well-rehearsed play. Carlos climbed out more slowly and walked around to the sidewalk, where they seemed to be waiting for him. "Walk in front of us, my friend," Rincon said, and Carlos knew then, from the tone of voice, from the sad-sounding *"mi amigo,"* from the fact that Jose absolutely could not make eye contact with him—he knew from all these things, and from the quality of the silence among them during the short ride, that Elena had been right. Rincon and the others had used him for their own ends. They were going to sacrifice him now like any beast of the farm. For one instant he thought of running—he even looked briefly down the sidewalk to his left. But there would be no running now. He would face what he would have to face with as much dignity as he could manage. At least, if they tortured him, there would be no names for him to give up, no one to betray . . . unless they forced him to denounce the completely innocent. Elena, Véronique, Julio.

They marched him up the walk, a prisoner who did not need to be handcuffed. The stone-faced guards at the entrance—D-7, both of them—saluted the second in command of the Armed

Forces as if it were graduation day at the College of the Defense of the Motherland. Carlos felt Rincon's fingers against his spine, a light steady pressure: where friends were concerned, you needed only fingertips, not the barrel of a gun. Jose held the door for him, eyes averted. They stepped out of the sunlight, into the disinfectant and piss smell of the stone lobby. More salutes, this time from the interior guards, the country boys, semi-innocent.

Rincon and Jose marched him down the corridor and up three flights of stairs, the screams and stink, the torment and death, echoing from every damp wall.

They proceeded at a brisk pace down the corridor toward Olochon's office, but before they reached it, Rincon used the pressure against Carlos's back to turn him left into the room where Ernesto had been killed.

The room had been cleaned, but it did not matter: Stepping into it, hearing the metal door close behind him, Carlos saw it as it had been on that day, the tortured man hanging there, the blood and tissue, the horror of Olochon's calm smile. He saw what he had done in a new light now. Elena was right again: You did not kill in the name of justice. There was the same scarred table with a chair behind it, the place where the interrogator sat when he needed a respite from his duties. Rincon moved him there, said, "Sit, please."

Carlos sat. He looked first at Jose, then at the general. "I did as you asked me," he managed to say from between lips as dry as sand.

Rincon nodded curtly. "Sit there," he said. "Keep your hands behind you as if they are handcuffed. For what it's worth, if we don't see you again, I'm sorry we had to do it this way. You are a man of courage." He saluted, his highest compliment, spun around, and banged through the door as if there were men all across the nation waiting for his word of command. Jose hesitated two seconds, then removed the pistol from the holster beneath his arm. Carlos understood that he was to be shot there, by his former driver and onetime close friend. His innards went loose and a sweat as cold as ice broke out on his face.

Jose turned the pistol around and handed it to him, butt first.

Carlos refused to accept it. "That's it, then?" he said. "All these years of friendship and what they amount to is that you'll allow me the privilege of killing myself, rather than doing it yourself or waiting for Olochon to do it?"

The flicker of an uneasy smile crossed Jose's face. "It's not that, Boss. Every chamber is loaded this time. When the Dentist comes in, wait as long as you can and shoot him at the closest range you can manage."

Carlos looked at the gun. It took him several seconds to understand. "Why . . . what . . . why was I chosen for this?"

"Because what was needed was a man beyond suspicion on the one hand, and with the brains and courage to do this on the other."

"And afterward, what?"

"Afterward, go outside to the front of the building. I'll be waiting for you in the car, at the corner, not directly in front. Rincon will take care of the guards at the front door. I'm sorry, too, for what it's worth. To put you through this. In the end it will seem right, even to you, but I'm sorry for the deception." He leaned down and tied a cloth gag around Carlos's mouth, then turned and was gone.

CHAPTER THIRTY*FOUR

—~w|hw—

A s the car sped through streets she could not see, Carolina had to use every ounce of strength and willpower just to keep her head turned so that the battered side of her face did not bounce against the carpeted floor. The man who had struck her reached his arm over the back of the seat and fondled the material of the dress, tugging it tight against her skin but not touching her through it. There was something utterly terrifying in the way he did it, as if he had possession of her now, body and soul, and an unlimited amount of time to bring her to deeper and deeper levels of misery. She had to urinate but would not let herself.

In a matter of minutes she heard the brakes and felt the momentum press her against the back of the driver's seat. Car doors opened and closed. The driver pulled her out as if she were a sack of coconuts. It was futile to resist, but she resisted anyway, by reflex, until the man who had been in the passenger seat, the hideous colonel, came around and struck her again, one iron finger pushed hard into her gut. She lost control of her bladder then, wetting her legs and sandals. The man cursed and stepped back and spat the vile word at her again.

Then she was being prodded up the walkway toward a stone-walled building that hulked and tilted like the abode of the devil himself, then up a set of stairs, her wrists cuffed, one powerful, merciless hand gripping her just above her right elbow. The colonel was striding ahead of them like a prince. A pair of mean-faced guards at the door snapped to attention when they saw him, offering sharp salutes. Her right eye had swollen closed. They passed through a foul-smelling lobby; more guards, desks, muted shrieks that became unbearably clear when she was brought through another set of barred metal doors. The stink and the raw fear made her want to vomit. She could hear the scrape of her breadfruit-leaf sandals on the floor but it was almost as if they were attached to some-one else's feet. People were wailing and moaning and screaming on all sides, a vision of hell. Through a curtain of absolute ter-ror it occurred to her that this place was the reason, the motiva-tion, that lay behind the whole project. For her at least. This was the reason she had come here, to help end this kind of thing in the land of her forefathers. Now she would pay her blood dues.

They led her up three flights of stairs and along a stone cor-ridor into which no daylight fell. They turned her sharply left, through a metal door, and as she stepped into a room that reeked of disinfectant her one working eye came immediately to rest on a man there. The man was wearing a suit, and he was sitting at a desk with his hands behind him as if he, too, were cuffed. He had been gagged, and his eyes followed them in des-peration. At the sight of him, the colonel with the terrible teeth stopped short. "What have we here?" he said, after a moment, in that awful taunting voice. "*Quién tenemos aquí?*" "What have we? Carlos Gutierrez, my good friend, come to give me his greetings in this room. What a gift, what a joy!" The colonel paused for a moment, drinking in the sight of the cuffed man, drawing the top lip back from his slanted, yellow teeth. "You shall be the observer first, my friend and former minister of health. An observer and then the participant. How wonderful. How wonderful to know that my intuition was correct all along. What a glorious day!"

Carolina was led to the wall where a set of iron cuffs stood at the height of her shoulders. The driver uncuffed her, then put her wrists into the thicker wall cuffs and handed the key back to the colonel, who was leering at her now. Now she would have taken the cyanide, if she could have reached her pocket. The man leered, savoring the sight of her. He turned to his huge assistant and said, "Give me my privacy. I want only Carlos to see this, our onetime minister of health. Only he and I will see what happens to *yanqui* whores who try to humiliate us."

The bodyguard nodded and left, closing the door tight behind him. For a moment, the colonel did not seem to know which of them to approach first. The man behind the desk had started to tremble now; she could see the sinews of his neck twitching. The colonel had one hand on her, just tracing the muscles of her right shoulder, where they were pulled back taut. "Let me speak with my friend here for a few moments," he said to her, almost in the voice of a lover. "Let these muscles start to feel the fire, and then we will begin."

He turned his back to her and took four steps over toward the desk. He said, "My good, good friend, the minister of health, how are you feeling on this glorious day? And who was kind enough to deliver you to me?" As he finished this sentence he leaned slightly toward his captive, as if getting ready to remove the gag, and at that instant the man behind the table somehow released his arms and swung them forward, and then there was a deafening sound, and the back of the colonel's head exploded toward her in a spray of blood and bone.

CHAPTER THIRTY‹FIVE

———–ᴧᴧᴧᴧᴧ–———

Volkes sat at a small table on the balcony of the Mandarin Restaurant, watching his comrade pace. They had requested privacy on the balcony, and his longtime partner and cofounder of the Orchid had walked the entire length of it and back probably twenty times. Volkes was nursing a martini. On the table beside his glass sat a cell phone, open so that he could see the screen. They had been waiting for it to ring for hours. "Calm yourself," Volkes said kindly, in the direction of his pacing partner. "It's going to be fine."

"She's my daughter," his partner answered. He had been saying it all morning. "She is the same as my daughter."

"We have people there who will help her."

"She fled the hotel."

"We know that. She's probably on her way home by now."

"Why haven't we heard anything, then?"

"There are always minor problems. Eddie called, our Eddie. Six Spanish freighters, said to be carrying cotton but in fact loaded with relief aid, are steaming toward Cuban waters. Slowly. One signal from us and they speed up. There will be an escort of U.S. Navy destroyers close by, if such a thing is needed. There will be planes dropping food. All we need now is one sign. Give us a sign, Lord."

"And the helicopter?"

"Hovering just beyond Cuban airspace."

"Wait ten more minutes and send it in."

"We can't, Roberto. Not until we know."

Anzar wrenched his wrist violently out from beneath the sleeve of a tailored shirt and stared at his watch. He paced to the far end of the balcony and leaned on the railing, looking across the Intracoastal at his buildings and the ones surrounding them. He appeared to be talking to himself. Volkes felt slightly sorry for him, but full of confidence, as always. At twenty minutes past two the phone sounded and he had it to his ear before the first ring was finished. "Yes," he said coolly, aware of the set of eyes burning into him from the other end of the balcony. He listened for a moment, then said, "Don't call again until you have found her" and hung up.

"The dose has been applied," Volkes said to the other man on the balcony. "Your niece, our brave girl, is missing."

"What about our boat?"

"Our boat never left the Port of Havana, for reasons we do not yet know."

"Then she's out there, alone, with every fucking D-7 animal searching for her."

"I don't think so," Volkes said calmly.

CHAPTER THIRTY⋆SIX

———⟋⟍⟋⟍———

Carlos tossed the pistol away from him as if it was poisoned. It went skidding across the cement floor and knocked against the wall. Once the weapon was out of his fingers he found that he could not move. He could not take his eyes off the scene before him, a spurting stew of gristle and bone where Felix Olochon's head had once been, the carotid arteries still pumping blood. He believed, now, that he had killed the devil. And become the devil. He no longer wanted to be alive.

"Get the key from his pocket," the woman said. It was, he believed, the third or fourth or fifth time she had said it. He could not move. "The key. *La llave.* We must go." Her Spanish was nearly perfect—it seemed to him an odd thing to notice, but he noticed it, watched one crimson rivulet trailing across the floor toward her feet. He saw then that her feet, half wrapped in tattered leaves, were blistered and cut, rubbed raw, and as if his professional self were rising up from a paralysis, that sight awakened him from his dream. He stood and wobbled two steps on rubbery legs. He leaned down, fished in the pocket of Olochon's uniform, and pulled out the key. Blood was still pouring from the ruined vessels, but at a slower rate. Coins skittered across the floor when he tugged at the key, coins and some kind of tiny doll. He thought, at first, that it was a Santeria idol, but when he picked it up he saw that it had belonged to, or been intended for, a small child.

"Quickly," the woman said. "*¡Rápidamente!*"

Carlos moved like an automaton, releasing first one wrist then the other. The woman did not even stop to rub them, but went for the pistol, lifted it, wiped it once against the peasant skirt, and pointed to the body on the floor. He saw that she was a beautiful woman. Cuban, Spanish, American, he could not be sure. One side of her face was swollen horribly, but you could see the beauty all the same, around her eyes, in the shape of her forehead and the cheek that had not been injured. "Take his pistol," she said through broken lips.

Carlos shook his head.

"Take it. Let's go."

He shook his head again. Then, as if in a dream, he bent down and, without getting too much blood on his shoes and hands, managed to remove the pistol from Olochon's holster. She urged him to take it, to go, but instead he put the pistol in Olochon's hand and tried to turn the arm so that it seemed the Dentist had pointed the gun at himself. He did not know what had given him the idea to do this. Olochon was dead. To whom would it matter how he had died?

The beautiful woman in the billowing peasant dress opened the door cautiously and peered out. She smelled of sweat and piss and the dress was stained behind her. He peered out, too, beside her shoulder. The corridor was empty. Jose had told him to do something, but he could not remember what that something was. They went along the corridor, crouching against the wall, the woman in front of him, holding out the pistol, Carlos staggering along behind. They found the door to the stairwell and looked down. There were cries, but it seemed to him that they were muted, as if the souls here already knew that Olochon was dead, and just that fact had somehow begun to ease their torment. Soaked in guilt as he was, if he'd had the key, Carlos would have let them all go, all of them, politicals and real criminals alike, all of them.

At the bottom of the third flight of stairs the body of Olochon's personal guard lay sprawled like a huge mannequin. Carlos glanced at it once then looked away, unable to ascertain how the man had been killed. The woman in the peasant dress opened the door carefully again and peered out. "There's another corridor," he said, as if she had not seen it. "Then there will be desks. Guards at the door. More guards beyond the door, at the top of the outside steps."

She moved out into the corridor and he was close behind. After a few steps they could see the desks in the lobby, but not a single person sat there. Word of the attempted coup had arrived; anything could happen now, in Cuba, anything at all. The clerks and the country-boy soldiers had fled for their lives. Carlos and the woman stepped forward cautiously, staying close to one wall. Through another set of doors they could see the two guards on either side of the entrance, D-7 thugs standing in the sun, working here because they enjoyed it, reveled in it.

"We'll never get out." He and the woman stood there, close together, breathing in what seemed to him a very loud way. A shadow stirred and cried out in the cell not far behind them. Carlos cringed but did not turn around. As they crept slowly forward along the wall, he suddenly saw a military hat appear through the barred glass windows of the front door. The hat rose up in quick jumps as its owner jogged up the steps. Another second, and the top half of General Rincon's face came into view beneath the hat. Rincon marched forward across the wide exterior landing, just as if it were any other day, but as the guards saluted him, he shot them, one after another, through the forehead. Once, twice, without emotion, without doubt. Carlos saw the raised arm, heard the reports. Saw one of the guards fall sideways, watched as blood spattered on the barred windows as if thrown there from a bucket. He watched Rincon march straight on, through the doors. "He is a friend," Carlos managed to say to the woman as she was aiming the pistol in her hand.

Rincon held the doors open with his body and motioned for them to come forward, quickly now. The woman pushed the gun down into the pocket of her absurd dress. Rincon's hand was on Carlos's shoulder. There was his car, there, at the curb, Jose at the wheel. Men in uniform were everywhere, but these must be Rincon's men. Vaguely, as if through layer upon layer of dream, Carlos sensed some sort of swelling, a movement on the streets beyond the tall iron gates, people sweeping in one direction with an urgency that had nothing to do with the everyday.

Rincon sat in front, Carlos and the woman in back. The radio was on, a familiar voice speaking there. Jose caught his eyes in the mirror and there was apology in them. Apology, admiration . . . something else.

"Central Committee building," Rincon ordered, and already it seemed to Carlos that the general's manner had changed. Why weren't they listening to the voice on the radio? Rincon reached his arm diagonally over the back of his seat and slapped the top of Carlos's thigh, hard, and left his hand there, squeezing him. On the radio, Fidel was going on and on. Fulminating. Waving a fist—Carlos could almost see him. "*Y los enemigos de la Revolución del Cuba, los enemigos de la humanidad son . . .*" And so on. He had heard this nonsense all his life. So Fidel was still alive, ranting about the enemies of the Revolution. The cream had not worked. Why were Rincon and Jose grinning then, like schoolboys?

"*Es una grabación,*" the woman said. "It's a recording. I know this speech. We heard it. We studied it."

The men in the front seat nodded, but Carlos did not believe them.

And then, after another thirty seconds, abruptly, as if the radio had heard her, the voice of the Maximum Leader went silent. Nothing came out of the speakers, only static. Jose tried the other two channels, but the result was the same. He turned the radio down but left it on. He met Carlos's eyes in the mirror and there Carlos saw a flicker of something new. Triumph, he thought it was. In a moment they had pulled up in front of the Central Committee building, or as close to the building as they could get. Already, people were milling about in a way unheard of during any normal day. As Jose pushed the nose of the Volga tentatively through the crowd, Carlos studied the faces near his window. Nothing was certain yet. Some of them would be outraged. Some of them would be celebrating, hoping. When they heard Fidel was actually gone, when they heard that Olochon was dead . . .

"What about Raul?"

It was the woman speaking. General Rincon turned around and faced her, brimming with confidence, bursting with it. "Raul Castro, unfortunately, has fled to parts unknown. But we will find him. My men have roadblocks on every road leading out of the city." He turned to Carlos. "Do you know this woman?"

Carlos shook his head, though, in fact, he felt as though he knew the woman in ways that he had not known anyone in his life, not Teresa, not Elena, no one. And that she knew him in the same fashion.

"This," Rincon said proudly, "is the woman who brought the lethal dose into our country."

"Carolina," she said, through swollen lips, looking at him, and then at the side of Jose's face, and then into Carlos's eyes. "Carolina Anzar Perez."

"Carolina"—Rincon was still squeezing Carlos's leg—"this gentleman here is our former minister of health, Carlos Gutierrez. Now head of the provisional government. This is the man to whom you ultimately delivered the dose."

"There are troops everywhere," Jose interrupted.

"Mine," Rincon said. The confidence was spilling through the skin of his face. "Hand chosen. There will not be a problem. Get as close as you can, and then Carlos and I will walk in and make our radio address, our appeal for calm, our announcement that the great Fidel Castro died peacefully at his desk today at one P.M., and Felix Olochon, upon hearing the news, took his own life. There will be supplies at the port, and we will announce that, too. All political prisoners will be released within the hour. Take Carolina to the port, Jose. In a short while you will see a helicopter, unmarked, come to carry her home." He turned now, looked her full in the face, and said, "From your uncle, Roberto Anzar. With love."

Carlos glanced at the woman, but could not manage a word. He looked into the rearview mirror at Jose. At Rincon's urging, he opened his door and stood up.

Blood on the cuffs of his sleeves, he was walking shoulder to shoulder with General Rincon toward the building that had once held Castro's offices, maneuvering his way through the loose spontaneous gathering, feeling Cuba seething all around him. Provisional government. A speech. Announcements. Anzar. He kept his eyes forward, forward, and did not stop.

CHAPTER THIRTY SEVEN

Once they had left the horrible building, once she recognized that the speech was an old one and understood that it meant Fidel was likely dead and she was safe, Carolina began to breathe again. The three men with her in the car were not going to hurt her. She breathed. She could feel the pain in her face and feet again. She could smell the sour odor of her soiled dress.

As the car moved forward, she began to try to work her way backward, piecing things together. The man to her left was still in a semi catatonic state. The man behind the wheel—he kept trying to meet her eyes in the mirror—was Jose Ulises. The man directly in front of her was the second-in-command of the Cuban Armed Forces, she knew that from his uniform and from his face. Rincon. Until the moment she had spoken her name she'd believed it was Rincon who had organized everything. And then Rincon had said something about the port, a helicopter, had said: "From your uncle, with love."

And she understood. All of it had been a test, a vetting, a charade intended to expose her to the roots of her soul. Roberto Anzar, Volkes, and Eddie Lincoln had orchestrated everything, tricking her into tiptoeing along the edge of the crevasse and hoping she would not fall in. She understood now. The false trip to see her uncle, the false meeting with Oscar in church, Volkes's lie that he knew who Roberto Anzar was but had never worked with him. It had all been an elaborate charade designed to assess her courage and loyalty while the plot—one of the plots—moved forward. Would she deceive her own uncle for the cause? Would she run away once she knew the organization had been infiltrated? Could she do what had to be done? The whole time she thought she had been deceiving the great Anzar, while he had been deceiving her.

Through the pain and the first sparks of exhilaration, a violent anger rose up in her. They had used her like a trained dog.

When the general stepped out of the car, she stepped out, too. He did not even notice. He and the other man, her fellow prisoner and apparently the former minister of health, Carlos, went pushing through the crowd, and the crowd, recognizing them perhaps, or just used to being shoved aside, was parting. She heard one or two brave people in the rear shout out a question: "What has happened? Tell us!" She could hear the anger and fear in some of the voices. But the two men moved forward, past the saluting guards, up the long set of steps, and into Cuba's future, leaving, as such men always did, bodies and blood in their wake.

"Get in, Carolina," Jose called, urgently now, she thought. He had leaned down across the front seat and was looking out the window at her. She realized how hideous she must look. She reached up and touched her swollen face. In the distance, she believed she heard the steady *whump-whump* of the helicopter that had been sent for her. All planned out so well. But instead of getting into the car, she turned and walked away, burying herself in the loose crowd, the Cuban woman's stolen peasant dress billowing around her, the side of her face throbbing, one eye closed, a pistol and poison in her pocket. Each step sent shards of pain through the bones of her legs, and she understood that she would not get very far before Jose caught up with her, but she moved into the crowd anyway. There was a peculiar energy there, a peculiarly Cuban kind of nervousness or thrill running in their faces. Somewhere off to her right someone had started to sing in a crazy voice. There seemed to be pockets of anger, bursts of violence in the heavy air.

What a sight she must be: People gave her strange, frightened looks, as if she had just walked out of the Torture House, ghost of all the souls who had been taken there. As if, battered, used, tricked, and dressed in bright colors, she belonged to them absolutely.

"¡Se ha muerto! ¡Se ha muerto!" someone was shouting now. And she could feel the reaction of the people around her surging in her own blood. There were more people singing, a fight breaking out somewhere near the fence of the Central Committee building, many defending Castro, mourning, others in rejoice mode. She could feel it all. "¡Ha muerto Olochon!" someone else bellowed, and a great roar of joy rose up and traveled through the crowd like a wave.

When it subsided, she heard Jose calling her name again, behind her, but she struggled on another few steps, wanting her uncle to worry, wanting things not to go exactly as he had planned them, wanting to disappear into the heart of Cuba and make them all sweat in their northern luxury, worrying about her. She pushed on a few more steps, thinking: Always the same here, on this island.

Always this hope and this music and this violence. Always the trickery from above laid over this hope, laid over this rich soil. May it end now, she thought. *May the misery end.*

And then Jose had a hand on her arm and was turning her toward him, roughly, urgently, as if something had gone wrong.

CHAPTER THIRTY EIGHT

Volkes took a sip from his martini, just the smallest sip, just to have the taste of cold vodka on his tongue. Not far from him, the great Roberto Anzar continued to wear out the balcony's floor with his pacing, and filled the air with mutterings about his daughter, his godchild, all his fear and negativity pouring out. When the phone rang again, Volkes had it instantly to his ear. The voice this time was rushed, almost panicky, and behind it he could hear sirens and shouting, and then moving air as if his source were running for his life along a city sidewalk. He listened to the words, made his man repeat them, and then heard the line go dead, and felt, in the center of himself, a caving in, as if the weight of age—held at a distance by his will—was now suddenly pressing down on his internal organs. He hit a button on the phone and three seconds later said, "Tell the pilot it is not the port. I say again, Not the port! Tell him to make a landing as close to the plaza as he can get. Tell them to get our girl out of there—I don't care who they have to kill. Get everyone you can over there, instantly. Get her out. Now!"

Before he'd even closed the connection he could feel Anzar beside him, practically breathing on his face. He made himself turn and look into the brown eyes, alight with a terrible fury now. He felt himself shaking inside, just the most subtle of tremors, as if an old oak beam that bore the weight of a building was beginning to fail. "There is the chance," he said, as calmly as he could manage, "just a chance, Roberto, that the cream either did not work, or worked only partially. Castro has been taken by ambulance to the hospital. The word I have is that he is gravely ill, and that Olochon is dead."

"Gravely ill?" Anzar hissed. "Not dead?"

"No, not dead. Not yet dead."

ABOUT THE AUTHOR

ROLAND MERULLO lives with his wife and daughters in Massachusetts. This is his eleventh book. You can read more about him at RolandMerullo.com.

A NOTE ON THE TYPE

THIS BOOK WAS SET in Sabon, a typeface designed by Jan Tschichold in 1964. It was named for a sixteenth-century type-founder, Jakob Sabon, a student of Claude Garamond. The type-face is a modern revival of a type issued by the Egenolff-Berner foundry in 1592, based on roman characters of Claude Garamond and italic characters of Robert Granjon.